THE PEOPLE OF THE LION

Book Eight

"The New Life Series"

By

LOUISE BOUCK

PERMISSION

COPYRIGHT

Register of Copyrights,
United States of America
Registration Number TXu 1-942-258
Effective date August 19, 2014
Copyright claimant Louise Irene Bouck

ISBN13 978-1-943984-07-7 paperback
ISBN 13 978-1-943984-17-6 eBook

Hisgivenstories LIB Publications

ACKNOWLEDGEMENTS

It is important to say thank you to all the people who have encouraged me. A special, "Thank you" goes to all the wonderful Christian family and friends who have continued to keep me and this work of love in their prayers.

A note of appreciation goes to Ray Shaw, who patiently taught me to use the technology necessary to create this series and make it available.

Thank you to the people at the public library. They have helped with finding research resources that I didn't know existed.

I acknowledge God's strength and favor that has helped me to continue to plod along on this ten book series. His precious touch is needed daily.

"Thank you Jesus."

DEDICATION

This New Life Series is dedicated to Jesus and to my family, those who have gone before me, those with me now and those to come and to all my brothers and sisters in Christ.

†

TABLE OF CONTENTS

INTRODUCTION

This is book eight in "The New Life Series." The Christian fiction in this series is written to offer the reader a wholesome entertainment, starting back in a simpler but not easier time. Their example of spiritual strength and "never quit" attitude is refreshing and inspiring. The adventurers follow the trail to a new land and challenges they never imagined.

In book one "More Than Survival," follow Benjamin Slater as he copes with the wild isolation of the new frontier and the lessons of self-preservation. He experiences the pain of loss and joys of accomplishment. He travels some of "Life's Many Journeys," in book two and learns to appreciate "The Land's Heritage," in book three.

In Book four, you will find out "The Story of Sarah"

As you read the books, Ben develops into a man of physical and spiritual strength. His problem solving mind is challenged many times.

When Sarah, his sister returns to him, they are finally "Together," in book five. You will find out how her life affected the Indians that took her and how they became "The Blue Stone People," a chosen nation in book six.

A change of scene takes you to the camp of the Sentu and three survivors enter the story, in book seven "Teewahpanyee the Boy, Two Feathers the Man," Willow and Water Bug bring new strength and young blood to an old people. With Willow at his side in book eight Two Feathers becomes leader of "The People of The Lion". They are chosen by the Lion of Judah to be rescuers, and are rewarded in book nine, by being allowed to discover "The Lion's Den."

In book ten, the land that Ben Slater's father chose has miraculously remained with the family as time has gone by and generations were born. In a day beyond today, the story moves to the final times after the rapture. A new heroine stands up bravely to the soldiers of the anti-Christ. She finds Ben's Bible, Mary Slater's journals and the gift of faith. Emily spreads the word and struggles to survive the time of tribulation as she finally realizes that this is "Just the Beginning" for those who believe.

Now please enjoy book eight.

CHAPTER ONE
TWO FEATHERS AND WILLOW

The camp of The Blue Stone People was quiet. The moon was high and nearly full. It lit the prairie and filtered down through the trees. The night guard had taken their positions as the sun had set. It was hard work to stay awake and alert until first light, but the young men had gotten used to it.

As he stood his position in the night guard, Two Feathers was remembering when he and Willow had joined the Blue Stone People.

Looking ahead at the column of people moving slowly across the grass of the prairie, I think I was a little fearful of what was ahead for us. I rode Friend. My Patches and the other horses were carrying our corn bundles and other belongings that day. I was riding beside Spotted Feather. He was from the Omati and Flying Eagle had taken him into his tent a couple years earlier, when he was left without a family. In a small way I think that makes him like one of us, The People of the Lion. I wonder if I will ever feel comfortable with these people. I didn't then and I still don't in some ways.

I can't see Willow or our tent from here. I couldn't see her that day either. She had pulled her horse up beside Snow Star, the Chief's daughter. Their people were traveling in their places according to status but I don't think Willow thinks much about status even today. They have all continued to be kind to us because of all that has happened. I wasn't happy when Chief Dark Wolf moved all the tents and put us with the unmarried young hunters. I have a family. That should count for something. He treats

9

the Abalinah as if they are married but they just choose someone. We have more loyalty and family than they do.

When the Chief invited us to stay in his tent during the entire summer council, I'm sure that gave us status with the people. Moonflower, his wife was good to us too, and the others saw it.

Someday, Willow and I will lead our own people. It may not be so very far in the future. When I think "Willow and I" like that, it sounds like she is my wife. I hope that one day she will think of me in that light. I couldn't stand it if she said yes to someone else.

I wonder what Water Bug will be like when he is grown. He is such a fun little fellow. I know that he will always want to live near water. He loves it. He smiled, when he thought about the little boy. He has grown so much.

Two Feather's mind continued to wander.

Debon was definitely interested whenever he saw the diminutive woman from his own people. They said she lost her husband a year before they came to our village. She could have taken a man at the summer council. She had proposals but turned them down. I wondered then what special skills she had that she thought she could remain self-sufficient. No woman should live alone. I am glad that Debon talked to Chief Dark Wolf about her. Willow liked her right from the start. They became friends on the way to the camp of the Blue Stone People. She told me about it.

Willow glanced back, noticing Sheltah riding alone behind the other women. She moved back near her, seeing that she appeared to be without friends.

"Hello, I am Willow," she said smiling.

The little woman smiled, but didn't reply.

"Do you understand our language?"

"Sheltah," she said with a smile, touching her chest.

"I wonder how long we will be riding. I am getting tired of being on this horse," said Willow. Sheltah smiled again, but didn't try to talk.

The caravan moved steadily to the edge of the tall grass and continued until they were nearly past it before they came to a place where circles of stones and an area of tall trees and a spring could be seen. Moonflower immediately took charge indicating where families should camp and guiding them to appropriate spots. She hadn't discussed this with Chief Dark Wolf, but thought that it would be best for now to place the Chief of the Choyinaw and his wife near their tent, but back a short ways. Their status had not been decided.

"Come Willow, bring Water Bug and we can fill our water bags with fresh water from the spring," suggested Moonflower.

"Yes, he will like to see the water. If I let him, he will sit in it and people will have to maneuver their vessels around him." Moonflower laughed at the image that Willow's words had created in her mind.

"That boy likes water more than any child I have ever seen. Did I tell you that our village is on the edge of a small lake? He will love that, but it will be a challenge for you to keep him out of it when you are busy. It amazes me, that you manage him so well."

"Thank you, Moonflower, but the woman, Sheltah isn't much larger than I am and she had a son of her own but now she is alone."

"Yes, she is small, but she is older than you are by several years, I am sure."

"Yes, I have been thinking about her. Let's go see if she is settled and has what she needs for tonight."

Willow greeted Sheltah with a smile but held back as she realized that Moonflower was speaking to her.

Sheltah smiled broadly and hugged Moonflower shaking her head no.

"She said she doesn't need anything."

"You have a gift for languages. How did you pick up so much of her tongue?"

"It is a good skill. It just happens. I don't have to work at it at all. I do think that all the new people should learn our language. It will help them blend into our people. She has been slow to learn our words, but seems to manage."

"I am glad that I don't have to learn a new language. All our words are the same, but I did notice that we say some of them a little differently."

"Willow, you and I get along so well, it is as if you were my daughter. I hope you always stay with the Blue Stone People."

"I hope we will always be near enough to be friends, but I know that Two Feathers plans to start a new people, with new traditions. That's when she told Moonflower that we are "The People of the Lion.""

Moonflower had said that we both are mature for being so young. She said to remember that it will serve us well to learn all we can. It is a funny thing about knowledge though, the more we learn, the more we realize that we know very little.

"Not you, Moonflower. I think you must know about everything," volunteered Willow.

Moonflower laughed at that remark.

The night camp was unusually quiet. It seemed strange to not hear sounds like conversations and movement. Moonflower was concerned and whispered to Dark Wolf.

"It is so still. It is as if the people are all listening."

"Yes, I noticed it. Perhaps, people are not at ease yet. I will walk through the camp and check on the new people."

Moonflower slid over to Willow and softly explained that they would not move on in the morning.

"It is a workday for everyone. The woman will cut the grain low to the ground so that it has long stems, then we shake the grain onto our blankets and weave containers from the stems to hold it. The men will hunt and hopefully we will have meat to dry and hides to preserve. It has become a tradition to do this. Three years ago we ran into a small herd of buffalo in this area. Since then we have taken advantage of the grain and good hunting on our way home."

Willow was pleased, she had wondered about passing by all that good grain. That gave her an opportunity to watch the women weaving. She still has a lot to learn in that craft, he chuckled. I hope I am never in a position where I have to do it again.

"Sleep well Willow," Two Feathers said to the dark night.

I had put my bedroll away from hers but still near enough that Willow could call out to me if she needed me. I slept well that night. I remember that I had said that I would never leave her alone again. I meant it. I want to be a comfort and security for her. I care for her. Our working together for survival has built a strong bond. We have become a family.

That morning, voices woke Willow as Water Bug tugged at the tie on his ankle. Two Feathers remembered taking him quickly behind a bush and returned him to Willow.

"We men are going hunting," I had said. That was the first time that I had been included with the hunters of the Blue Stone People.

"Be safe and have good luck," she said as I hurried to find Spotted Feather. It is good for us to have others to work with and learn from. I feel happy now. We have friends.

Silently she had prayed, thanking God for the people around her and the good feeling of protection. I promise I will work hard and learn all that I can. Father, please watch over Two Feathers and all the hunters. Please keep them safe and help them to be successful in the hunt.

Willow was learning the rhythm of cutting the grain. She held her father's knife at an angle. Step, cut, step, cut, she held the grain in her left arm with the heads up trying to collect as much as she could hold.

Late in the afternoon the men returned less than jubilant. Collectively they had just one large deer and three rabbits.

Wisely the women praised the size of the deer and prepared it for the campfire. They would have a communal meal and move out in the morning. The women had worked hard all day and had sacks of grain ready to be transported.

Although a little disappointed by the poor hunt, they were glad not to have to stay while meat was drying. They were all eager to get back to their village and the new members of the people were curious to see where they would be living.

I better quit letting my mind wander and be more watchful, thought Two Feathers.

*****

The lake seemed a bit smaller. The corn was short and dry but the crop was good. It would have to wait a few more days to be harvested until the people were settled and rested.

Soon after their arrival, Moonflower glanced up at the knoll expecting to see Chief Dark Wolf and Chief Sky Fire there, but he was not in sight. She could hear men's voices in the communal tent, a few yards away and decided to see what was going on.

"I tell you, it is the right thing to do. As long as he is called Chief, their people will look to him for direction. They will never completely accept your authority."

"They have been through so much. Growling Bear, how can I take away his title?"

"Think about it, my Chief. We will talk again."

Moonflower had hesitated to enter when she realized that a very serious tone filled the air. She had her answer anyway.

I didn't think they would address that issue the moment we arrived, but I suppose that it is good to get it resolved soon.

It will be good to have the new people settled and comfortable, she thought.

Two Feathers and Willow set up a camp site near the communal tent, just a short walk from Chief Dark Wolf's.

Chief Sky Fire, had helped his wife, Rippling Water, to erect their tent very near Two Feather's camp, but he had edged it between theirs and Chief Dark Wolf's. Moonflower didn't like it at all.

"It is too close, Morning Dove, I don't like it there. It is as if he is trying to be a co-Chief. They can hear every word we say."

"Don't worry about it, Moonflower. You are probably right that he would like to be a co-Chief and share the leadership. He has lost nearly all his people but not his desire for power. The men will have a meeting and they will solve it."

"We will be too busy anyway, said Moonflower. "We need to harvest the corn and anything left in the garden by the lake, before weather ruins it. We can get the new women to help, so they will learn our ways, and that includes Rippling Water and Okallah."

Morning Dove laughed out loud as the two women parted company.

Moonflower frowned as she scanned the village. We have added so many people with different ways and strange beliefs, First the Abalinah walked into our meadow from the north, bringing their Chief. Poor Sweet Grass was upset that she couldn't help him enough. He died soon after they arrived.

Then we found the young people camped and growing corn near the spot of our summer meeting. I like Willow and Two Feathers. They are so mature and respectful in their thinking. Having to send their entire village to the spirit world and care for that growing baby boy at the same time would certainly be more than most grownups could handle. I find it hard to believe that the Sentu are all gone. Many loved ones in their camp will never smile and talk with me again. My heart is heavy.

Our summer meeting wasn't at all what anyone wanted or expected, with the Choyinaw attacking. Chief Sky Fire has very few of his people left. That was a bad decision he made, sending his warriors against the many at the summer meeting. What did he hope to gain? Now he is here, with his wife, his son and daughter-in-law and their

16

one girl. Standing Bear and Dancing Willow took Smiling Moon into their family. She was from the Choyinaw but I don't think she is related to Chief Sky Fire. It is a good thing that other villages accepted several of the families that he brought back with him. Two women with children were married to young hunters of the Omati. I am glad. They will do well there.

Chief Dark Wolf approached her.

"Moonflower, what are you thinking about? You were frowning and looking off into the camp, but I could tell you were not watching anyone in particular."

"Oh, I was thinking about the many new individuals and what we must do to blend them into one people."

"Don't worry about it. That is my job. Now, have you forgotten that you still have a husband to feed?" They laughed together comfortably and entered their tent.

In the months to come, Debon had gotten permission and had chosen Sheltah according to the custom of the Abalinah.

He knew the added responsibility would give him status among the hunters. She was a complex person with many talents. She made useable, strong water pots and decorated storage jars that she fired in a large oven she built among the big rocks.

Father Bob was not happy with some of the customs that the new people brought to the camp. He tried hard to strengthen the acceptance of the Christian faith and continue the work Sarah had started.

Two Feathers and all the unmarried young men were assigned positions in the night guard. The territory of the Blue Stone People was well guarded both day and night.

The Jesuit priest, Father Bob, was well liked and was accepted in the camp as a friend. He had come several years back; before the earthquake and built a small church on the other side of the lake. The people cherished his stories from the bible and they had accepted that his God was the Great Spirit. With the help of Brave Sparrow, Moonflower's adopted daughter, the people had learned about Jesus and referred to God as the Great Spirit. Brave Sparrow, now asked to be called Sarah. She had left the people and found her brother, Ben Slater, with a growing family and ranch.

It was Sarah who found the turquoise and encouraged the people to use it to trade with the white men.

With the passing of time, a trading spot was established and the Winahatah were converted and became The Blue Stone People. They prospered. While other tribes fought with the soldiers and with each other for hunting grounds; the people grew strong in numbers and were known as peaceful and they were the only ones that traded the blue stones.

Chief Dark Wolf had decided that he would not tolerate his authority being challenged by the remnants of other tribes. He gave an order that the entire camp was to be rearranged, not by status, but the tents were to be placed so that hunters and warriors were in close proximity to each other. He placed the night guard at the edge of camp and designated an area behind the big tent for a group of tents that were home to older couples. These men became his council. It had been almost a year since he had organized it that way and it had worked well.

Now, he had noticed that the young men of the night guard were developing into a unit of their own making. They guarded their positions at night as directed and attended meetings when necessary, but he sensed a growing allegiance not to the oldest member of their group, but surprisingly to the youngest, Two Feathers.

Willow had decorated their tent with a painting of a lion on the right side of the doorway and flames on the left. She had learned to color the grease paint with dye she made. From a distance the red and yellow flames appeared real. The white lion seemed made of mist. She is very clever, he thought. Even their horses are easy to recognize in the herd. She has braided yellow cloth into the mane of every one of them.

The first time one of Two Feather's horses became heavy, and ready to deliver her foal, he had moved her from the herd to a place near his tent and she was pampered. He rode a big black stallion and that too was always near and ready for his use. He acts like a leader, setting himself apart, not by distance, but by appearances and the way he carries himself. It draws respect.

When the new brown and white foal was born, Willow braided yellow cloth and tied it around the new foal's neck just close enough to stay on when she tipped her head down. She gave her as much attention as she did Water Bug.

The boy was growing fast and swam like a fish. She had given up worrying about him going near the lake because he was always there. He caught fish with his bare hands and netted them in a quantity large enough to make a meal, when asked to do so. Water Bug had learned on his own that he could lead the horse they called Grandmother, to a tree, where he would climb up and slide onto her back. He was riding a year earlier than any other child his age. Two Feathers had made it clear that Grandmother was the only horse that he was to ride. They talked about it one night and decided that he was probably about four years old that first spring that they were in the camp of the people.

*****

Willow and Two Feathers had formed their family unit out of necessity, after their entire village of the Sentu was raided and nearly everyone was killed. With time, they had developed an affection that added strength to their bond. They lived as brother and sister, yet neither of them entertained the thought of choosing a mate. It was as if they already had one. They functioned as grown-ups and in the time that they had been together, they had formed a real family. They had matured into responsible, good looking adults.

Sheltah had traded with Willow, for one of the largest floor mats she had made. Willow was pleased with her new water pot. She carried it to the side of the lake and dipped it in filling it. It was heavier than she thought it would be. She carefully poured some of the water out and then lifted it to her shoulder and carried it back to their tent. Hondor, the oldest of the men from the Abalinah, had watched her from a distance. He smiled at his thoughts as he entered the big tent for a men's meeting.

CHAPTER TWO
ABSENT WITHOUT LEAVE

Father Bob slipped in at the last minute as Chief Dark Wolf stood to speak. He had observed Hondor's lustful looks and immediately knew he had to speak about more than the acquisition of beef for the people. The men needed to hear about faithfulness and morals at this meeting.

"I have called you all here although I know that my night guard is tired and their responsibilities have kept them up all night. Our camp at this moment is unguarded for the first time by my choosing, in two years. I need to come directly to the point. Although we prosper with trade goods, our people are greatly in need of meat. The buffalo herds do not come to our hunting grounds and the deer are so few that our most seasoned hunters have no luck in finding a fresh trail to follow. Father Bob has a way to bring us meat."

Father Bob stood and was trying to count the number of missing men as he explained that he would purchase cattle from a Christian man and they would be brought to the prairie side of the big rocks by the white men. I believe that it will be at a fair price and perhaps he can arrange a regular supply that we will be able to count on. His mind was focused on their need for meat until he glanced at Hondor.

Without Chief Dark Wolf realizing it, Father Bob had decided that he needed to turn this men's meeting into a lesson on morality and the faithfulness needed for a good family relationship of one man and one woman. He transitioned into a lesson abruptly.

"Now, I need to tell you of something else of importance. When you choose a woman, you should choose her to be a wife, it should be forever. A good wife is a blessing from God. You cannot set aside a wife or take someone else's mate. These are rules in the Holy Bible. I know that some of you have never heard this before, but as you go about camp doing your work, think about it. This is one of Ten Commandments that the Great Spirit has declared. We must all honor Him by obeying them."

Father Bob said he would talk more with Chief Dark Wolf about the arrangements for the cattle in the morning. The meeting soon ended and the men went to their tents.

Chief Dark Wolf walked straight to the tent of Growling Bear and scratched near the flap. Big Flower wrapped a fur around her shoulders and stepped out.

"Where is Growling Bear?"

"He is not here. He did not return to our tent since he left this morning."

"Where has he gone?"

"I don't know, my Chief. He said he would be gone for a while and maybe overnight and that I should not worry. He made sure that I had everything that I needed before he left."

"That's good, don't be concerned. He probably forgot to tell me. He has been teaching some skills to the night guard. Did he take anyone with him?"

"Yes, I saw Two Feathers ride out with him."

"Is Two Feathers the only one?"

"He is the only one that I saw."

"Thank you Big Flower."

The Chief was frowning as he walked down the row of empty tents that should have held the sleeping night guards.

"Willow, where is Two Feathers?" He scratched on her tent and asked the question before he saw her.

"He has gone with Growling Bear."

"Many of the night guard were not at the men's meeting. How many went with them?"

"I don't know. I just saw Two Feathers ride out with Growling Bear."

"Thank you Willow, Oh and I noticed your drawings. They are interesting." He smiled at her hoping she couldn't read his mind. They were well executed but he viewed them as another sign of undeclared separation.

"Thank you," she said softly as he hurried away.

Father Bob was sitting on the little knoll again. He was waiting for the Chief.

Chief Dark Wolf joined him carrying a leather pouch, decorated with beads. This should be more than enough to pay for thirty of the cattle.

"Chief, you look worried. What is bothering you?"

"Growling Bear, Two Feathers and many of the night guard have left camp. Didn't you notice they were not at the men's meeting?"

"Yes I did, but I thought you had given them something to do." The Chief was deeply concerned. He wasn't sure when they had all left, and he wondered why they had dared to leave the camp unguarded during the night.

"Father, when will you be leaving?"

"I thought that I would leave sometime tomorrow. I have a couple chores to do and then I will go. Is it alright with you, if I release my mules and horses that I won't be taking, inside the fence so that they will be safer?"

"You can put them in there anytime."

"That's good."

"The sooner that things can get back to normal the better it will be and I thought you should suggest that the cattle be brought to the trading spot. That way the men of our people will feel they have earned the cattle by mining the stones. It will be just another trade, only a very sizeable one."

"Chief Dark Wolf, that's a great idea. The people are used to white men at that location. They won't feel that their arrival there is a threat."

After a few minutes, the two men went their separate ways, each deep in thought. Father Bob was planning his visit to the S. and J. Ranch, while moving Rudy, and Mabel into the meadow through the gate. He stopped to talk to Singing Wind for a few minutes and then went back to collect Father Pete's two pack horses and turned them out into the meadow. They look happy to be with the herd, he thought. I should have done that long ago. I just didn't want to overstep my boundary.

Meanwhile Chief Dark Wolf paced back and forth through the center of camp. It was as if he expected to find the absent men there and in their tents each time he drew near.

"Chief Dark Wolf, please sit down and have some tea with me," said Big Flower. "You have walked passed this tent several times. Checking will not make the men return sooner. He told me he would be gone a lot with the young men. He wants them to improve their skills."

He listened but was not going to stay for tea, until he found a cup of tea being pushed into his hand.

"Your sons, are they all sleeping?"

"No, the story mothers have Little Cub and Blue Stone and Dancing Willow took the babies for a little while.

Smiling Moon is there too. They are all under the shade pavilion."

"Yes, I can see them." He smiled at her and decided that Growling Bear was a lucky man. Are you cooking the meal for Growling Bear? Do you expect him back soon?"

"No but I always try to keep things in place and food ready so that when he returns he can eat and rest. I know that he will be tired. His duties as top hunter have kept him very busy lately."

"Thank you for the tea Big Flower. I am going back to my tent now and check on Moonflower. Her leg has healed well but for some reason it stays tender. Perhaps she would like some help with something.

The rest of the day seemed to play out in slow motion. That night, his mind would not let him rest although the moon was high in the sky. He was sure that he would have to confront Growling Bear for taking the night guard without his permission. Why do these people have to create so many problems?

After sending Bending Grass for a jar of fresh water from the lake, Moonflower settled in front of their tent with her sewing to enjoy the sun, while the tent blocked the cool breeze. She was puzzled to see Hondor slip into Sky Fire's tent and Rippling Water hurry away toward the shade pavilion. I wonder what he is doing in there. He hasn't been around Sky Fire since they arrived in camp. I am sure they are not close friends. She couldn't possibly guess at the conversation that was going on.

*****

"You are doing well old man. You have nothing to fear as long as you continue doing what you are supposed to do. Keep that wife of yours in check. She has a mouth on her that I will permanently silence if she says one word about any of our people. Remind her that she has one son left and his family, including a granddaughter that she enjoys. You told the story just right. They believed every word and now they treat you with kind respect. Just keep it that way."

He stepped out as swiftly as he had entered. Sky Fire had not responded. Rippling Water sat with the story mothers just long enough to see Hondor cross the camp and then she returned to her tent.

"What did he want? What did he say?" She asked.

"He said we are doing well, but he threatens Young Blood and his family; if we say anything about the Abalinah raid on the Sentu or why they are here. You must never speak of it, not their raid on our camp or the slaves they took. Say nothing. Do you understand? He will kill Young Blood and the last of our family and then probably us."

Her face turned ashen and her legs became weak. She slid to the furs on the floor of the tent.

"Yes, I understand. I have never spoken of it. I even left the dinner with the priest and the Chief when his wife asked questions about the bead stories on my clothes."

"Look, I am making a new shirt with designs I have seen on their clothes here in camp. Morning Dove told me what they mean and they are simply symbols for rain or sun, and birds or animals. I am being very careful, Sky Fire."

Tears slid silently down her face as her trembling hand showed him the work.

"You must not cry anymore tears for our people. We cannot save those that live, or bring back the ones that walk in the spirit world. Now dry your face, Rippling Water, and put on a smile for me. I am tired, so very tired. I think I will rest awhile. Will you lay here with me? The camp is quiet today. Perhaps I can sleep."

She curled next to him, covering them both with a colorful blanket. Her body rested but her mind was at work trying to figure out a way to expose the Abalinah without the retaliation that would follow if she was found out. Her heart ached for her daughter and son that had been taken as slaves. Many of our young people were taken away. I can't help but long to see and hold my children again. I fear to think of the dreadful life they live with those wicked people. That is why I sewed the beads to show they are dead! I know that I will never see them again.

They made our warriors attack the summer council while they held our camp hostage. They knew most of them would be killed. They pretend to be victims here asking refuge. I can't stand to look at them. Tears spilled onto her furs as Sky Fire slept beside her.

*****

In the early morning light Growling Bear and Two Feathers had headed out of camp. It was just light enough to travel. That was two days ago, now Two Feathers began to worry as they traveled along with the cattle. This is wrong, he thought. This will bring trouble to the camp of The Blue Stone People. He looked at the wide trail they were leaving in the prairie grass. Anyone could follow the tracks these heavy beasts leave. I wish I had not taken part in this. Willow will be disappointed in me and Chief Dark Wolf will be furious with all of us. I should not have listened to Growling Bear. This was his idea. The man that owns these cattle is sure to be angry and he will report it. If the soldiers come, many of the people will be killed.

Two Feathers regretted his role in this, more than anything he had ever done.

When he looked up, he saw a single rider coming. It was Father Bob and he didn't look happy.

Father Bob had talked with the Chief about acquiring beef for the people. He was on his way to the S and J Ranch to buy some beef cattle when he met the men from the village bringing the small herd of cattle.

He instantly knew that they had stolen them. There was no other way for them to acquire cattle here on the prairie. What should I do Lord? He felt a pain in the pit of his stomach as he imagined soldiers riding into the camp with guns pointing at people he had learned to love. This is such a mistake, he thought.

CHAPTER THREE
DID YOU TRADE?

Growling Bear pulled his horse up and stopped, motioning for the rest of them to continue on.

"Growling Bear, what have you done?"

"Hello, Father Bob," he said with a wide smile. "We are bringing meat for the people."

"Did you trade for the cattle?"

"We took what they have taken from us. They have taken away the deer and the buffalo. That was our meat, until they came with their fences. Now we take the meat that our people need for winter."

"Oh Growling Bear, this is not the way to get meat. You have endangered our peace and have opened the door for war. The Great Spirit says you must not steal. He will not bless the people if you do not honor His rules."

"You are soft, Priest. We do what we must." He kicked his horse and rode swiftly around the herd to the guard at the opening to the big rocks, causing a stir in the small herd. He ordered Night Hawk, the man on guard at that position, to ride through the big rock area and open the gate to the meadow.

As the big rocks loomed ahead, the cattle slowed and stopped. They began to mill around, uncertain of the path.

"Two Feathers ride through and show them the way," signed Growling Bear silently.

He moved slowly to the front of the small herd of cattle and walked his horse in the opening of the path making a small whistle to draw the attention of the animals. When he looked back he was astonished that it had actually worked. The cattle were following! The night guard stayed close gently crowding them to the opening.

Chief Dark Wolf sat on his knoll worrying. He was shocked when he saw the first few cattle enter the meadow.

As more came in, his face began to display his disbelief. How could they be so senseless? This is going to cause us big trouble. At first he had seen Two Feathers come through the path in front of the cattle.

At that moment he thought that this was his doing but he knew differently when Growling Bear proudly entered the meadow last, following the men of the night guard that he had taken. The man on guard closed the gate noticing that the horses had all gone to the far end of the field. Coyote and Falling Stones were concerned. They feared that the big horned beasts would injure the horses.

Chief Dark Wolf knew that it was far too soon for Father Bob to have arranged the purchase of cattle for the people. He had left only a short time earlier.

"White Grass, tell Growling Bear that I want to see him in my tent, now!"

"Yes my Chief."

White Grass hurried along the outside of the meadow motioning to Growling Bear.

"The Chief is in his tent. He wants to see you right away," said the young man.

Growling Bear glanced in that direction and saw Moonflower scurry away from the front of her tent when her husband approached. Behind him in the meadow she could see the cattle. The look on Chief Dark Wolf's face was enough to tell her that she did not want to be there just now. He didn't have to ask her to leave.

Morning Dove stood outside her tent with Roaring Water. She joined them.

"The Priest has not had time to go purchase these animals. Growling Bear has brought us meat but with it I fear he has brought death to this camp. I am going to talk to some of the other hunters. Chief Dark wolf will call a meeting in the big tent soon. He will want us to be ready to defend the camp," said Standing Bear.

He walked toward the edge of the big rocks where Night Hawk and Snapping Turtle stood talking animatedly.

Growling Bear responded to the summons joyously. He was not thinking clearly. He expected praise.

When he scratched on the tent flap of Chief Dark Wolf, he was not ready for the harsh words that met his arrival.

"Growling Bear, you are a fool! What you have done will bring the soldiers here for the first time! I can't believe that you think that this is the way to feed our people. Have you lived here with us and not learned the moral code that Sarah and the Priest have taught our people? We do not steal! You have taken the lives of our people in your hands and their blood will pour over you!"

Growling Bear stood silently. He did not respond. I had to get meat, he thought. He only half heard the words the Chief was saying. He felt anger wash over him.

"Is this how you thank me for bringing food for all our people to last the winter? I have taken back what they took from us! They took the buffalo and the deer!" He was shouting and Chief Dark Wolf couldn't believe that even now, Growling Bear could not understand the harm in what he had done.

"Who gave you permission to leave our camp unguarded?

Who said you could take the night guard and leave camp? Are you now an authority here that answers to no one? Growling Bear this was wrong on so many levels that I can't begin to explain it. If you can't see it, then you are no longer capable of being my top hunter and warrior. Your skills have always been a strength that I could count on, but now I cannot believe the poor judgement you have used. Go to your tent and stay there until I send for you. Do not leave your tent! Do you understand?"

"Yes my Chief," he said humbly as he backed out of the flap and went to his own tent swiftly. He knew their words had boomed over the immediate area.

As tongues wagged; everyone would know his disgrace in a few minutes. He wondered how he could survive this humiliation. His anger boiled on top of his crushed spirit. For the very first time since he had become leader of the warriors and hunters, he felt that the Chief no longer had respect for him.

Big Flower saw him enter the meadow with the cattle and then she watched as he went to the Chief's tent. She was aware of the concern that he had caused by taking the night guard without telling Chief Dark Wolf. She thought that was the issue at hand. She didn't realize that he had stolen the cattle and the possibility loomed that soldiers would follow.

Her first instinct was to try to comfort him, but when she saw the blood red of his angry face, she darted out and went to the shade pavilion where her children were being entertained.

Smiling Moon greeted her cheerfully as she bounced Happy Song on her knee making her laugh. Dancing Willow, Blue Stone, and Moonflower walked across the center of camp starring in the direction of the meadow. Snow Star was already there with Watching Owl. The faces of the women revealed concern and fear as the story of stolen cattle and soldiers had reached their ears.

"Mother what will we do? There is no way that Father can make this right. He is Chief and the soldiers will hold him responsible for what our men have done. I am so glad that Flying Eagle wasn't with them." Snow Star understood the gravity of the situation.

When Father Bob had left just shortly before the cattle had arrived, Chief Dark Wolf had given a sigh of relief; but now he saw stolen cattle in their meadow and an urgent problem. He had lost respect for Growling Bear and knew that this was a significant challenge. He sent Bending Grass and White Grass rushing to tell every man in camp that they needed to come to the big tent at once.

"Tell all the other men, but don't stop at Growling Bear's tent."

"Yes my Chief, we will hurry."

He dismissed Sweet Grass with the wave of his hand and sent her away from the big tent.

"We will not need anything for this meeting. You may go."

The men came. They responded instantly understanding the urgency, both young and old, until the tent seemed nearly full, without the women and children. We may need to make this tent larger, if we all survive this, he thought.

"Men of The Blue Stone People, we have a meadow that holds cattle. We did not trade for them. We did not hunt them. They are not wild animals, from our hunting ground. The soldiers will soon follow. We have promised the white men that we are a peaceful people. They come to our trading spot and we need the goods they bring to trade there." He paused to think.

"Now they will feel they cannot trust us! They will not come to trade. Soldiers will come to retaliate! I fear for the

33

well-being of our village. Many years have passed since we lived the way of the Winahatah. We are a new people. We know the ten rules of the Great God. He has blessed our people with the blue stones and shown us the way to an excellent life. This one foolish act could bring death to this camp." He paused trying to decide what he should have his men do. His declaration brought chills.

"My night guard, it is good that you have come to this meeting! You missed the last one! Night guard members stand now." They hesitantly stood, wondering what their punishment would be, knowing they deserved one. "Each of you left your position and went away from camp leaving women and children unguarded. What do you say for yourselves?"

He waited, but no one spoke.

"Two Feathers, you seem to be the self-appointed leader of this group, can you say nothing? Did you not have any awareness that what you were doing was wrong?"

"Yes my Chief, I did, when I became informed of Growling Bear's plan; I knew you would be angry and I feared that it would bring trouble to our camp, but I was not advised of what he had in mind; none of us were, until it seemed too late to turn back. He gave directions as he had when we were hunting and it seemed natural to follow them. He has been our teacher; but we are not children. We knew it was not the right way. We are as responsible as he is. Maybe we are guiltier. He was in charge and felt the pressure of the growing need in camp. He believed it was his duty to fill that need. He said it was the only way to provide meat for the camp, because the deer can't be found and the buffalo do not come. We all deserve to answer for our actions. I am remorseful for leaving my guard position, and I am even more regretful that I have disappointed you and for putting our village in danger."

"Thank you Two Feathers, I appreciate the explanation and your apology." He paused again, thinking.

"Now you inadequate example of guards, you may all leave here and take your weapons to your positions. Take food and water and stay there, awake and alert, until you are relieved!" He shouted.

The young men left the tent hastily and gathered what they needed in record time. They rode swiftly to their posts.

"Now that the children are out of here, we men must decide what is to be done." His hunters recognized the disrespect in his comment, but at the same time it seemed that he was at least in part, allowing their youth to excuse their actions.

"Flying Eagle what do you think should be done?" The young man had not projected an aura of leadership since his return from the Omati. He was surprised that the Chief had called on him first.

"I heard Cat Claw say that they met Father Bob, on their way here with the cattle. Maybe he will be able to act in our behalf and calm the anger of the man that owns these cattle. You indicated that he was going to attempt to arrange a trade with The Blue Stones. It is my hope that he can still do that after the fact."

"I hope you are right, Flying Eagle. Meanwhile, we sit here uninformed and vulnerable. Standing Bear, what do you think should be done?

"As you said my Chief, the night guard is made up of very young men. They are for the most part, trustworthy, but it might be wise for the village to be guarded by additional men with more experience until this is resolved. I know that I will be glad to take extra shifts so that my family is safe." Others murmured approval and agreed that they too would be willing to stand guard more often.

"Sky Fire, what do you think should be done?"

"I think you should go to the fort and pay for the cattle before it is too late!" He spoke loudly and with stern and strong conviction.

"I don't think I want to go to the fort just now, but I would be happy to speak to the man that owns the cattle if I knew where he lives."

Is there anyone else that has an idea? Does anyone else wish to speak?"

"I do my Chief." Growling Bear stepped into the big tent boldly. The men were silent.

"I cannot sit in my tent while decisions are being made that affect me and my family. I understand that most of you do not embrace the old ways of doing things. We did not always try to please the white men."

"When we called ourselves by our real name, the Winahatah, we were strong and proud. Now we have to apologize for taking back what has been stolen from us. Who do you think took our meat away? The white men have driven the deer and buffalo from our hunting grounds. They cut the land into pieces and fence it and call it theirs. How can a man own the earth that is walked on by men, and animals and guarded by the spirits of the unseen world? Chief Dark Wolf, you did not apologize to her parents when you brought a white child here and called her your own. Can none of you see what is happening? We are becoming weaker and depending on the things that the white men bring to the trading spot. Now the priest says he will buy and bring cattle. What happens when he no longer can bring cattle? Who will we depend on then?"

Chief Dark Wolf stepped closer to Growling Bear. He understood the heart and mind of this experienced warrior.

"Growling Bear, you and I are from a different time. We are not the only people in this land. We must change as the land changes or we will all be lost. We are outnumbered by the white men. Their soldiers carry powerful weapons and have the desire to remove our village from this world. Only by learning their ways and respecting their God, will we be able to survive. Father Bob is right. We must obey the ten rules of the Great Spirit. If we do not, we will be punished and we will perish."

"If we do, we will starve!" Growling Bear left the tent as quickly as he had entered.

Several men stood. It seemed to Chief Dark Wolf that Growling Bear had not been there to learn the decisions of the men but more to defend his actions.

"Please sit back down. I will talk with him later. It is important that we know that our camp is protected. We need to double our guard both day and night."

Hondor stood, wishing to speak.

"What is it Hondor?"

"You talk about guards but my question is why do you wait for the camp to be attacked? Can't we protect the village better by placing our warriors on the prairie? We know where the fort is. If soldiers are coming, they will come from that direction. Let's form a line of defense out away from the camp. There are natural places, like small hills, bushes and trees that we can hide behind. They will be riding in a column in the open. We will have an advantage."

"There is merit in Hondor's suggestion, but we must not leave our village unguarded. It is never a good thing to have many of our men gone at one time," said Standing

Bear. He was also one of the older warriors and he was slow to trust the new people in camp.

Although the plan would take a possible battle away from camp, he considered that Hondor might have another reason that prompted his advice.

"Flying Eagle and Sky Fire, I would have you stay for a few minutes. The rest of you go eat and rest. Prepare yourselves and your families for the possibility of war."

The Chief felt a trace of resentment in Sky Fire as the other men filed out of the tent.

"I propose that the two of you recommend a schedule that we can live with for the days ahead. Talk it over and I will be back in a few minutes."

He walked to Growling Bear's tent and asked him to come with him. They moved to his favorite spot on the knoll and sat overlooking the camp.

"Growling Bear, my friend, these are very difficult times. I want you to know that I understand why you did what you did. Not everyone appreciates what you were going through. Some here do not yet grasp the seriousness of our dependent situation." They sat together not speaking for several minutes. "Go let Big Flower feed you and get some rest. We may need your excellent fighting skills in the days ahead. We will talk again."

"Yes my Chief," he said softly, feeling the weight of the danger his actions had brought on the people.

Hondor slipped back into the big tent as the other men left the area. He knew that both of these men could in some way challenge Chief Dark Wolf's authority.

"It is good that you are both willingly taking this problem onto your own shoulders. While you figure out what can be done, he sits with his old friend on his knoll and has done nothing to curtail Growling Bear from creating a similar threat again when he decides it is called for. I find it hard to identify the value in Chief Dark Wolf's leadership. Either of you would have dealt swiftly with Growling Bear and made sure that every man here knows they can't go off on their own authority. Chief Sky Fire is there anything I can do to help you. Your plan to go to the fort was a good one. I would ride with you if you still feel it is necessary to go, and Flying Eagle you were right to think that the people need to offer to pay for the cattle, but do we have an ample supply of the blue stones to do that?"

"Yes of course we do, but I don't think our Chief wants us to work out a plan other than a schedule for additional guarding of the camp until Father Bob returns," said Flying Eagle.

"I guess I was hoping that he was ready to realize that you men were offering the best advice." Hondor quickly left, not wanting the Chief to return and find him there. He had done what he intended. He left both men with the feeling that they had given suggestions that had not been taken seriously.

Hondor retrieved his riffle and horse that he kept at the ready, behind his tent and boldly rode into the north woods without being stopped or questioned.

*****

By noon the next day new additional positions were being guarded and men were standing guard and changing posts often. Kier, another of the Abalinah men, had entered the woods behind the lake and slowly walked his horse along the wide path that led to the area where the blue stones were extracted. He stopped his horse, using the cover of the brush and trees, he watched the men as they worked the blue stones loose from the pit they had made in the cliff.

"I am telling you that I don't see anymore. I have moved rocks in every direction and there just aren't any more blue stones here," said Running Deer.

"That can't be possible! Let me take a look," said Roaring Water. I'm going to knock a big piece of the gray rock out and maybe we will see the start of it again."

His face showed the concern that Kier heard in their voices. It can't be, he thought. Just when we finally get a chance to find out where they get the stones, they are running out! That's not possible. He almost gave himself away in his frustration.

Roaring Water hit the rock as hard as he could and a large chip flew, hitting his side while smaller chips flew at his face causing two tiny cuts. He did it again and again until his face was bleeding in several places and he was sweating profusely.

"There just isn't anymore! What are we going to do?"

"Do you think that God is punishing us because of the stolen cattle?"

"No Running Deer, but I think the timing of this is going to cause our people even more trouble! We need to look around. Try over there." Their voices sounded panicked.

They worked the rest of the morning looking for a new location in the area that would yield the blue stones, but when they finally felt defeated; they took the small satchel that held the last of their harvest from the bluff, and went to Chief Dark Wolf's tent.

The Chief's smile of greeting faded as the two men entered with their small quantity of stones. Roaring Water looked as if he had been in a fight. They were exhausted and worried.

"Sit down men. It is obvious that we need to talk." Moonflower placed a clean cloth in cold water and wrung it out. She handed it to Roaring Water as she left.

CHAPTER FOUR
PROBLEMS AND BLESSINGS

Kier sat in his tent with Gamier talking very quietly. He didn't want to believe it himself.

"I know Gamier, it is hard to believe, but I heard it with my own ears. They can't find any more of the blue stones in the bluff. There is no reason we should stay here and wait to be shot by the soldiers. We need to get Okallah, Debon and Sheltah and leave here tonight."

"Kier, are you sure? Hondor has gone to report to Chief Gray Fox about the possibility of the soldiers coming. He will be furious that we somehow didn't find this out before he left."

"It can't be helped. They just discovered that they couldn't get any more today! Besides, he didn't even tell me he was going. Okallah told me this morning that he had left. Can we tell Sheltah and Debon?"

"They have adjusted well here. I wonder if they will want to go back with us," she said.

"Maybe we should leave them and just go."

"No, we can't leave them. They will be questioned by the Chief when he discovers we are gone, or worse they will be killed when the soldiers come."

"What can they tell the Chief? Debon was not on the raid of the Sentu. They were never in the camp of the Choyinaw and they don't know where the slaves came from. They can't speak the language of the Choyinaw. They have kept our secret long enough that it is just history now."

"Once we are gone there is nothing to stop Sky Fire from speaking, or have you forgotten about him?" Gamier felt apprehensive.

Kier was firm in his decision.

"He can do nothing. He is powerless."

"I don't know Kier."

"The soldiers will take care of our worries. They will wipe out this village anyway, so stop thinking about it. You find Sheltah and tell her to come here at sundown. I will tell Debon."

"We have accumulated a lot of nice things. I hate leaving it all."

"Yes, but we must."

When Debon and Sheltah were told to prepare their horses and have them ready to travel, they objected strenuously until Kier explained why it was necessary to leave immediately and the real danger in staying.

"Our reason for being here all this time was to take over this village and the blue stones. Now we know there are no more blue stones. They will soon be a poor and starving people. The game is over. They have taken cattle and that will bring the soldiers. We need to get out while we can."

Okallah gripped the large piece of turquoise on her necklace for just an instant before deciding that she would not leave empty handed.

As moonflower and several other women sat under the trees weaving or sewing and voicing their concerns, for the future, Okallah went stealthily to the back of Chief Dark Wolf's tent. She slit a seam in the outer layer and an opening in the lining. Quietly she slipped through, entering the empty tent. Silently she searched for the blue stones. When she found a large pot covered with a mat, she knew that she had found some. She looked further. A large basket with a lid held more. Pushing first the heavy pot and then the basket out ahead of her, she left them tucked close to the back of the tent.

"Kier and Debon come quickly and quietly. I need your strength."

She led them to the containers and had them carried to the trees where their horses stood concealed.

"Fill your packs and satchels. Tuck them in anywhere. Then let's get out of here," she said with a grin.

They headed deeper into the north woods, away from the camp, avoiding detection. The many men on guard duty were talking to each other and looking only for soldiers.

*****

Father Bob rode along on Macho heading across the prairie with good news for the people. They would not have to worry about soldiers coming or about the scarcity of meat in the territory anymore. The Slater family was making sure of that. Thank you Lord, my Indian friends will not suffer hunger because of the generosity of that wonderful Christian family. Thank you for blessing them with the gold. Now they have the means to provide the cattle.

He was thinking of the gold discovered in the Hickory River and planning all the wonderful things that it would make possible. Free land for a church on the river and a mission school is certainly a blessing, too. God you have blessed me in so many ways. I wish I could tell my family and I should let the church know about all this and about Father Pete's death. I wish there was a way to send a letter.

He wasn't hurrying Macho. He had stopped twice to rest him and give him water. He sat in the prairie grass eating his roast beef sandwich that Beth had packed for him when he discovered the tasty piece of cheese she had tucked in the pack. This is delicious, he thought. I wish there was a way to provide milk and cheese to the village and eggs, too. The children need to have milk.

Maybe I can arrange to get some milk cows and then Beth or Mary could teach the women of the village how to make cheese. No, that isn't a good idea, but Sarah could teach them. She is accepted even though she is white. She knows how to milk the cows and all about the chickens. There are so many possibilities now that I have the gold. I want them to have everything! That's silly. They already have a good life and they like it the way things are. I must move slowly and introduce new ideas gradually. First I must concentrate on their souls.

As he looked ahead at the big rocks and the woods to the right, he realized that he could see more guards than before. The people are afraid, he thought. I am glad that I can bring them good news.

When he entered the gate and closed it, he continued on moving timidly around the cattle in the meadow. He thanked Falling Stones for opening the gate near the church. He rode on slowly passing the church and lake, to the tent of Chief Dark Wolf. Dismounting, he scratched at the flap before he realized that the tent was empty. It was then that he heard a man's voice coming from the big tent.

As he stepped inside and allowed his eyes to adjust to the dim interior, he saw Chief Dark Wolf, Sky Fire, and Young Blood seated on the furs. They had been having an intense conversation.

"I am sorry. I didn't mean to interrupt you. I will go to the church. Chief Dark Wolf please will you send a messenger when you have time to talk with me? I have news." he said with a smile that quickly faded as he observed the serious expressions on the men's faces. Chief Dark Wolf acknowledged him only with a slight nod.

Father Bob was puzzled. What could be more important than my news?

He returned to the church and turned Macho loose in the meadow with the other horses and cattle. He had a feeling of home when he entered his little personal area in the back of the church. It smelled wonderful from the bountiful supply of cinnamon candy. I haven't given them the cinnamon candy yet, he thought. I will do it at the next celebration fire we have. I wonder what problem Sky fire and Young blood have brought to the Chief. He has had more than his share of trouble this year. I hope it is nothing serious. He was preparing to say his evening prayers when Bending Grass came to say that Chief Dark Wolf wanted to talk to him in his tent.

"Thank you Bending Grass. You are getting so tall. Aren't you nearly thirteen?" The priest asked, as they walked down the path to the camp together.

"Yes I will be when winter takes the leaves from the trees. I will take my three day journey next spring. Father said that I can choose a horse for my birthday. I really like that black and white paint that I have been riding lately. He belongs to the people but Father said that he will talk to Chief Dark Wolf and that perhaps he can be mine. Father Bob, are you bringing news of the soldiers?"

"Bending Grass, I am sure that you will have a good horse when the time comes and now I think I need to give my news to the Chief." He started to scratch on the flap of the tent but Chief Dark Wolf was standing near the big tent with Moonflower and Morning Dove, Roaring Water and several others.

"This is awful," said Snow Star. "Mother you must feel terrible knowing that someone was in the tent. Are you sure they didn't take anything else?"

"Yes, I am sure. They couldn't have been in there very long. They didn't find the polished stones, only the jar of rough small ones and the basket of rough large ones."

Flying Eagle stepped close to Chief Dark Wolf and said that he had checked his tent and all the trade goods were still there undisturbed.

"Good. We will need them," replied the Chief.

"I still don't understand why they left like that," said Flying Eagle.

Father Bob stood there looking puzzled until Chief Dark Wolf turned and greeted him.

"I am sorry Father Bob. We have had a strange occurrence. Come in the big tent and we will talk. I'm sure that you have much news to tell me. I hope that it is good. I have had enough bad news to last me a long time." He said it with a heavy sigh as he stepped up, and into the big tent.

Sweet Grass stood nearby.

"Come woman," he said. "Make us some tea that will help us sleep tonight. We have both had several difficult days."

"Yes, my Chief," she said.

Once the pan of water was prepared with the herbs and starting to simmer near the fire, she placed two cups near it and a ladle on a small wooden tray with a bowl of honey and two spoons. She left, knowing that they would appreciate the privacy for their conversation. She wished that she had gone to the back and slipped into her area that Sarah had used. She wanted to know what Father Bob had to say.

Instead she went the few yards to Moonflower's tent and helped her and Snow Star stitch the damaged seams in the back of the tent.

Although Father Bob had confidence in Ben and his promise to set up a regular supply of cattle, he skipped over that and just told the Chief that the cattle were to be accepted as a gift from God's bounty and that the people should use them as needed.

The Chief explained that the six people from the Abalinah had left and he was sure that they had taken the supply of the unworked stones.

"Is that what you and Sky Fire were talking about when I arrived?"

"No Father Bob. He was telling me that he had been afraid to speak the truth while they were around. The Abalinah warriors were in his camp while he talked with me at the summer council. It was their warriors that forced the raid on the summer meeting. That was their way of eliminating most of the men of the Choyinaw. They took his twin daughter and son as slaves along with four other young people. He said that it was not the Choyinaw but the Abalinah that raided the Sentu camp. He said he isn't sure where the Abalinah camp is, but that it is somewhere northwest of here. It is their way to use slaves to do their work. He fears for the life of his son and daughter and the lives of the other people taken as slaves."

"Oh, Chief Dark Wolf, that is horrible. Those poor people had no choice but to lie. I am sure that they threatened him with the lives of his remaining son and his family if they disclosed any part of the truth! It is no wonder that Rippling Water left the church when Moonflower questioned her about her children and the designs on her clothing. She was telling the truth. In her mind, her daughter and youngest son are lost forever. We have to do something! We have to get them back. Somehow, we must free all the slaves they have taken."

48

"I know Father, but I need to make a plan. I haven't had time to think about it yet. I did remember that Willow said that the raiders took her cousin and Water Bug's mother. They might still be in the Abalinah camp, if they haven't sold them by now."

"I am going back to the church to pray. Is there anything else that you want me to pray about?

"I heard that, Roaring Water and Running Deer came back after working the bluff and said they could not find any more of the blue stones there. They were devastated, thinking that we would no longer have a way to trade. I have been praying steadily about that."

"Father Bob, I know where there are more blue stones, but I hesitate to tell anyone else just yet. There are too many things going on. Please pray and ask the Great Spirit to give me wisdom in all this. I think that the Abalinah left because they somehow overheard the men telling me. That's why they took the unpolished stones. They thought that was all that was left. I never really gave any of them my full trust. I kept them away from our trading spot and the location where the stones were gathered. With the possibility of the soldiers coming here, they quickly grabbed what they found and ran."

"It would be my inclination to say let them go, but with the added knowledge about the slaves, it changes things. Do you think that your hunters can track them?"

"Yes, it shouldn't be difficult. There are six people riding with heavily burdened horses, all in the same direction. I think Growling Bear or Night Hawk will be able to find their trail easily, but we need to know more about their camp, where it is and how large it is. How many warriors do they have?"

"I think you will need to send some men to carefully follow them undetected and get the information that you need. Chief Dark Wolf, your camp and people are not the only ones that have been affected by the Abalinah. Could you ask the help of some of the people that were at the summer council?"

"Father that is an excellent suggestion and I think I need to have a meeting of all my people to tell them what has happened."

"Let's both get some rest and pray tonight," said Father Bob. "God will guide you in the way to proceed."

As Father Bob returned to the little church on the opposite side of the lake, his mind was racing. He knew that again he was going to be joined in a battle against evil. Kneeling on the loose grass that covered the floor, his prayers filled the church with intercession for the people held as slaves by the Abalinah. His heart was pounding with pain as tears spilled from his eyes and his mind created before him the anguish, suffering and demeaning drama of their daily existence. He felt the misery as surely as if he were there experiencing it himself. Hours had passed as he continued to pray.

Finally a revelation so strong and sure presented itself that it could not be denied. I must go with them! God will free those people. I am not the warrior that Growling Bear is, but I know that God wants me to go and He will lead us. He rose and walked slowly, the few feet to the small altar where his cross knife stood in a block of wood. His fingers traced the figure of Christ on it.

"Again, Holy Spirit, I acknowledge that I will need your power going before me. Give us wisdom and an unwavering faith in you. Give us a victory that will change the hearts of all of the people involved in this battle. We will go for You Lord, and we will win because you will lead us!"

In the morning, he still knelt on the floor at the foot of the altar. The cross blade from the altar was still in his hand. He was gripping it so tightly that the sharp blade had cut his palm.

The morning sun filled the church with its golden early morning light as it reflected on the floor from the open door and window. He stood up stiffly; replacing the cross on the altar.

Brushing the grass from his clothes, he pulled them off, down to his long johns and dove in the brisk water of the spring fed lake.

He could see the smoke curling up from a few cooking fires as women of the camp began to do their usual daily routines. He pulled on dry clothes and felt it necessary to wear his priest's robe today. Most days he wore the leather trousers and shirt that Moonflower had provided. They were worn, soft and comfortable. He had a second set that he had made, copying her work, but they were not as comfortable. He couldn't figure out why.

Today, I must talk with Chief Dark Wolf and tell him all that God has revealed to me. He started the prayers of the mass and was joyous when he realized that Chief Dark Wolf had slipped in the door of the church. Soon Sky Fire and Rippling Water came in with Moonflower. Young Blood stepped in with his wife, Meadow Lark and their daughter, Rain Drop.

People continued to come until the church was overflowing and they stood on the grass surrounding the door and window.

Father Bob felt such joy that he had trouble voicing the prayers of the consecration. He raised the host and then the chalice, and finally it was time for the blessing. He blessed the people gathered there and knew that he was finally starting to fulfill his assignments. The first from the seminary and now the one he was given last night by the Holy Spirit. I will go with you anywhere you lead me," he said.

Father Bob walked among the people and hugged each one and thanked them for coming. He was embarrassed by the tears that continued to stream down his face.

"We need to get all of you baptized," he said happily. A voice inside him told him that it was crucial to do it before the battle.

"We need to expand this church," said Chief Dark Wolf. "It is good to start the day with prayer, to feed the spirit of a man but we must also feed our body. Come, you will eat with us," he said putting his arm around the shoulders of Father Bob as they walked back to camp.

The Chief had also been wide-awake most of the night; walking the center of camp and praying to the Great Spirit.

When he finally gave in to exhaustion and lay on his furs beside Moonflower, he slipped into a deep sleep that brought him a dream so clear in every detail, that he remembered it completely when he woke. He knew that it had not been an ordinary dream. He could see the shine of metal on shields that his warriors carried. He could see the cross emblazoned on them shining so brightly that it hurt his eyes.

What troubled him the most was that he could not see Growling Bear. He was not leading his warriors, but Father Bob in his simple black robe, rode ahead of them. In his hand he carried the cross blade, as he rode to battle against the Abalinah!

As they neared his tent, Chief Dark Wolf realized that they were not going to be left to talk over breakfast. Women of the camp were coming with huge pots of food they had hurried to prepare, urged by their men. A communal feast was being laid out before them. He was amazed when he learned that many of the men in camp had experienced the same dream and Sky Fire and Young Blood were among them.

"Father I don't think we are supposed to include people from other camps. I think we are to go and you are to lead us."

"No, you are wrong. God will lead us, under the banner of the cross. Our warriors must all be believers, baptized in Christ. Only if we follow His plan can we be victorious!"

Sky Fire stood and looked at the faces of the people gathered there.

"I am no longer a Chief, I am an old warrior, but I was given the dream. I believe that the Great Spirit will lead us. I will be baptized and I will ride to bring my son and daughter back!" The people cheered and applauded and danced, as one man after another declared that they had experienced the dream and they wanted to be in the group of warriors that went.

No fire burned but the people were gathered around the fire pit in their usual way as the morning progressed. The night guard expected to be relieved, of their duties at sun-up but when no one came to replace them, one by one they wandered into camp and asked permission to eat and stay at the strange celebration. None of them had slept, so none of them had dreamed. They were puzzled by all the talk of baptizing warriors.

*****

Two Feathers sat down with a plate of food beside Willow and Water Bug.

"Tell me what has happened," he said.

"Many of the seasoned warriors have all had the same dream. They believe that they were chosen by the Great Spirit to follow Father Bob into battle against the Abalinah. They believe they will be able to free the slaves that the Abalinah have taken from other camps. They took people from the Sentu and the Choyinaw, and maybe even from other camps that we don't know about. Father Bob says he will ride, led by the Great Spirit and that all the warriors that go, have to believe and be baptized."

"What is this baptized?"

"It is a washing in the water that takes away sin. It is a declaration that God, The Great Spirit, is in that person. It gives them the power to follow Him, as you have followed the Lion of Judah. Two Feathers you must do it and know in your heart that the Lion of Judah is a name for the Son of God. You must go. This is very important. I have felt a stirring inside my heart for two days and I didn't know what it was until now. This will be the start of our people, "The People of the Lion of Judah." The Great Spirit will be with you on this journey. Tell them that you will go."

Two Feathers leaned over to Father Bob and spoke quietly.

"Is it necessary to have the dream to be one of your warriors?"

"No, Two Feathers, but it is crucial that you believe in the Great Spirit and be baptized."

"I will go," he answered.

Father Bob smiled and praised God silently that something so good could come from such wickedness.

Father Bob baptized men, women and children in the lake, most of the afternoon and early evening.

There were very few left in the village, that did not profess their faith in God that day.

CHAPTER FIVE
IT IS LIKE HOLDING OUR BREATH

Chief Dark Wolf spoke often with Father Bob and joined his prayers with those of many others as the days of waiting stretched into the chilling cold nights of early winter.

The trackers, Flying Eagle, Night Hawk, and Young Blood had left the next day. They followed the Abalinah and were still gone.

Snow Star was eager for their return. She had been without Flying Eagle too much. She was sure she was pregnant again and wanted to tell him and have him near.

Father Bob was certain that the three men would be gone for several weeks. He decided to take some work horses and return to the S. and J. Ranch. He had thought when he was there that he would be able to return right away.

When I tell them all that is going on at the village, they will understand why I couldn't return sooner

As long as the ground doesn't freeze and stay that way, I should be able to pull a few stumps on the land. These big guys need to work. I hope they are still capable of working hard. They are rather fat. He looked back at the string of four work horses plodding along behind him and laughed out loud. I wonder if I could take back a load of lumber to expand the little church. I can leave these big fellows at the ranch and ride into the settlement to see if Tom can make it happen on such short notice.

He stopped midway to give the horses water and to let them rest, while he enjoyed a light lunch he had brought. I need to buy a strong wagon. It will be indispensable with the projects I have in mind.

As usual he was greeted at the river crossing. Johnny had been on the bluff as sentry. It is amazing how you always have a lookout and know that I am coming before I get here," he said in between hugs.

"Father we knew you were planning on working on the new land when we saw you bring the big work horses. We were wondering what had kept you though. Sarah has been fretting for days."

"Ben, it is so good to be back. I feel at home here. Sarah, you should not worry over the people of the village. Last week I baptized almost all the people in camp. They are safe in the palm of God's hand."

"That is wonderful Father. I wish I could have been there to see it."

"Much has gone on and the Blue Stone People will need the grace and protection of the Holy Spirit more now than ever before."

They walked along the path to Ben's house and Father Bob commented on the small field that contained white mares and foals.

"They are beautiful Ben. You and Jed have something wonderful and special here. It only could be accomplished under God's blessings."

"I agree. God has blessed everything that we have worked on from the building of our houses to the seeds in our gardens. We know that this ranch is His. We just work and live here."

As they filed onto the front porch, Father noticed the yellow and orange and rust colors still in the flower beds near the steps.

"Mary, how is it that you still are having flowers? It must have frosted here. It has at the camp of the people."

"Yes it has been cold at night. Those are straw flowers and I leave them in the beds until they begin to dry and then I cut them. They make pretty bouquets for winter. I will send some back with you and you can put them on the altar in your church."

"Thank you, I never thought of drying flowers. To tell the truth, I have never picked wild flowers and put them in there either. I should. It will be nice to see them when there is snow outside."

"That's good, and we have some other things we will send with you too that you can share as you see fit. Our garden produced so much food this year that we had trouble trying to keep up with it."

They all settled around the table. It seemed like that was always where people gathered, in Ben's or Jed's house. It was a warm and loving atmosphere that welcomed everyone. Mary started a big fresh pot of coffee and Josh slipped out just before dark to make sure they had an all clear at the lookout.

Jed's face appeared to be all business as they talked.

"Father Bob we have a lot to talk about. We followed the plan that we made that day, in my barn. We dug the caches out in the field. There is one on each side of the old horse. We sat for several nights, weaving the grass into strong sacks, and then we went down making sure we got there just before lunch and worked until the shadows covered the river. We stripped the top visible layer of gold from the water. First we did Sarah and David's land but then when you didn't come back in a few days; we went ahead and stripped yours because the river was getting pretty cold to work in. The visible gold went more than halfway across your land. There is probably a lot more, but our goal was simply to remove what might be spotted by a casual glance."

"I just had to make small signs. I couldn't stop myself," said Josh. "We knew that Father Pete was Irish, so, since we didn't know the horse's name I put "Pete's Shamrock" but I wanted to mark the spots where the gold is and I was playing with words and I decided that the gold from the church land should be "Chum" and ours is really God's so I wrote, "R.I.P. Goldie". I figure God always brings peace when we do what we should."

"Josh, I don't get it. Why did you put Chum?" Father Bob asked.

"Well, Chum means friend and you are our friend, but really it is a word I made by taking the first three letters of the word church and the first letter of money, so church money became Chum."

"That's amazing and a peaceful end for three good horses," said Father Bob laughing heartily. "Thanks to all of you, for your hard work weaving, digging, and picking rocks out of that freezing cold river."

Just then Lily slipped up into Father Bob's lap and with a big yawn; she placed her head against his chest and stuck her two middle fingers in her mouth.

"It looks like she is ready to go to bed. It is late," said Beth. She said Goodnight and took Lily home, but Johnny wanted to stay there with his father. He didn't want to miss anything. Soon Mary tucked Eli and Natty into bed, too. The house grew quiet as only the sound of the conversation at the table continued.

Sarah slid from the bench and pulled a willow chair up next to Father Bob.

"Father I am wondering why you said that The Blue Stone People will need God's protection more now than ever before. I won't be able to sleep tonight until I know what is going on."

"Well, Sarah, I don't know that you will sleep any better when I tell you. Did you meet the people from the Abalinah? No I'm sure you didn't. I'm glad you didn't, but maybe your spirit of discernment would have revealed their deception."

As Father Bob related the story as accurately as he could, he could see the shock in the faces of his friends. I think I should have saved all this until tomorrow. I wish I had. I want to assure all of you that God has the situation under His control and it is going to be alright. He brought the Israelites out of Egypt and although I am not Moses, he will lead the Blue Stone Warriors to the camp of the Abalinah and we will free the slaves."

"David and I are going to go with you. You can't do this alone!" said Sarah, almost in tears.

"You can't, Sarah. You weren't in the dream. I feel in my heart that it is required that we follow every step that we saw in the dreams. The only thing that has me puzzled is how to make the shields with the cross on them. They have to be strong, light weight and very shiny."

"You should ask Matt at the blacksmith shop. He will know," said David. "He is a very good man, and he will help if he can."

"Yes, I agree. I liked him right away. He put shoes on all six of my animals."

"Father, how soon will you and the Blue Stone warriors leave? It will be winter before long. You say their camp is north? You could find yourselves trudging through deep snow. That's a problem that Moses never had to face."

"I don't know for sure David. I know we have to get the shields made and then wait for our trackers to report back.

We need to know how big their camp is and how many warriors we will be facing."

"I feel strongly that I should go with you," said Ben. You will need all the men you can get. No Ben, I would like your company tomorrow when I go to the settlement, but I know that I must just take the few warriors that the men saw in their dreams. The Holy Spirit will fight this battle, not men. We don't want to get in His way. It will be His victory not ours."

"You can't stop us from praying for all of you," said Sarah.

"I cherish you and your prayers Sarah. Until this thing is over I will treasure the thought that believers are praying for us."

"It is very hard to focus on other things that need doing. It is like a huge cloud in front of my face. Everyone in camp feels the same. It is as if we are holding our breath."

Josh had not spoken for a while, but he had been listening to every word.

"Father I tied the big work horses on long leads along the river so they can reach the grass and water. I put Macho in the field where he used to be a lot. He looked comfortable there. I brought your pack in. You didn't bring much. Your water bags are down by the crossing."

"Josh, you are such a helpful young man. I appreciate all the things you do for me when I am here."

"That's fine, I wanted to do it. Do you think I could ride along with you to the settlement in the morning? I haven't been there in quite a while. Dad is it alright if I go with you in the morning?"

"Sure Josh you can go. Are you going to take some more of your carvings to the store?"

"No, I don't think so. I just want to look around and see what has changed and spend the day with you. I have never been to Tom's lumber mill. I would like to see it."

"We will enjoy your company Josh," Said Father Bob. "Maybe next time Johnny can ride along. I know I can't take all the good help away at once."

Mary came out of the bedroom with her arms full of blankets.

"That's for sure Father Bob. Johnny will have to help more with Ben and Josh gone. Josh if you don't mind, I think you can make yourself comfortable here on the bear rug with Rascal. I made up your bed for Father Bob."

"Sure, that's fine Mom. He went over and patted Rascal and told him to move over.

"This is the quilt that Dad had up in the tree his first night here. Grandmother Slater made it. I remember that story every time I see it."

Ben's face showed that he remembered it, too. His smile was for his son, but it was touched with the sad recollection.

Father Bob stood and stretched.

"I heard you say that there is a bed waiting for me. I think I am ready for it."

Jed said that he and Johnny would head home and that Ben could relax and know that all the chores would be done while he and Josh were gone.

"You might want to take the wagon in, loaded with some more of the garden produce from my barn and on the way back you could stop and cut some wood from those old cherry trees near the crossing of the Silver. We would be glad to have it for carving this winter."

"Jed, that's a good idea. Father, do you mind waiting a few minutes in the morning while I get the wagon ready and hitch Sundown to it?"

"Of course not, but do you think there might be enough cherries left on those old trees for a pie?" It has been years since I had cherry pie. When he mentioned that, it made my mouth water. I am going to remember to take my gathering bag in the morning, just in case. Goodnight and God bless you."

Goodnight Father Bob, we are glad that you came back. I need to be sure to take the hatchet and the hand saw," Ben said to no one in particular. He was planning his coming morning.

Mary was also planning her morning. She would make dried cherry pies while the men were gone.

*****

Silverville was bustling when they arrived in front of the trading post. The boat had just delivered its small bundle of mail and a few treasured packages for folks and was heading back up the Silver when they arrived.

Josh rode Little Mouse down the trail past the four fingers of the Silver so that he could get a good look at the boat before it had labored its way up-river and out of sight.

Father Bob was amazed to find out that he could now mail a letter. Ben hadn't thought to mention that mail service was now available. His letter going back to his family had been mailed nearly two months earlier. He wondered how much longer the boat would be able to come before the weather made the trip impossible until spring. He hoped he wouldn't have to wait that long.

Sam was glad to take all the produce in the wagon but was disappointed when they said they had not had time to do any carving. He had no trouble selling the things that they made.

Father Bob bought a tablet, two pencils and some envelopes and a nice writing pen and some ink. He was glad that there was mail service here and he would write a letter to his family and one to the bishop at the seminary.

The small wagon was stashed behind Sam's store and after they had spent the very chilly night, bundled in their small tent, they got up early and Father Bob said he was looking forward to visiting the little Café that Cookie had open on weekends. He spotted the sign that read Steak and Spirits, but it was dark inside.

"I wonder what day this is."

"It's Friday, said a man that walked by, tipping his hat to the priest.

"I guess we came on the wrong day. It is a shame. We would have enjoyed eating there. We may as well head out to the mill."

Ben reached in his saddlebag and pulled out several big pieces of jerky and handed one to Father Bob and his son and held one in his teeth while he put the sack containing the rest away.

"This ought to hold us for a while," he said.

"That's got a nice flavor to it. What did you put on it?" Father Bob asked.

"The women experiment and it is a little different each time, but I can tell it has pepper and salt and something else."

"It's good."

"I see Tom coming our way. He has quite a large load on that wagon. I thought by now the weather would slow his work. Who would be building this time of year?" The priest commented.

"Hi, Tom, we were on our way to the mill to talk to you."

"Well hello, to all of you. Father I didn't think you would be back here this soon. Zack go ahead and take um on down to the fort. The soldiers will unload it," he said as he climbed down from the big freight wagon.

"Sure Tom; Hi Ben, and Josh, look at you. I didn't recognize you. You have gotten tall!" Wish things weren't so busy; I would bring my family to visit."

"We understand Zack. We have been well occupied, too. Tell Rachel and Margaret that we said Hello, when you go home tonight."

"I will. It was nice seeing you." He snapped the reins and clacked his tongue and the big work horses shouldered into the harness and the load of lumber was on its way.

Ben slid off Sundown and walked beside Tom. Soon Father Bob and Josh had done the same. The walk to the mill was further than Josh thought it would be. They chatted and Father Bob explained that he needed lumber to build a church, but he also needed to buy or use a big wagon.

"Father, I have several wagons, but sometimes I need all of them. You might talk to some of the new settlers that have built houses. They might part with their covered wagons and you could modify it to work for you."

"That's a good idea. If I can get a wagon, how long would it take you to get a load ready, like the one we just saw? I have a team of four big work horses at Ben's ranch. They are doing nothing but eating him out of every blade of grass in sight."

Tom laughed at that remark and rubbed his chin while he thought about it.

"If you can get a wagon and the rigging, I can get you a load by mid-week."

"That's great. Is the price still what we discussed? Yes it hasn't changed."

"Tom I will let you know as soon as I find a wagon."

"That's fine Father, but you better pray hard that it doesn't snow until you get that lumber where you are taking it. Horses can't pull a load on the prairie through snow drifts."

"That's good advice, thank you Tom. I'll be seeing you soon."

Just then a bell clanged and men walked by heading for a large cooking fire in the center of the lumber camp.

"Have you men eaten yet?"

"No as a matter of fact we haven't. We stopped at the Café but it was closed."

"That's Cookie's place. He opens on the weekends. Come eat," said Tom.

"Cookie, it is good to see you again."

"Father Bob, hello, you want steak and beans? No fried potatoes until tomorrow."

"That would be wonderful, Cookie." He smiled broadly while handing plates to each man that came near.

"This man needs lots of food. He is tall but thin as blade of grass. Come you have more beans." He piled extra beans on the plate that he handed Josh.

"Dad, I don't know if I can eat so much."

"Thank you, Cookie," said Ben laughing.

Finally the loud singing of the saws in the building had stopped and several more men came out near the fire to be fed.

When they had finished eating, Tom invited Josh into the building to see the powerful saw blades slice through the logs. The bark had already been stripped and as they watched, the tree became large planks for someone's new building.

"That was exciting! I am so glad you let me see that." Tom pointed to two men on the edge of the clearing. The tree they were working on started to shiver and tremble as they shouted "Timber!" It snapped and cracked loudly, then, whoosh, it landed in rolling clouds of debris, of broken branches and dust. "All the work you do here is so noisy!" With the saws running again, Josh had to shout to be heard.

"You get used to the noise after you are here a while."

As they rode back into the main part of the settlement, Father Bob kept his eyes open for a wagon. Finally he turned Macho down Second Street and found a house that appeared nearly finished. The people were still using their wagon to store things, but after a bit of haggling, Father Bob had bought the wagon and all the tack for his team. They were happy. They had money for some much needed supplies and materials to finish their house before the coldest part of winter.

"God is so good. He supplies all our needs. I knew I would find a wagon ready for me. I just had to look for it. Now I need to talk to the blacksmith. While I do that, Josh, would you do me a big favor?"

"Sure anything Father."

"Would you tell Tom that I will take that load of lumber and that I have bought a wagon?"

Josh was pleased to be trusted to deliver the message. He rode back the way they had come, grinning all the way. This was more fun activity than he saw in a month at the ranch. He was having a good time.

Matt was pleased to see them when they stopped at his shop. At first He was puzzled by Father Bob's first project.

"I have never tried to make a shield and you want it to shine brightly?"

"Yes and it has to have a large cross on it."

"Matt, I will need more than one. I need thirty."

"What? That sounds impossible. Let me think about it for a few days. When are you coming back?"

"I will be returning to the church mid-week. I will stop and see you before I leave the settlement, but that's not all I need. I have purchased a covered wagon from the folks building the new house down at the end of Second Street. Could you pick it up and modify it so I can use it to take a large load of lumber to my church when I go. I have a team of four big work horses, and I also bought the tack from them to use with it. Please check that and make sure it is in good working condition."

"Do you really think I can do all that by the middle of next week? You must think I can work miracles," said Matt.

"No but I know someone who does," said Father Bob as he pointed up. They laughed together at that and then Matt said he would go get the wagon right away and think about the shields while he was working.

"It is always good to have a challenge," he said. "Father, are you doing a play about the Holy wars?"

"No Matt. I need these to be real shields that can stop an arrow or bullet."

He shook his head in bewilderment.

Josh had joined them and they prepared to leave for home when he reminded Ben that he should get some candy for the children.

"They will be disappointed if you forget."

"You are right. Take this money and spend it on a couple of different flavors. It will be nice to have it in the house when the snow is blowing."

"Thanks Dad."

"While you are doing that, I will go hook our wagon to Sundown."

As they traveled down the trail next to the Silver, Ben felt bad that they really didn't have the time to stop and visit along the way. He didn't want to seem unfriendly.

It was dusk when they crossed the Silver. They camped on the home side and in the morning, they cut down an old cherry tree for its soft carving wood. The twisted old branches no longer gave fruit, but they would be used for something beautiful. Its wood filled the wagon to overflowing.

CHAPTER SIX
NO SENTRY

By mid-day Father Bob seemed very tense as they traveled across the prairie at an angle, skirting the mud bog and seeing the peaceful field of cattle on Mary's land, from a distance.

"Ben I have a bad feeling. Something is wrong. We had a productive trip and the people were all very nice in Silverville. I can't discern what is bothering me. I hope I'm wrong, but I think we should hurry."

Suddenly, Ben could feel it, too.

"Father, will you let me take Macho? You and Josh can bring the wagon."

They switched places and Ben rode away quickly on Macho.

As he neared the crossing at the oak tree, he knew immediately that he was right. There was no one at the river to meet him. He splashed through the Hickory and stopped on the path to look right to Jed's and then left. He saw two horses in front of Sarah's house.

Something has happened, he thought. Macho was tired from his fast run when Ben led him to the rail and tied him. He burst through Sarah's door without knocking and found his whole family there.

"Ben! I am glad you are back. We have had a little accident," said Sarah in a soothing tone, as she continued to wrap Adam's arm.

"What happened?"

"I fell, Dad. I fell when I was coming down from the lookout. Aunt Sarah says I broke my arm. My side hurts too." He was being brave and fighting back his tears. "Aunt

Sarah put a patch on my side but it still hurts something awful."

Ben put his arm around the boy's shoulders. He had tears on his face.

"I am so sorry Adam." He kissed the boy's forehead and wiped away his tears with his thumbs while he told him that Aunt Sarah has special medicine. "You will feel better very soon."

"He caught his arm in the rocks when he fell. He has some bad scrapes on his ribs but they aren't broken. He will feel much better in a few days and his arm will be like new before Christmas."

"Christmas, that's a long time, Aunt Sarah."

Jed had gone to help Father Bob cross the Hickory with the big raft, and when they arrived at Sarah's he pulled Father Bob's saddle from macho's back and turned him loose in the field where he had water and lots of grass.

As Macho drank, Jed rubbed him down with a burlap sack until he was cool and comfortable.

Beth came from Mary's walking along the path with Lily and Eli holding hands as she carried Natty.

"Jed is Adam going to be alright?"

"Yes but he has a broken arm and some very sore ribs. Here let me take Natty. He is getting so big." They entered Sarah's house together with Father Bob. Josh had taken Little Mouse and Sundown to Ben's corral and made sure they had all the attention they needed. He filled the water hole and on impulse he swung up on Ginger, riding her bareback without even a set of reins. She followed the path and stopped by the other horses in front of Sarah's.

"You are such a good old girl. We all love you, Ginger," he said as he opened the gate and let her enter the field.

Josh stepped inside Sarah's door just as Ben lifted Adam down from Sarah's table.

"Thank you Sarah for helping him. It is so nice to have our own healer on the ranch," said Ben.

Father Bob placed his hand on Adam's head and prayed.

"Father God, we are grateful that Adam is healing. We know that you protected him when he fell. Thank you for always being here for us and thank you for giving Sarah the skill and knowledge to be able to help. Amen"

"Amen," said everyone present.

"Ben, I think this young man was too excited coming down from the lookout, because he could smell what you have in your saddlebag."

"Father, I am sure you are right." Adam smiled in spite of his injuries.

"Dad I rode Ginger here, I will take her and get the sack for you if you want."

"That's good, son, she needs the exercise. Just go slow." Josh laughed as he answered.

"Dad, you know that is her only speed now, very slow."

Adam enjoyed his treat when it finally arrived, holding it with his left hand. His right one was cradled in a sling.

Later when Mary had tucked him into his bed for the night, she sat near the window in her rocker and she found that there were tears in her eyes. Lord I am so grateful that my son will get well. I have always felt concern when he went up on the bluff. Thank you for protecting his head and back. He is a precious boy and very smart, but a dreamer. Sometimes he is doing one thing and thinking about something else. Please help him to focus on what he is doing so he doesn't ever get injured again. Then she remembered how she had worried about him falling, the first time she had seen him lying on Sandy's back.

Now that horse comes across the field and stands against the fence so that he can climb up and get on her back. I know that I need to trust you. You are in control. She was glad that Ben had not seen her tears. She tried to always be strong. With four sons, she had to be, but sometimes it was very hard.

Father Bob spent the next few days getting used to working with the big horses. Jed went down with him and together they had managed to cut and pull several of the huge trees to the side of his property.

When he became aware of the big oaks and maples in the center of the land, he said he didn't have the heart to cut them down.

"Jed, now that I have a better knowledge of the layout of this land; I will go back and give it some serious thought, and draw a plan for the buildings. Maybe I can figure out a way to build and still preserve most of these wonderful old trees."

"Don't you want to take a couple days to rest before you take these horses to town for the lumber? We have been working them hard and they will have to work even harder, pulling that load all the way back to your church."

"Yes Jed, you are right but I just got an idea. If you shot into one of these hard wood trees, How far do you think the bullet would go?"

"I'm not sure, but we can experiment at the ranch if you want to. Are you thinking about making the shields of wood?"

"No, but I think we should line them with wood. I am eager to talk to Matt again. I know my idea will work!"

"What are you saying?"

"The shields, Jed, we need to line them with wood. I am sure that by now he has figured out what to use for the outer layer. I am so eager to see one made, that I don't know if I can wait until Tuesday."

They returned to the ranch and Father Bob patted the big horses as if they were favored new foals. He loved that they were so strong and willing to work hard under his inexperienced direction.

When he left for Silverville, it was early Tuesday morning. The family had gathered to wish him well.

"If this goes the way I hope, I won't be able to stop back here on my way home. I will go down the Silver and use the wagon crossing and stay on the wagon trail. I think it will be a better route. Please pray that the weather holds, and thank you again, for the wonderful meals, especially the cherry pie, Mary and soft bed, Josh and the fellowship. This ranch is so wonderful. It feels like it embraces me when I come. It will probably be spring before I can come again. Adam you will be all healed by then and I am guessing that you will be the one that sees me coming. You are a good lookout. Just always look where you are going to step. Goodbye, everyone," he said.

They all said goodbye and waved from the crossing near the oak tree as he rode away on Macho, leading his string of work horses.

*****

Matt had done an excellent job of converting the covered wagon to a freight wagon. He had Liz help him and together they had folded the big canvas top and he had lashed it to the seat to form a thick pad. He removed boards at the back of the wagon that curved up and replaced them with flat ones and made sure the entire wagon was strong. The leather tack had all been oiled and checked. It was ready for the team.

Father Bob was impressed but more excited about the shield that he saw leaning against the wall. Matt had used half of a steel drum and shaped it with heat and his hammer. He had lined it with hardwood and attached a wide leather strap on the back with bolts, to provide a way to hold it. The bottom of the shield would rest on their saddle. He had created a gentle curve that would follow the shape of the saddle. The top edge was straight across, and it had a wide slit for the warrior to look through. Matt had buffed the steel to a high gloss and then painted a tall white cross in the middle. The whole shield had a high gloss from a coat of varnish that had been further polished with paste wax.

Father Bob stood looking at the shield. It was identical to the ones that Chief Dark Wolf had described.

"It's heavy," said Matt. "I hope your thirty men are strong."

"They are and the shields can be transported separately until they near the battle so their mounts are not overburdened. Matt you have been inspired by the Holy Spirit."

"I don't know about that. I just used what I found available. Sam had lots of these drums behind his store. He gets supplies in them. He was supposed to send them back on the boat when it went but he forgot to. He sold them all to me. They are out back."

"How many can you make?"

"Each shield takes half of a drum and he had fifteen. That is just right to make thirty shields."

"I'm glad that he was forgetful," said Father Bob. He attempted to pick up the shield from the side with just one hand and found that it took a concerted effort with both hands. "This is heavy!"

"It will do what you need it to. I tested the steel and wood together and it will stop a bullet or arrow. Anything lighter might not."

"How soon can I get them?"

"That is a good question. They take a lot of time and hard work and I am going to have to charge you for the barrels that I bought from Sam. I will have to get some more oak from Tom.

"Just say when I can get them, and how much."

"Father what are they for? Why do you need them?"

At that moment Liz entered the shop bringing Matt a sandwich and some coffee.

"Hello Father, I will go back and make you a sandwich and bring out the coffee pot. Are you pleased with the wagon?"

"Yes, I certainly am. Matt did a fine job on it."

She darted back with another sandwich and more coffee and then left again explaining that she didn't want to leave her children for more than a moment.

Matt and Father Bob sat on bales of hay along the wall and ate their meal while he told the story of the Abalinah and what they had done.

"That's nearly unbelievable. I can see why you and the Blue Stone warriors feel you must fight them, but why are you taking just thirty shields?

"I won't wear one and there will only be thirty warriors with me. God will lead this army. He has lain on my heart that he wants only thirty. The whole confrontation will probably be very short. I believe that we will not lose one man."

"It is amazing that so many had the exact same dream on the same night." Matt was trying to wrap his mind around the whole situation when he suddenly blurted out that he would make the shields for nothing. "Just pay for the supplies. I have little to do in the winter. I will try to get them all done by early spring. That's when the kings in the Old Testament would go to war."

"Yes, you are right. Thank you Matthew, for being willing to work so hard for us, that will be perfect. I will come for them with the first greening of the grass. Now let's see if these big fellows know how to pull a wagon." The work horses had been tied near the Hickory and they had done a good job of cropping the grass there. They all seemed to know they would soon be working because they drank and ate like they were storing up energy.

Matt gave him a few instructions on the use of the reins and the brake and with Macho on a long lead he headed the team to the lumber mill.

Tom did not disappoint him. He had plenty of lumber cut to fill the wagon. His men loaded it while they talked about getting some windows and doors and a load of wood shingles for roofing. The load was tied on tightly before Father Bob slowly pulled away, gently coaxing the team to pull the full wagon. He breathed a sigh and was able to relax a little after he had maneuvered the turn from Main Street onto the trail as he headed up the Silver. He worried about the crossing until he saw Tom and three of his men riding along behind him. They followed, stopped with him and took a break and then followed again until they had seen him safely across the Silver.

Tom had taken the reins when it was time for the team to enter the water at the crossing and his harsh whistle and crack of the whip in the air above the horses brought a sudden response from them that surprised Father Bob. Their powerful muscles took the wagon across without incident.

"Tom I am so grateful to you and your crew. I am a novice at all this."

"You are doing fine. I respect what you are doing for The Blue Stone People and I hope that you can accomplish what you have planned Father. We are going to head back to the mill now. Just remember to give these big guys some time to rest now and then and give them a drink from the barrels on the side. The nails are secured there, too.

If it starts to rain or turns to snow, you better keep moving until you reach your destination. They can't get the traction they need in snow if it gets deep."

"Thank you for everything Tom." He waved at the men that had come with Tom and one of them was making a circle with his hand and pointing at the wagon wheels. He is reminding me to put the grease on the axles near and in the wheels. He picked up the big grease pot and brush from beneath the seat and held it out so the man could see that he understood. Father Bob waved until they had all turned and were riding away, back toward the settlement.

"Father God, you have blessed me with so many good friends in this settlement. Thank you for the help you provided all along the way. I would have been stuck in the river. I wouldn't have known that these horses could pull like that or how to ask them to do it. That was amazing. All your creation is marvelous."

As the wagon rocked back and forth uncomfortably on the bumpy trail; he knew that each turn of the big wheels were taking him closer to the camp of the people. I can't take this wagon through the big rock path. I'm not sure what I will do when I get there.

The guards had spotted him coming and he was met by an astounding number of men, all willing to hand carry the cut lumber to the church. He instructed them to stack it neatly inside. He wanted to protect the wood during the winter weather. They did an incredible job.

Once the wagon was completely unloaded, Growling Bear stepped forward and told Father Bob that he had been working with Cat Claw and Pine Berry and they had removed bushes and even some trees where needed.

"If you go slowly, you will be able to take the wagon to the sheep hill behind the church by going through the trees beside the bluff.

The path had not ever been used for anything bigger than a saddle horse, and Growling Bear's efforts were just enough to allow the empty wagon to scrape through in several places, but with the many enthusiastic hands helping, he was finally back home. He thanked the men over and over.

When he had a chance to look around, he noticed that everyone had been working very hard while he was gone. Drying racks once again lined the village side of the lake and half of the cattle were missing from the field. It was then that he noticed that a new section of fence held the remaining cattle and a channel had been dug to form a small pond for them.

Hides were pegged out and being worked.

Chief Dark Wolf greeted him warmly and said that the hides were going to be used to expand the big tent.

"That's good," said Father Bob. "I want to use it for church this winter. This small church that I built is nearly full of lumber. The men brought it all in and stacked it neatly. I am planning to use it to build a bigger building in the spring when the weather permits."

Chief Dark Wolf looked in the doorway of the church in amazement.

"The wood is so straight and smooth. I would like to see how this is done."

"I have seen it." They chatted about the work at the lumber mill as they walked the path to the Chief's tent. Moonflower had a snack ready and some tea which she served and then quickly left. She was aware that they would soon be discussing the serious possibility of war with the Abalinah.

"Have the three men that left to follow the tracks of the Abalinah returned? Have you had any word from them?"

"No; I am very worried. They have been gone so long. I hope they have not been discovered. Of course we have no way of knowing how far they had to travel. Two Feathers told me that the warriors that took the Chief of the Sentu rode west of his camp for a way before stopping. I think that might be a clue to the direction of their camp."

"I don't know, but after Night Hawk and Two Feathers got acquainted, they came to me and said that Night Hawk had made an error. It was the camp of the Sentu that he had found when he rode out alone. He had no way of knowing, but when Two Feathers described the little stream near the woods and the shelter he had built on the edge of the trees, Night Hawk was certain that was the camp he had seen."

"It is shocking to me that six people could live with us for over a year and conceal such a staggering deception."

"Have the people continued to pray while I have been gone?"

"Yes, Willow and Sweet Grass have prayed with the people every day. They are praying for the safety of the slaves and for the protection of our camp and the men that will be chosen to fight for them. Willow reminded Moonflower that one of the women taken from the Sentu camp was her cousin and the other was Water Bug's mother."

"I'm sure she has strong feelings about giving the boy back to his real mother after caring for him so long," said Father Bob.

"Somehow if we are blessed to find them and get them back, I'm sure that everyone will be glad to help them adjust, but I can see that our success will be a painful problem for Willow and Two Feathers."

"Chief Dark Wolf, do you remember the men talking about seeing very shiny shields in their dreams? I took the challenge of making the shields, to the blacksmith in Silverville. I described them and told him they have to stop a bullet or an arrow. I drew it in the dirt of the shop floor, the way you did the drawing of the camp when you started the night guard. He has made one already. It is quite heavy. The outside of it shines brightly, like silver jewelry and he painted a tall white cross on it. I think we will have to take extra horses to carry them until we are close. He says he will work on them all winter. He is only charging us for the supplies to make them.

When I told him the reason we need them, he was stunned. He will have them for us to pick up at the first greening in the spring. He is a good Christian. He considers it sacred work."

"Father, I think it is inspired work, because some of our men have had the dream more than once. It is always the same to the smallest detail. They are eager to go. I think that is good but we must be patient and wait until spring. I don't want our warriors heading north in the winter."

"This thing weighs heavily on me. I will be glad when it is over," said Father Bob.

"All of us will be. We are all glad that you are back safely. We feel that our camp is incomplete when you are gone."

"That is nice to hear. I always feel that I am going home when I head back." He stood and stretched thinking he still had work to do before he could relax in his little room at the back of his church.

"When the meat is totally dry I will have someone bring enough to fill the church cache."

It was then that Father Bob finally realized that he was respected and held in high regard by the people. He felt humbled.

*****

In the morning, Spotted Fawn and Blue Stone had noticed the priest struggling to spread the huge white canvas near the back of the church. They were puzzled but walked over and offered their assistance.

"Father, do you need help? What are you trying to do?"

"Well I thought that if I greased this canvas, and then spread it over my wagon and tied it on really well, that it would protect it from the damage of winter."

"It looks big enough to cover it." Blue Stone took the pan of grease to the center of the canvas and began to smear the grease on generously. Spotted Fawn had gone back to her tent and returned with a similar supply. She started to copy Blue Stone.

Soon the entire canvas was well coated. The nearby Shepherds joined their hands to the effort and helped to lift it and before long the wagon was concealed in greasy canvas that was tied securely in place.

"Thank you, good job, God bless you," said Father Bob, laughing and a chorus of four voices, said it back to him, followed by laughter as they each went to the edge of the lake to scoop sand and water on their hands until they had rid themselves of the grease. Then each went back to what they had been doing earlier. Now that they understood the language, they appreciated his words and it was a fun way to part.

The village was covered with a dusting of snow during the night and the women were glad that their caches were full of good dried beef. The hides had been dragged in the big tent. They were stiff from the cold but softened in the warm tent interior.

The horses stood clustered together in the morning sun.

*****

"We didn't build them a shelter, but it isn't too late," said Growling Bear. We all need something to do while we wait for the scouts to return."

They took the idea to the Chief and with his enthusiastic approval they started building immediately. Standing Bear suggested that they make it a roof with just two walls and poles the rest of the way. We can put the walls to the west and north where the storms come from. The men now appreciated the big work horses and used them to pull the downed trees to the meadow gate where they were able to drag them to the far corner of the meadow. One group of men were splitting the logs while others cut more or cleaned them so they were ready for use.

In the next few days a long shelter appeared running parallel to the north fence. The morning sun shone in and warmed the horses.

As soon as the men quit pounding nails and left the field, the horses strolled over one by one. They were grateful for the shelter and windbreak.

The celebration for the building of the shelter was held in the big tent as the first real snow of winter came down creating a thick layer on the ground. The people sang songs and the Chief spoke of the cooperation of his men's efforts, but he could feel the heavy hearts of his people. They longed to see the three missing men.

"This is a good thing," said Chief Dark Wolf, praising his men's work. "The games have taught you all how to work together to achieve something good. I am proud of you. Now our animals can get out of the snow and harsh winter winds."

"The way you have built it, the summer winds will cool it and the roof will offer shade." Standing Bear was proud of his design. The people thought it was a good one.

"When our scouts return, I know you will all be feeling more like rejoicing," said the Chief, but we will also be happy when we have enough big hides to increase the size of this tent next summer. We are all in here, but it is a little too cozy," he said laughing.

Father Bob knew this celebration was to distract the people from worrying. It was a hard thing to do since most of them had heard that the bluff held no more of the blue stones, so necessary for the people to flourish.

Father Bob stood and the many conversations, buzzing around him, quieted.

"I just wanted to say that I am glad that so many men in our camp are willing to work hard for the good of the people and their horses. I have much to learn about the horses, but when I went to the blacksmith in Silverville to have the metal shoes put on my animals, I learned that they need the same things we do. They need food, water and shelter. He told me that if a horse has worked, carrying on his back beyond his prime, he may develop a painful sickness in his back. He said the one thing we can do for him to ease his discomfort is to offer shelter from the extreme cold. This is a kindness you have done for the herd. I am proud of the men that worked on the horse shelter."

"Many of the men in this camp met me as I returned. They greeted me and helped me to bring the mill cut lumber to the church to protect it from the winter weather. In the spring, I plan to add on to the church so more of our people will be able to fit in there comfortably." The people cheered and applauded.

"I know that you all are wondering what will happen in the spring, and so am I. I am thinking that winter is long and it conceals the mystery of when our trackers will return. What news will they bring? We do not know. One thing we do know is that "John 14:27 NIV" tells us this. "Peace I leave with you; my peace I give you. I do not give to you as the world gives. Do not let your hearts be troubled, and do not be afraid."

"Know that they are on a mission for God and they will return and by the power of God, we will succeed!"

CHAPTER SEVEN
PRINTS IN THE SNOW

Young Blood stood over his wounded traveling companion wondering if they would ever make it back to the camp of the Blue Stone People alive.

They had traveled north through the hunting territory of the Sentu. The camp was devastated just as Two Feathers had described it. The tracks of the six people they followed had continued on, riding beside the little stream as it grew wider. They expected them to turn west but they hadn't. Many days had dawned and dark had come sooner as the season grew colder, but still they traveled.

The water of the stream became hot and their horses backed away from it. It is not good here. The mountain has brought fire into the trees and the ground has been made unstable. It is unsafe here.

Those they followed had decided it was best to skirt the mountain and their trail led them through the heart of the burned trees and the ash was stirred by the horse's hooves. As the day warmed the melted snow became black mud.

When the snow fell, it was welcomed by the fleeing Abalinah as well as those that tracked them. The snow was the only useable water they had seen since they entered the burned area. It was difficult to gather, with a layer of ash beneath it.

The three men kept their fire low as they melted the snow to refresh their horses and fill their water bags. Night Hawk's softened meat as the water heated for the men. They needed a warm meal as they camped for the night.

"I think tomorrow we will be out of this black area and we may find that they have finally led us to their camp," said Flying Eagle.

"I hope you are right. It puzzles me. How did they learn about our people and the blue stones, when they live so far north," said Night Hawk?

"I am not comfortable here. I fear they may discover that we follow. We should leave a greater distance between them and us. It is not our goal to overtake them. We need only to find their camp and get information for our Chief."

Young Blood was very concerned. He had seen firsthand the vicious ways of the Abalinah. He felt he and his little family had been spared only because they were being used as leverage against Chief Sky Fire, his father. They all knew that discovery meant that they would fail in their mission. It could also mean death or being forced into slavery.

The next morning the sun warmed their faces when the trail they followed turned east and a foggy layer floated above a beautiful still lake. A horse whinnied in the distance causing them to abruptly stop. To the left of the trail in the sand and gravel, loomed huge rocks and a tall gray formation that signaled the start of a large mountain range in the distance.

"I think we should wait until we can see. This fog makes it impossible to know how far ahead they are," said Flying Eagle.

It was at that very moment that an arrow hit Night Hawk in his chest, sailing through his coat, shirt and sticking out below his shoulder blade. His companions swiftly carried him into the rocks seeking cover.

"Well, someone knows we are here," whispered Young Blood, "And that arrow is coated with something. We need to clean the wound immediately, or he will die." Without a discussion; he clamped his left hand over Night Hawk's mouth, while he forced the arrow farther through with his right hand.

"You can cut the tip off of it with your knife while I hold it steady, but don't pull it out yet. I need to find an icicle!"

He found one hanging from a snow covered rock.

"I needed one that was long enough to go all the way through." Cautiously the arrow was pushed forward as the ice was introduced into the wound and forced to follow the channel that the arrow left.

"I'm hoping that the ice will slow the blood from taking in the poison and as it melts maybe it will dilute it and wash the poison out."

"Where did you learn to do that?" Night Hawk asked as he struggled to keep from crying out. The pain was excruciating!

"Don't move. Rest now, we can't go out there until we can see anyway."

Young Blood darted out again and disappeared into the dense fog. He was gone a long time and the two men left behind the rock were worried.

"He just told us to stay here until we can see and then he leaves. Where do you think he went?"

"I don't know but if he doesn't come back soon we need to get out of here. For all we know, when the fog lifts we could be surrounded."

"This is hurting like all fury! I think the ice was keeping the pain down but it is melted now. I am lying in a puddle of mixed blood and water."

"I hear footsteps, Night Hawk, be quiet."

"It's me. I found a willow tree on the edge of the lake and got some bark. I couldn't see anyone out there. I don't know where that arrow came from." Quietly he crushed the bark between two stones and added a handful of snow. "This isn't as good as a cooked poultice but it will have to do. We can't make a fire." He packed large handfuls on both the entry and exit wounds. One on Night Hawk's chest and the other was on his back and then with his rope he bound Night Hawks shirt tightly to his body to keep them in place. "I wish I had something soft to wrap around as a bandage, but that's all we have right now."

"Young Blood, I am grateful. If you had not known what to do, I would be dead by now. Keep that arrow. I want to show the people back in camp."

"I will put the end with the feathers in your saddlebag, but the tip with the poison is not safe to carry. I tossed it in the bushes."

As the day warmed a bit, the fog lifted and the full beauty of the large lake was revealed. Unfortunately it also showed that the people they were following had ridden on in the edge of the water leaving no further trail to follow.

"What should we do? We can't give up and we can't just blunder on until we stumble into their camp."

"Well, I think they are smart enough to have discovered that we were following, but while we were hiding, they were riding. We can pick up the trail again. They can't stay in the water forever."

"You are right Night Hawk, but maybe you should stay here hidden and we will go on. We will come back and take you with us when we go back to our camp."

"No Flying Eagle, I don't want to stay behind. I can ride." He gritted his teeth and swung up on his horse.

They headed out cautiously staying close to the scrub brush and trees that lined the lake. All of them kept their eyes on the edge of the lake trying to find the place where the riders had left the water. They were on the backside of the lake before they spotted a strip of disturbed sand and then another.

"This has to be where they came out," said Young Blood. They could see a partially concealed small trail leading into the trees. They slid from their horses silently and tied them behind some bushes. It wasn't until then that Flying Eagle and Young Blood realized that Night Hawk was very ill.

"It's the poison in his blood. I can't help him. We need to hide him in the bushes and let him rest," said Young Blood in a harsh whisper. "He is burning up. I am going to soak his clothes. That's all we can do for him right now." He poured the contents of his water bag onto Night Hawks chest and legs. "That will help him fight the fever. Let's go."

When the trail broke from the trees, they saw that it led to the edge of a large herd of horses being guarded by two riders. Beyond the herd, they could see a walled in village. The wall was higher than a man's reach and appeared very thick and strong. It was surrounded by open grass land.

"This looks impenetrable," said Flying Eagle. "It is worse than I thought. There is no way that our warriors can get in there."

"Let's go back and stay with Night Hawk until dark. Then maybe, in the dark, we can find where they go in and take a look at the inside and how it is built. We need to know how many warriors live in there. It looks huge from here. They have deliberately built it in a way to create that impression."

When they crept back to the spot where they had left Night Hawk, they found that he was sitting up against a tree. He had untied the rope and managed to pull off his shirt.

"Night Hawk, how are you feeling?" Young Blood could tell that the fever had come down some, but Night Hawk was covered with blisters. He was scratching wherever he could reach.

"I'm miserable! I itch from head to toe and these blisters are everywhere."

"Maybe if you sit in the lake it will give you relief."

"I am willing to try anything!"

They led their horses to the water and filled their water bags with the fresh water while Night Hawk eased slowly into the very cold water. He sat there until his teeth were chattering. The blisters seemed less irritating and a few appeared to have gotten smaller.

"You have strong blood. Your body is fighting the poison and I think you will be much better in the morning."

Young Blood's prediction was right, but they insisted that he rest near the horses and stay hidden.

Night Hawk greeted them with a smile when they crept back through the trees as the first light of morning filtered through.

"Tell me what you saw. How hard was it to get in?" Night Hawk wanted to know everything.

"They are still building the wall. It is unfinished. We were able to sneak in the back part of the camp undetected. They have many warriors and many slaves. I don't think the slaves would fight us if they knew we were there to help them. We saw a circle of tents that is as large as our entire camp and also a separate area with about twelve tents. I wish you were well Night Hawk so you could have been with us," said Flying Eagle.

"I am getting well. I feel much better. Do you think the tents that are separate are for the slaves?"

"Yes I could see their outlines through the tent walls. Their tents are not lined and they are not dressed warm enough either. The tents in the main circle are lined, and the few people we saw were guards. They were bundled in furs."

"Flying Eagle, draw the camp on the hide and our map will be finished. We can leave here and know that we have done our job."

Night Hawk was frowning.

"I made a mistake and thought that the raided camp of the Sentu was the camp of the Abalinah. How do we know that this really is their camp? Did you see anyone that you could recognize?"

"No, I told you, that all we saw were two guards."

Young Blood was annoyed but he knew that Night Hawk was right. They had followed tracks to the water and farther on had found disturbed sand near the path to this camp. They needed proof that this was the Abalinah camp.

"Let's move away from this path, to the back of their camp and keep a close watch for a while. We can hide our horses in the woods and make sure they get some water before we leave them."

Once they had managed to stash their horses and find a place with sufficient cover, they settled in for a long vigil taking turns napping and watching. Flying Eagle finally decided that it was time to share a large supply of travel cakes that Snow Star had placed in the bottom of each of his saddle bags as he was preparing to leave their home camp. He had waited until now, knowing that there would be a time when they would need food badly. The cold winter sun did nothing to ease their aching fingers and toes. They tucked them into their armpits or sat on their feet in a pile of gathered grass. They needed the richness that the travel food would supply.

The broad smiles of his companions were thanks enough when he broke large chunks off of the mixture and handed them each some.

"This is good. I have been so hungry for so long that I think I have lost a lot of weight. My trousers are hard to keep up," said Young Blood. "I must remember to thank your wife when we get back. She did well packing this for us."

"Snow Star is a good woman. I know that I must do better by her and our people."

"Look, isn't that Debon?" A young man had ridden out and headed for the herd.

"I think it is," said Night Hawk. "I wish I could get closer to be sure."

"Look at his clothes. He is wearing the trousers that he wore in camp with the white circles of beads on the sides. I'm sure that is Debon."

"Well, I think we have all the proof that we need. In a couple hours it will be dark and we can get out of here and head home," whispered Young Blood.

"Home sounds good to me," said Night Hawk.

"You have had the worst of it Night Hawk. I know that you will be glad to get back." Flying Eagle offered the fresh water bag to him and then settled down to rest until the cover of dark would make it safer to leave.

Their horses greeted them with a stomp and frosty blow of their breath. They would be happy to be moving too. Small flakes of snow drifted down. It would soon cover the prints of their horses. They were glad for that.

At the lake they drank and filled their water bags and let the horses have their fill, knowing that it would be a dry camp ahead.

Toward morning, with the aid of the full moon, they found a place where they could light a fire. Finally they could warm their hands and feet near the campfire. Another meal of the travel food was welcomed before they hunkered down to rest.

They didn't swing wide of the mountain but carefully took their nervous horses past it, hearing rumbles and strange eerie sounds from inside its smoking façade.

"I'll be glad when we are past this thing and the camp of the Sentu. I think it spooks me almost as much as this big beastly mountain," said Night Hawk.

"None of us like riding near it, but it cuts a day's ride off our trip to go straight through. I know what you mean about the Sentu camp. It feels like it is full of spirits," said Young Blood.

"Two Feathers sure has been through a lot. Willow is amazing. It is hard to believe she survived that raid and has been raising that little boy. She won't have to, if we find his mother."

"She may not feel that way about it. He and Two Feathers have been her family since the raid. They both are adults now. I don't think it is right to split them up unless they really want it."

"What are you saying Night Hawk?"

"Well I just know that they are closer than any family I ever saw. She gets what Two Feathers needs before he knows he wants it. She acts like his wife, not his sister."

"He better make her his wife before someone else does. She is a good looking young woman."

Flying Eagle laughed at them and said they sounded like a couple of old women gossiping. All conversation ceased as they hurried through the area of the Sentu village. None of them wanted to linger.

"Another day of riding and we will be home," said Night Hawk. "I am eager to get back and this poor horse is as tired of me as I am of him."

Without warning Flying Eagle had sent an arrow flying through the air to the heart of a young deer that had been standing in the weed covered cornfield.

"We will eat fresh meat and take the rest home." They traveled just far enough to be away from the area of the Sentu village. There they enjoyed their camp and the wonderful smell of cooking meat and the heat of a generous fire. The next day the deer was deboned and wrapped in its own hide to travel on the back of Flying Eagles horse. His bedroll was tied on with Young Bloods.

It was nearly dark when they rode through the trees and greeted the guards watching the north woods of the Blue Stone Camp. Falling Stones cheered loudly and before they knew it they were surrounded by people from the camp.

The return of the three trackers had been anticipated for weeks. They now took the liberty of slowly riding all the way into camp. People poured from their tents wrapped in blankets or quickly pulling on coats as they hurried out not wanting to miss what was happening.

Snow Star ran from her tent, with Watching Owl in her arms. Neither of them had a coat on but they didn't seem to care as Flying Eagle hugged them and held them close.

He took the boy and wrapped him inside his coat as he hugged Snow Star again.

"I have missed you Snow Star. I am very glad to be home." Spotted Fawn and Meadow Lark came running from their tents behind the big tent. They greeted their men enthusiastically, but all of them knew that it would still be a while before the three men could come to their tents to relax.

Chief Dark Wolf came out of his tent smiling broadly and his three trackers were met with praise.

"We have all been praying for your safe return. We are thankful that you are finally back. Do you bring us good news?"

"Yes, I think we do," said Flying Eagle.

He pulled off his coat and wrapped it around his wife and son before stepping up and into the big tent. Night Hawk and Young Blood followed.

Other men of the village entered too, seating themselves in the many soft furs that covered the floor.

Father Bob also arrived within minutes of their return. It was easy to guess the meaning of such a commotion in the camp.

A messenger was sent with permission to all the night guard so that they too could be present. Two Feathers came hurrying in and sat down next to Father Bob.

Sweet Grass and Moonflower had been busy providing food and hot tea for the men, making sure that the trackers had been given more than enough. They knew with a glance that this absence had been a time of discomfort and hunger for the men.

"Thank you Moonflower and Sweet Grass that is plenty. Most of us have eaten recently." Moonflower took that as her signal to leave, but this time Sweet Grass quietly slipped behind the hanging separation in the back and settled comfortably on her bed of furs. She wanted to hear what the trackers had discovered.

The three men devoured all the food that they could hold, giving it their full attention, until the others grew impatient.

Finally Chief Dark Wolf asked.

"Did you find the Abalinah camp?"

"Yes, my Chief, we did. It is much farther than we had imagined. We are certain that this is the route to their camp." Flying Eagle unrolled the leather chart they had drawn holding the edges so that the men could study it. They slid forward crowding each other until they had all had a good look and settled back where they had been. Some were quiet but others had questions.

"How could people that live that far away know of us or that we had the blue stones?"

"You ask a question that is a good one. The answer was not in their tracks," replied Flying Eagle. The men laughed. Perhaps when we raid their village, we can ask them," said Young Blood.

"What is the thick line that you drew around their camp?"

"They are in the process of building a very high, thick wall. It overlaps with a gate near their horse herd. It is partial on the back side of the village. That is where we slipped in. It's not finished back there yet. They have a large camp, like ours plus an area that is set aside with twelve tents that hold the slaves. We saw Debon come out and go to the herd. They keep some horses near their tents like we do. There is a large building in the center of their camp. The roof looks like it is thatched. It starts at the ground and curves up and over to the ground on the other side. It seems to be all roof. We couldn't see how it was built in the dark, but I believe that many people were inside. We could hear them."

"What were they saying?"

"I don't know. I don't speak their language," said Flying Eagle.

"I think that is something that we must work on during the winter. Those who go in the spring will need to be able to communicate with them somehow," said Father Bob.

"Night Hawk, you have marks on your skin. What happened to cause that?"

"Let me show you!" He jumped up and went out to his saddlebags that now rested near the doorway of the tent. The horses of the trackers had been relieved of their burdens and taken to the meadow.

Night Hawk came back with the arrow in his hand. The men passed it around. He opened his shirt to show where it had hit his chest.

"If Young Blood had not known what to do, I would be dead. The tip of it was covered with poison!"

"What did you do Young Blood?"

Sweet Grass leaned against the separation trying to hear every word. It was poisoned! This is important. I need to know what he did, she thought.

"I just pushed an icicle through the hole after we cut the arrow off and pushed it out. It washed some of the poison out, but he was very sick for a few days. He had a high fever and got a nasty rash all over. That's what left the brown marks on his skin."

"Let me see that arrow," said Two Feathers. "Yes, I thought so; I have one in my tent that matches this. We found many like it in the camp of the Sentu."

"Vengeance belongs to God, Two Feathers. We are going to their camp in the spring, only to set the captives free," said Father Bob.

"What do you plan on doing with the rest of them?" he asked.

"That will depend on the circumstances and on how they react at the time. It isn't our intention to go there to slaughter their people. Do we want to become like them?" Chief Dark Wolf found that he was standing. With a glance, he could tell that many of the men in the tent were glaring at him. Some had lost so much and they had been hurt so deeply that it was understandable that they would want to lash out. It is good that Father Bob will have the final say on who should go, he thought.

"How many days' ride is it to get there?" asked one of the men.

"It is five, or six days to the other side of the lake. If we ride straight through it takes a day off, but I didn't like riding so close to that talking mountain. On the way, when we followed them, they went away from the mountain, through the trees so it took longer," answered Flying Eagle. It wasn't until that moment that he realized that he felt no hostility coming his way from Growling Bear. He seems different.

Father Bob stood and stretched. I would like to pray with all of you, if you will stand with me. His prayer was simple and brief.

"Father God, Almighty Spirit, we thank you for bringing our men back safely and for healing Night Hawk from the poison arrow. We thank you for showing them the route that they will need to take to set the captives free. Watch over them Father. We ask you to continue to bless all our men and everyone in this camp. We pray for wisdom for our Chief and the blessing of peace for our camp during the cold winter months ahead. Amen."

As the men filed out, Chief Dark Wolf spoke softly over Father Bob's shoulder.

"Come talk with me tomorrow, whenever you have time."

He nodded, but didn't reply. They had much to discuss and plan in the months ahead.

CHAPTER EIGHT
THE QUIET TIME OF WAITING

Since their time on the trail together, the three men found themselves together often. Young Blood was capable in many skills that the average person might not expect. He sat with the craftsmen and gently wrapped the silver around the polished stones, creating exciting and beautiful new designs.

Flying Eagle bemoaned the loss of their last raw stones as they worked together in the big tent. Only Father Bob had been told that the Chief was keeping a very big secret about the location of more stones.

Spotted Feather had begun to show an interest in carving. Most of his efforts were in adding beauty to items that were useful. He shaped bowls that were covered with flowers and leaves on the outside. He made a comb for Snow Star that looked like a small bird had settled in her hair. It was beautiful.

He wished that it was possible to carve during his long hours on guard, but since he was on night guard, he couldn't see to carve. When he asked to be changed to day guard, the Chief asked him how he could look for the approach of a rider and not cut his fingers. The subject of a shift change was forgotten.

One day, Sky Fire came and sat beside Father Bob as he was cooking a meal. He wanted to talk and hoped that he could influence him in his selection of men to go on the campaign in the spring.

"You know that it will be an emotional struggle for any man that goes. You will need experienced warriors that can conduct the operation with skill and fight fearlessly."

When Father Bob looked over at him, he noted that Sky Fire was not the man he was describing. His fists were balled as if ready to fight and his face was red with rage.

"I know that our success will mean more to you than most of us can imagine. You have invested your heart and it is wounded. God will lead us and if it is His will, we will bring your son and daughter back with us."

"Are you telling me that you don't intend for me to go?"

"I haven't been given the names of the men that God will select yet." Sky Fire stomped away, feeling that once again something had been taken from him.

Father Bob shook his head in dismay, knowing that not until it was the right time, would God give him the names of the men to go. Sky Fire wasn't the first to approach him and he thought that he probably wouldn't be the last. I think that Flying Eagle and Growling Bear will be the hardest ones to leave behind, but I feel certain that they should not go. They have given no indication that they are true believers, and they are not baptized either. I think I will go talk to them and see if I can make any headway.

Winter stretched on and Chief Dark Wolf had hung the charted route high in the big tent for all to see. Having no explanation, some parts of it puzzled the women, but they understood that it represented a long route to a destination that could mean death to the men that went.

One day Sweet Grass got an idea. She took a feather and a pot of dye and painstakingly copied the map to a second hide. She included every detail. Having heard the men, she better understood what she was seeing and drawing.

Most of the women showed little interest in it, but dreaded the thought that their men might be leaving to go to war in the spring.

*****

Father Bob anticipated the Christmas season with mixed feelings. No one in this camp had ever experienced Christmas as a child or been at high Mass at midnight or on Christmas day. They had never seen a Christmas tree or exchanged Christmas gifts.

He missed his family at that moment more than he had in years. I can't allow myself to get feeling low. I have a family here. This can be my best Christmas ever. I wonder if I can pull it off! I am going to show these people the joy of Christmas! I'll get a tree and decorate it. I can get the women to help me make some decorations, and Sweet Grass will help me decorate the inside of the big tent. I will hold midnight Mass in there! I can have the children sing and the homily will be the Christmas story from Luke. What can I do about gifts? I wish I had thought about this before I went to the settlement. Ideas were all filling his mind at once. I need to make a list, he thought and talk to Sweet Grass about helping me.

When he stepped into the big tent and saw the map that Sweet Grass had made, he was amazed.

"You have artistic talent, Sweet Grass. This is very nice."

"I have a challenge for you. I would like you to make a drawing for me, like this, of a woman with a baby in her arms and with a blanket up over her head, sort of like this." He held a fur up wrapping it around his head and shoulders.

She giggled at him.

"You look funny," she said. "Can I ask Willow to help me? She is good at drawing things."

103

"Yes of course. Do you need me to get you a hide?"

"No Father, I have several. This will be fun to do, but why do you want it?"

"You will see later," he said with a grin as he left."

I wonder if Moonflower would be interested in getting involved. He walked to her tent and scratched.

"Yes, I am here," she said.

"Moonflower may I speak with you for a few minutes?"

"Come in Father. Would you like some tea?"

"Thank you, I would. It is going to be very cold again tonight." He settled on the furs close to her small fire and realized he had never before been in there without Chief Dark Wolf. He wondered if it was appropriate protocol and decided to speak quickly about the reason for his visit.

"Moonflower, I need your help and ideas, if you are willing. I would like to make a very special celebration for the people. It is called Christmas. Christians; people who believe that Jesus is the Son of God and that He died for all of us so that we are saved; celebrate his birth on a very special day. They make beautiful decorations and sing songs and sometimes they give each other gifts. They have a big feast and it is a happy time to thank God for his Son and for all the blessings he has given us. Do you think you would be willing to help?"

"What could I do?"

"I was hoping that you could get some of the women to make some pretty decorations. I would like stars, lots of them in many sizes." He reached out the door and drew a five pointed star in the dirt with his finger. "Could you make them out of grass?"

"I think we could. What else will you need?"

"I don't know yet but I will think about it and get back to you. I can promise you this that it will be inside, warm, fun and joyous. Thank you for the tea and for being willing to help. We will talk again soon."

She was smiling when he left.

"I saw that you had company so I waited. If I had known that it was Father Bob, I would have come in. What did he want? Was he waiting for me?"

"No not this time. He is planning a new celebration for the people and he said it will be fun."

"Doesn't he have enough to think about without planning feasts?"

"He said it is called Christmas and that people, who believe in Jesus, celebrate his birth. He asked me to help him get ready by making stars out of grass. See, that's where he drew one to show me."

"Are you going to make them?"

"Yes I don't understand what they are used for, but I am glad to help him in any way that I can. Morning Dove and Blue Stone helped me bring lots of weaving grass in the big tent before the first snow. It is along the back wall. I think I will ask them to help me."

"When is his celebration?"

"I don't know. He didn't tell me. He did say that he had to make a list so that he wouldn't forget anything. He is like a whirling wind, go here, do that, pray here and say the mass then go over there. Since he put the wood in the church he is in the big tent a lot more and I see all the trips here and there that he makes."

"Don't worry about it Moonflower. He is fine. Just make the stars that you promised and I'm sure the celebration will be a good thing."

That particular night was very cold. Everyone had gone in their tents earlier than usual, building up their inside fires to compensate for the chill.

When Moonflower peeked out she thought that the village was a pretty sight with the yellow glow warming the many tents.

"Chief Dark Wolf was glad that Two Feathers had encouraged the night guard to build the little shelters at each position. He didn't want them to build fires but they could dress warm and keep extra blankets there to wrap themselves in. He didn't care as long as they stayed alert and awake. They were out of the cold wind. The night sky offered no light. The stars were hidden by a layer of heavy winter clouds that threatened to dump snow soon. Most of the night guard had discovered that bringing their horse in under the roof of the shelter was a benefit to both of them. Its body heat warmed the air and it gave them protection and companionship. The horse's keen senses, offered a warning from predators that the guard could not see in the dark.

Winter seems so long this year, thought Two Feathers. I am tired of being here alone and cold all night every night. I think we should stop this night guard after we go to the camp of the Abalinah. No one travels in the dark. The Abalinah sure made fools of all of us. It takes a lot to mislead Willow, but Sheltah did. We all liked her and Debon. I thought Hondor and Kier were alright. Just shows us that we have to remember that people like that are out there. I guess we do need to guard our camp at night.

Moonflower was awake, thinking about Sarah. I wish she would move back now. I know that she has found a brother and lives near him. I always thought she would marry Sharp Knife one day. I am glad. He is a good man. It was astonishing that she came when she did. That ground shaking ruined our camp and I don't think my leg and ankle would have healed as well as they did, if she had not come.

Poor Father Peter, he was doing all that he could, but he just didn't have the skills that Sarah does. It has been a year and a half since she was here. She may have a baby by now. I want so much to see her. Maybe she will come in the spring, when the weather makes it better to travel. That's when the men will go to the Abalinah camp. The thought of it makes my stomach hurt. They are such wicked people. How could they fool us like that? I feel so bad for Rippling Water and Sky Fire. They have been through so much, but at least they enjoy Rain Drop, their granddaughter. She is a beautiful, sweet girl.

Moonflower turned her thoughts to prayers. She prayed for the people she was thinking about.

"Great God, look at our people and heal their hearts. Bring my daughter back so I can see her and watch over our men. Help Father Bob to choose wisely. I know he says that only thirty are needed, but I think if I were a warrior going into that camp I would want all the men with me. Protect those that will go and all the rest of us that will stay behind. Also I want to thank you again for the believers that promise to send us meat when it is needed. Please give them a special blessing." With the end of that silent prayer, she drifted off to sleep.

*****

"What are you doing Father Bob?"

"I am thinking that with a little change inside; this oven can be used to bake food. I don't think Sheltah or any other Abalinah will be back making pots in it any time soon."

"I certainly hope not," said Falling Stones as he watched Father Bob fit a shelf in on top of four stones that would support it over the fire in the bottom. "What are you going to try to bake?"

107

"I will need to practice, but I want to make some special treats for the Christmas celebration."

"I didn't know we are going to have a special celebration. When will it be?"

"I hope that it will be sometime soon. The harder I work, the more things I think of to do."

"What do you need? I will help."

"Falling Stones, that is wonderful! I need someone to go into the woods and bring back a whole little pine tree. Not a big one. I want it to be one like that one over there, only small enough to actually stand up in the middle of the big tent and not touch the top. Remember it also has to fit through the door flap."

"Why do you want to put a tree in the big tent?"

"I can't tell you now, but it is part of our special Christmas celebration. If you can get someone to help you cut it down and bring it beside the church that will help me a lot."

While they talked, Father Bob lit a small fire in the oven and rolled the door shut.

"Now I need to go get the dough that I made. I am going to have to borrow some cooking stones too. They will stick if I put them on the stone shelf. I'll need to experiment."

He hurried away looking around in the back area of the church until he found a large crate that contained Father Pete's cooking utensils that they had never used. He spotted a cook book in the bottom. That will help, he thought. Then he found the very treasure that he needed, a cookie sheet.

"Thank you Jesus! This is going to be a really fun celebration. I am beginning to think so myself." He was getting excited about it. With the greased cookie sheet in one hand and his bowl of dough in the other his trial and error process began. Each failure coming out of the oven was met with many volunteers to taste and comment. He read the cook book and found a simple sugar cookie recipe that he could make. He tried again. Next he had to figure out a way to time the batch so it would be done but not burned. With encouragement, they found that if he put the tray in the oven and walked the path through the big rocks, to the prairie and back, it was just time enough. The men were making strong bonds, good smells and having fun as they helped him. He wrote everything down so he wouldn't forget anything, down to the number of small pieces of wood he had used to make the fire. He would not make the big batch for the whole camp until the day before he declared it was Christmas. The cookies would be his gifts this year, but he hoped that next year others would have gifts to give and receive within their own families.

*****

He had purchased paper when he was in the settlement with Ben and Josh and had mailed two letters when he returned to pick up the lumber. He had sent a letter back to the Cardinal who had ordained him. He also had written to his family, hoping that one day next spring he would get an answer from one or both of them. He hoped that the Cardinal would be inspired to send another Jesuit to help him.

As he settled at the crude desk he had made, he opened the Bible to the book of Luke and prayed for God's guidance.

As carefully as he could, he wrote chapter two, verses one through forty, in words that he hoped all the people would understand. It was a major undertaking and he labored late into the night.

109

The morning came but he was not up at his usual early hour. Moonflower worried that he might be ill and was considering sending someone to inquire when she saw him in camp talking to some children.

Later she heard him and all the children talking and laughing as they trudged into the woods behind the lake. I wonder what they are doing. She considered the sound of their laughter and knew that whatever it was, it was fun and would break the monotony of the cold winter days for the children and it gave their mothers a short break. She didn't see Singing Wind enter the woods just before them.

Their rosy cheeks and bright red noses told that it was very cold in the woods, but the sparkle in their eyes said that they had enjoyed the outing. They had been sworn to secrecy. None of them would tell what they had been doing. They just giggled a lot when they saw each other in camp. Father Bob would laugh right along with them when he saw them.

One morning after Mass in the big tent he was treated to a private, small art show by Sweet Grass and Willow. They had each created a drawing of the mother and child that he had requested. Neither was what he had pictured in his mind but quite lovely in their own way. The mother in Willow's had long dark hair, pulled to the side with a silver comb. The child in her arms looked a lot like Water Bug had when he first came to live with the Blue Stone people. The blanket he had asked for was around the mother's shoulders and tucked protectively covering the child's arms and legs. Willow had taken it one step farther by tinting her drawing with natural dyes. He couldn't take his eyes from it.

Sweet Grass had wrapped her mother and child in furs. The drawing was minimal and yet all the details were there. It seemed to show the pain that Mary felt when she allowed her mind to acknowledge the cross in her little son's future. It was drawn as correctly and proportionately as the map. It was a haunting depiction that stunned him.

"Ladies, these are far beyond what I could have hoped for. They are extraordinarily beautiful. This is a wonderful job! Please, would you sign them? I know that they will be here in this village long after we are all in heaven. Your work will outlive all of us." After they had each made a simple mark of their choosing in the corner, he carefully rolled the hides up and tied each one with a strip of cloth. "May I take them to the church? I want to write on the back of them and put the date. We will hang them and the people will see your work at the Christmas celebration. You have made my heart sing! You have such talent that I am humbled by your work. Thank you so much."

He unrolled the hides when he got back to the church. The day was nearly gone. He lit the new lantern and placed it carefully on the stacked lumber looking from one Madonna and child to the other. Who would think that such beauty could be found in the artistic ability of a couple of untrained Indian girls? He turned them over and wrote for them, "This was painted by Willow of the Blue Stone People and of the People of the Lion, in winter in the year of our Lord, 1878." On the other one he wrote, "This drawing was done by Sweet Grass, the healer of the Blue Stone People, in winter in the year of our Lord, 1878."

After a light meal, he said his prayers and prepared to go to bed. With the hides safely rolled and placed in his private area, he turned the lantern off and edged his way back carefully.

When he looked out the door of the church, he could not tell which of the animals in the meadow were his. The snow was blowing and biting his skin. That shelter is not big enough for all of them and the snow is so deep they won't be able to find feed under it. He bundled in his warmest clothes and trudged out. He slipped ropes on his animals. They plowed their way back to the animal shelter he had made. Macho stomped and immediately started to eat the dry grass piled against the walls in thick rolls.

"With you guys here that will leave more room for the other horses to get under the horse shelter. I wish I could feed all of them." That was when he remembered the four big bags of grain he had, two of corn and two of wild seeds. He slid one of each to the shelter, by pulling them on an old hide. Once he got there, he opened the bags and spread the grain all along the two walls. "That is just a snack for so many of you, but it is good feed and will help you stay warm until the snow stops and the sun melts the snow enough so you can get to the grass underneath; so, Merry Christmas, my beautiful hardworking friends."

"Father Bob, I saw you out there with the horses. What were you doing?"

"I was giving them a Christmas treat. Growling Bear, what are you doing out in this harsh wind and snow?"

"I came to talk to you. Big Flower says that I need to believe and get baptized so that I can go with you in the spring to fight the Abalinah. She is nagging me about it night and day. She thinks that if you don't choose me, I will surely lose status as top warrior and will never be able to get it back!"

"I never thought that Big Flower would be the type to nag. I am sorry Growling Bear. I know in my heart that every man should learn about our God and His Son. I think at times when I talk with you that you believe there is a God above all the other spirits, and I think you feel that the Great Spirit hears our prayers. What has stopped you from believing in His Son Jesus, and the salvation and forgiveness He offers?"

"I'm sorry Father but it all seems like women's stories. I can only believe in what my senses show me."

"Growling Bear, if you can believe in your sight, that's all you need. Look outside."

"The snow has stopped. Did your God do that?"

"He did, but that is not what I am talking about. Look at the snow on the piled wood, next to the wall. Look very closely."

Growling Bear smiled broadly when he realized that the dusting of snow that had landed on the frozen bark was actually tiny little geometric flakes, which formed stars and flowers. No two were alike.

"That's wonderful! It's marvelous! I never noticed that before. Is all this snow made up of little patterns like that?"

"God makes every tiny flake and they are all different. Can you imagine how many it takes to fill our meadow?" Growling Bear shook his head looking again with wonder.

It's thundering around in my head. That has to be a number too big to ever count!"

"The snow has stopped, and tonight you will be able to view the stars that are the floor of heaven. He made all of them just so we would have a beautiful sky when it is dark. He made the moon and sun, the trees and grass. He made all of us including your baby boys. Do you remember that prayer answer?"

Father, I know that he did that. I forgot that night for a while, but not anymore. I do believe in God, and His Son. I don't like the part that he let His son die on the cross, but I think it is alright now because he woke him up and he is out of the cave and up in heaven with The Great Spirit."

"Growling Bear, do you believe that God's Only Son took away the punishment for our sins when we are sorry?"

"Yes, I really do. He is a good God!" Growling Bear looked again at the snowflakes.

"I am so happy for you and Big Flower. Would you like me to baptize you?"

"The lake is frozen over. I am not crazy!"

"We can do it in here, right now. It is easy and quick. I will just pour a little water in this bowl." As he said it, he was doing it. "I make the cross with it on your head and say, Growling Bear, with this water; I baptize you, in the name of the Father and of the Son and The Holy Ghost. Growling Bear you have chosen to come from death to life in Jesus Christ. Do you believe in Jesus Christ?"

"Yes I believe."

"Growling Bear, congratulations, you are a Christian and you are baptized, but you must remember that I have not promised anyone that they are chosen to go."

"I know, but now maybe Big Flower will quit nagging me. I have done all I can and when God gives you the names, I know mine will be one of them." Father Bob reached into the bowl of water and splashed a bit on the front of Growling Bear's hair and coat.

"What did you do that for?" he asked.

"That was for Big Flower," he said laughing.

Growling Bear left soon after and went straight to his tent to tell Big Flower what had occurred. Then he tracked snow into Moonflower's tent to tell the Chief.

Father Bob asked Moonflower to tell all the women that if the snow continued to melt, they would have a big communal fire and a feast in two days and that is when it would be Christmas. He said that they could make any food they wanted to make and he hoped they would be able to eat outside by the big fire.

"What are you going to do with these, she asked?" She had enlisted help and together they had made dozens of stars in several sizes.

"Moonflower, you have done a magnificent job! I am not going to tell you yet, but they are very important to our celebration. Here I will carry that big basket for you and put it in the big tent. We will use them in there. Thank you so much for your hard work and please thank the other women for me that helped you."

He nailed a base on the nice tree they had found for him and hoped that they could get it in the big tent without being seen. He and Falling Stones were going to take it in after dark.

The wonderful people at the S. and J. Ranch had given him a big bag of popcorn. He planned to make some at the communal fire for everyone to enjoy, but he also had to pop his largest kettle full several times to get enough to string for the tree. Another night of lost sleep and deep prayers went by as he allowed his mind to pray for anyone that came to his thoughts.

Suddenly he was jolted by the lovely face of the girl his parents had wanted him to marry. Joanne was a good girl, but I didn't love her enough. I hope that she has a good life. He didn't know that she was now married to his older brother, David and that they had two growing boys. I had fun as a child, at Christmas. We were not rich but we always had enough to share.

"Father God, I desire to have contact with my family. Please move them to answer my letter. Bless them all and give them your joy and provision. Amen"

The busy work of stringing the popcorn had not required concentration. His mind had wandered into doors that he normally kept closed. He was sad when he went to bed. Tomorrow is Christmas Eve. I must cheer up, he told himself.

CHAPTER NINE
THEIR FIRST CHRISTMAS

Since the big communal tent was Sweet Grass's home, the preparations couldn't be kept from her, but everyone else was asked not to go in.

The Christmas tree stood in the center of the tent. The fire pit was empty and cleaned of ashes. Another piece of Father Peter's small white tent was cut to make a blanket of white for a tree skirt. The women were bustling to make quantities of their best dishes. Some of them had not worked this hard in years.

The men that had reaped the benefits of the trial and error on the cookie making were enlisted to bake the cookies once the big batches of dough were made. Falling Stones said that he would make sure they were not eaten. Father Bob took special care to measure the ingredients carefully. He wanted these to be right. He took down a big bowl of white sugar and asked them to generously coat the top of the hot cookies before they cooled. The cookies were carefully stacked in the old crate that had also been lined with the white tent canvas.

Growling Bear had helped Father Bob move his altar to the area of the communal fire. The wood was piled high ready to warm the area and a big stack nearby had been collected so that the fire could easily be fed. The altar table stood bare for now, but just before Christmas Mass he would cover it with the white linens and place the candle holders and other objects necessary on it. He smiled when he thought of the straw flowers that Mary had given him. I will put them on the altar, too. The women will be amazed to see flowers in the middle of winter. I wish I could serve communion, but they aren't ready for that yet. Maybe next year we can do that in our enlarged church.

He went back to the church and smoothed out his vestments and retrieved the candle stubs that he had been treasuring and kept in a basket. In his pocket he had a roll of soft wire and a pair of clippers.

Back in the communal tent, he and Sweet Grass fastened the candles to the tree, carefully trimming away any pine needles that were too close. They wrapped the popcorn strings around and around until the tall tree was completely decked. Sweet Grass was clever at fastening the stars on with stems of grass. They were constantly conscientious about keeping things away from the candles.

"Now Sweet Grass we can hang both the beautiful drawing, and the painting. I want to put one on each side of the tent."

They stood inside the doorway admiring their work and just then Falling Stones brought the crate, covered with the white canvas.

"It was hard to keep from eating some of these," he said grinning. "The dough you made was enough so we have more than one each."

"Thank you for your help and thank you for not eating them!" They laughed together.

"What is in there," asked Sweet Grass? "That crate smells delicious."

"No peeking!" Father Bob was pleased with the way things were getting ready. He placed the crate under the tree, and wagged his finger at her. She giggled.

"I won't touch it, but it doesn't mean that I don't want to."

Chief Dark Wolf strolled over and Sweet Grass giggled and barred his entry by turning around and lacing the big tent shut.

"You mustn't look, it will spoil the surprise," she said.

"If the women have the food prepared and done enough so they can pull it away from their cooking fires, I think we can spread the word that it is time to light the fire and gather."

Moonflower was glad, for she had eagerly been standing near; waiting to get the signal. She sent two messengers. The first one, Bending Grass, was stopping at every tent while the second one, Cat Claw, rode to the guard positions and called the night guard in.

The Blue Stone People sensed that this was a celebration that was different from any they had ever attended. A lovely sound came from the flutes of the shepherds as they walked around the people gathered there and stopped near Father Bob at the altar.

They started their music again and all the children of the village looked to Singing Wind for direction. They sang, "Silent Night, Holiest Night, all is quiet in the fires light, "No one in the village knew this song except one young woman. Willow stood and joined in the singing, "Gentle virgin, mother and child, God's own Son," tears streamed down her face as her mother's voice echoed in her memory. She could not continue, but the children did. Softly they sang the words that Father Bob had explained to them. Everyone seated at the fire was moved by the moment and the beautiful hymn.

Before he started the prayers of the mass, he briefly explained it to the adults gathered there. They nodded, understanding that this was a feast for the birth of God's Holy Son, Jesus.

At the proper time, at his homily, he read from the pages that he had so carefully transcribed in the simplest English possible. Now they further understood the meaning of the song.

When the mass was ended, he asked Singing Wind to please lead the children in the new song again. They sang with joy and Willow sang with them all the way through this time.

"Now, Chief Dark Wolf has something to say."

The Chief smiled broadly and asked the women of camp to bring the hot food. "Let the feast begin!"

Until now the hunters of the Blue Stone People had never considered bringing a turkey to camp to be used for food. They thought of them as vultures. Father Bob assured them that they were not and that they had been passing up a bountiful delicious food supply available in the woods. Five big birds had been roasted and now were added to the feast.

When everyone thought they had eaten all that they could, he slid three huge pans near the fire and had men shaking them until the popping sound drew attention to another treat being prepared. He signaled when to pull them off and shook salt on the hot corn. It was dumped into big baskets and three more pans were made while the baskets were sampled and started to empty. Laughter and happy chatter filled the air. The aroma of the popcorn was a new scent and added to the delicious moment.

Finally, when all the popcorn was eaten and the fire had burned down to a soft glow, people started to notice how dark it had gotten and that it was getting very cold.

"I think it is time for our last surprise, but first, the children have another new song! We need all the grown-ups to stand." Flutes and drums and children all started at once, singing "Jingle Bells, Ringing Bells, Singing on this day," as they danced all the way around the fire, shaking cans on strings with suspended stones inside. The homemade bells didn't sound quite the same as real bells, but they were all having fun.

When Singing Wind and the children had gone through the verse many times, they finally stopped singing but they still stood.

"You can leave your blankets and the food for a few minutes. We will come back and get them later. Come with us now into the big tent."

Father Bob quietly led the people in, directing Moonflower and Chief Dark Wolf to go in first. Sweet Grass stood holding the lantern high so that it lit the right side of the tent and shone directly on Willow's painting. The left side of the tent was not dark but dim. The people made sounds of appreciation; oo's and ah's as they filed in and saw the lovely painting. Father Bob took the lantern and stood nearby until everyone in the village had settled into the very full tent.

"This is a painting that Willow has made for us. It is a mother and child, like The Mother Mary and Baby Jesus." More pleasant comments and praise for her work filled the tent. Slowly he made his way through the seated people and stood near Sweet Grass's drawing.

"Over here we have a second picture. This wonderful work was done by Sweet Grass." Applause and cheers followed with murmurs directed to her, showing how much the people appreciated her artwork.

While that was going on, Two Feathers had slipped out to the fire and lit a bundle of long straight twigs. He brought them in handing one to Father Bob, and another to Sweet Grass. Willow stood close to the tree and took the fourth.

Soon the candles on the tree were all lit and the twigs were safely placed on a rock outside the tent and put out. Father Bob turned the lantern down low and at that peaceful, awesome moment, as the candlelight reflected and flickered in the eyes of the people: the children sang Alleluia and the grown-ups joined in softly in a true observation of their first Christmas and their first Christmas tree.

With tears, Father Bob regretfully turned up the lantern and asked the adults nearest the tree to carefully put out the candles.

"Christmas is a beautiful and sweet celebration. It is remembering the birth of God's only son, Jesus and His gift to us of salvation and eternal life. Other Christians around the world celebrate this feast as we have, but they add other traditions. I have one thing more. My family gave gifts to each other. Gifts they had made or purchased. These gifts aren't important. Jesus is important and what He did was His gift to us."

Next year, you can celebrate the last part of Christmas by giving a gift to someone special. This year, I have a small token gift for each of you. Falling Stones would you help me?"

Together they carried the full crate and handed out the cookies, making sure everyone received one.

"These are called sugar cookies. When I was a child, my mother and Grandmother made them in shapes of stars and animals and bells." He reached over to one of the tin can bells and shook it. Everyone laughed. She colored the sugar red or green. It is a wonderful time to tell people how much they mean to you. I want you all to know that you are my family and I love all of you. I will do anything I can for you. I would give my life for you."

He stepped quickly from the tent. That was not a very happy note to end on. Why did I say that? He stuck his head back in the doorway, just long enough to say that the pictures should stay here on the walls of the tent.

"When the church is empty of lumber we can hang them in there. The tree can stay here for tonight. Tomorrow we will put it out by the other trees and the animals will enjoy the popcorn. Moonflower would you and some of the ladies like to keep the stars for next year?"

"Yes, we will take them off in the morning."

"Good, and Sweet Grass would you please save the candle stubs for me?" He smiled as he watched the people file out of the tent, but they didn't hurry to clear up the food, or take away their blankets, it was as if they didn't want the celebration to end. They lingered near the warm embers of the communal fire. Talking in small groups, they gathered their things. One by one they came to him, thanking him for the best feast ever. Two Feathers, Willow and Water Bug came as a family.

"Father Bob, you are very special to us. Thank you for tonight. We will never forget it or the lesson that this feast teaches. Now we must trust that The Great Spirit will send His Lion of Judah to lead us," said Two Feathers.

"He will," said Father Bob. Willow gave him a quick hug and said a quiet thank you. She wasn't sure if it was appropriate, but she loved and respected this man. All the people did.

"Thank you for the Christmas hug," he said chuckling as Chief Dark Wolf and Moonflower walked over near him.

"This has been a night to remember. You continue to amaze us with all the things you have in that holy book. We all have so much to learn."

"Yes, my Chief and I have the most to learn of anyone."

It was snowing softly when the common area of the camp was empty and the tents each glowed with their small fires inside. Falling Stones and Coyote had quickly helped to dispatch the stars from the tree into an empty basket and the candles were placed in a second. The tree was lifted out of the tent and carried to the edge of the woods. Sweet Grass was grateful to have her fire pit back and lit a small fire in it, moving her sleeping furs close to it for the warmth.

In the morning, the people found that the wind had blown the snow into drifts in some areas while others were totally bare. The horses and mules were glad to find the grass easily accessible in some areas.

Weeks of winter crawled by as the people enjoyed each other and activities in the big tent. Always there was that thought in the back of their minds that spring would bring a time of war. The women dreaded it as much as the men.

When the first change in the weather told them that spring was on the way, they wished that they could stall it. Usually spring was looked for with joy, but not this time.

Father Bob looked out of the church door at the soggy ground and wet animals nearby. They walked near the fence, sticking their heads through to eat the grass standing on the other side. It was last year's growth, but soon the roots would send up new shoots. All this day needs is a clear sky and warm sunshine to declare it spring, he thought. He turned and walked to the small area on the back wall where the altar stood. It had been carried back and forth to the big tent or the communal fire many times during the winter. Since the arrival of the wagon load of lumber things had changed here in camp. He knelt and began his prayers, but his mind wouldn't allow him to say the usual litany of prayers, he was troubled and concerned about the need for guidance for the coming days.

It seemed that the only answer he received was "Soon, very soon." It didn't satisfy him.

He decided that as soon as the ground dried and the days grew just a little bit warmer, he would take the wagon and go to the settlement. He felt sure that by now Mathew Morgan had completed his work and that when he arrived, he would find thirty shields neatly stacked against the wall of his shop. He grew excited at the thought of it. He had never pictured it quite that way before.

Within another two days, Father Bob couldn't stand to wait any longer. He found that the canvas was dry covering the wagon. He untied the cords that held it in place and just as they had before, extra hands came to help him remove the big canvas and fold it neatly for storage.

Now that his animals were back in the meadow, he had more room. He tucked it in the back of their lean to. With brush and grease pot he painted the axles and stuffed as much grease between the wheels and axle as he could. He refilled the pot and placed it in its spot under the seat.

Chief Dark Wolf saw him working on the wagon and asked if he needed help.

"I just hope that I can convince the same four big horses to pull this thing again. I'm not even certain if I remember how to hook all the straps and buckles. I'm really not very good at this, but with God's help, I hope to leave in the morning."

"You will do fine. Falling Stones will bring the horses in the morning and Night Hawk can help you hook them up. He knows all about horses and their rigging. I brought this to add to your supply. You will need to pay the man that is making the shields." He handed Father Bob another pouch of polished blue stones.

"No, really, I don't want to take them. Matt said that all I need to do is pay for the supplies that he purchased. I have more than enough for that."

"Father Bob, take them. We have lots more. You will see that we do, when I tell our craftsmen where they are. I will come back in the morning to see you on your way.

CHAPTER TEN
FAITH AND PREPARATION

Macho strolled along beside the rattling, freight wagon as they headed for Silverville. At the last minute Father Bob had asked for help to cover the wagon deeply with big bundles of grass. He knew it would help to cushion the shields on the way back. The big canvas was tied on to hold the grass in place.

The people had cheered and waved as he pulled slowly across the sheep hill and into the woods. He questioned their cheering until he realized that they were encouraging a necessary step in the righting of a terrible wrong that was on-going.

Once again Growling Bear had shown his initiative and willingness to help. He had cleared the path through the woods again. It hadn't been used since Father Bob had squeezed the wagon through on his return in late fall.

Several rocks had fallen into a new position at the foot of the bluff. They were just enough to make it impossible for the wagon to pass. Growling Bear had moved them and noted the unstable spot. We will check this spot and remove any other rocks that are loose, he thought.

"Father Bob, do you need me to come with you to help load the shields?" He sat on his horse beside the trail where he had worked.

"Hello Growling Bear, I am sure that Matt will help me load the shields, but I would enjoy having your company if you want to come along, but before we go any further, please ask the Chief if it is alright and let Big Flower know that you are leaving. You need not hurry. It is early and we have plenty of time. I will wait right here."

Growling Bear laughed loudly.

"I know enough not to leave without the Chief knowing it. He made that very clear. I told him I would go if you would have me and Big Flower was content knowing that I would be with you. She has packed us enough food to keep us fed for a whole moon!"

"That's wonderful Growling Bear, then let's be on our way." With the large dark brown mare tied on a long lead near Macho, Growling Bear slid up on the seat and they moved cautiously down the trail through the woods and out onto the prairie. Growling Bear noticed that Father Bob was smiling.

"I am very glad that you came with me, Growling Bear. Since Father Pete died, I get lonesome sometimes having to do things alone. I am not complaining. I know God has a plan, but I just wish I knew what it is and when He will send me a new co-worker."

"I understand. I felt like that. My wife and baby died with the white man's disease and even when I was with my hunters, I still felt alone, until I got Big Flower."

When the sun was in the middle of the sky, they stopped for a break and watered the horses and had some lunch.

"Father Bob, when do you think you will know who will be going with you to fight the Abalinah?"

"God will tell me, when he is ready. I don't know any more than you do."

"You know I want to go. All the men want to be chosen. It will be a disgrace for me to be left behind. I am top warrior. You ask the Chief. He will tell you I am!" Growling Bear was getting himself riled up and Father Bob knew it.

"Growling Bear, if God asked you specially, to do something, would you do it?"

"Of course I would do it. Who dares to say no to God?"

"If He asked you to go, would you go?"

"Yes, I would," he said excitedly.

"If He asked you to stay and guard the camp would it be any less of a request?"

"I see what you mean. I won't ask you again. I will try to wait patiently."

"Thank you Growling Bear. I consider you a very good friend," he said with a grin.

With most of the trip behind them, they made camp for the night in the pleasant area at the base of the waterfalls.

"It is too late to do anything in the settlement now. All the stores will be closed. We can go the rest of the way after we wake in the morning."

With their horses tied where they could enjoy the grass and water they bravely decided to enter the cold water for the first bath they had taken since winter had frozen the edges of the lake. Growling Bear dove in the center of the deep pool and took a long time coming up. Father Bob was getting concerned when he finally popped up holding a rock from the very bottom.

"You are a better swimmer than I am. I don't think I will accept the challenge to try to reach the bottom. Just jumping in the cold water will take all the grit I have!"

Growling Bear was laughing loudly as he stretched out in his soggy long johns in a last spot of sunshine warming the gravel bank.

Timidly Father Bob forced himself to enter the icy water with a shriek. He bobbed his head under the surface and scrubbed his hair and body. Like his companion he was wearing his winter underwear, but when he came out, he pulled them off and covered up with a dry pair and then pulled on his leather clothes quickly. In the morning he planned to trade them for his black priest's robe, but for now comfort and warmth was what he wanted.

"If you think it is best, maybe I should not go into the settlement. Would you rather I wait for you in the trees."

"Growling Bear, you came to help me load the shields. How can you do that if you hide in the trees?"

"The people of this white men's village have already learned a lesson about judging people. Don't worry. We have come for a purpose and it is a good one. If everyone knew what we are going to do, and why, all the men here would be like you. They would want to go when the time comes. They are good men, but very different."

When they reached the sectioned bridge, spanning the forks of the Silver River, Father Bob could see that Growling Bear was very nervous.

"Do you think we should take this wagon across?"

"It should be fine now but we will go back on the trail beside the Silver to the wagon train crossing. You will be surprised at the way these big horses can pull a wagon load through the river and up the other side. When Tom showed me how they could do it last trip, I was shocked to see their power!"

"Father Bob, I need to tell you something. I came here once before, wearing war paint. I had a war party with me, and if these bridges had been in place, this settlement would not be here today."

"I know, Growling Bear, but you were a different person then. God has made your heart new and you are learning that He lives in you and also in your white Christian brothers and sisters. Be proud Growling Bear and walk tall. I am honored to be with you."

Father Bob was very pleased to see two men walking toward them on the bridge. One of them was Mathew Morgan.

"Would you like a little help coming over the bridge Father?"

"Yes, thank you. I was hesitant to start across. It looks very narrow. Will we fit?"

"Yes, and it will take all of the weight, but just to be safe, I think we should unhitch the front pair of horses and take them over first and then let the back pair bring the wagon."

"It is so good of you both to come to greet us. Good Morning Matt and Sam let me introduce my friend. This is Growling Bear. He is head warrior and top hunter of The Blue Stone People. He is also a baptized Christian. Please make him feel welcome." Matt Morgan stepped up and offered his hand to assure the leathered Indian that he would be friendly. Sam did the same.

"I own the store over there. I am not great with horses but I came to say hello, and see what Father Bob was bringing in the wagon."

"It is just bundles of grass covered with the canvas. Sorry Sam, I didn't bring anything to trade."

"Stop in before you leave," he said to them as he turned and walked back to his store. He hoped that if they bought any supplies that they would do it with the beautiful turquoise stones. He had made a handsome profit on the ones he had accepted from Father Bob last time.

With the first team unhooked, Matt led them and tied them to the railing along the Hickory. They were happy to be off duty and immediately started to crop the sweet grass near the water. From the habit of his trade, Matt checked the shoes of the big horses and shook his head.

"You poor guys, I guess Priests and Indians don't think about horseshoes. I will see what I can do to convince them that you need a little work done." He patted a big fat brown rump as he walked back toward the bridge. Father Bob was carefully leading the horses pulling the wagon. Growling Bear had gotten off the wagon and onto his mare. He didn't want to be responsible if something went wrong. Matt took the second pair to the rail and checked their feet.

"Father Bob, all four of the work horses need shoes. Do you want me to check Macho and the brown mare while you are here?"

"Matt, I am sure you are right. I trust you to do whatever should be done and I will pay you, but right now I am not thinking of horseshoes, I am thinking about the shields for the warriors. Please tell me that you were able to finish all thirty."

"Yes, they are done and I am quite pleased with them. I hope that you are satisfied when you see them." He walked into his shop and immediately Father Bob noticed the bulging canvas that covered a major portion of the area.

"I worked myself right out of floor space. I will be glad to get my shop back," he said with a chuckle as he pulled back the canvas revealing the rows of shields. Each one was made the same, matching in every detail.

"These are perfect!" The expression on the Priest's face showed that this was serious business. Growling Bear touched the top of one, and then stooped to examine it closely.

"What are these made from? It feels like metal."

"It is metal from heavy storage drums, and then I backed it with hardwood and affixed a strap on the back to help with holding it in position."

Turning the first one around, Growling Bear investigated the back and how it was made. With one hand he lifted it with the strap and held it at arm's length.

"It is heavy."

"It will stop an arrow or bullet."

"How can a man shoot an arrow when he is holding this?"

Matt swung up on Macho and reached for the shield placing it in front of his body, resting on the saddle. He slid his arm through the strap and then pretended to place an arrow on a bow and pull the string.

"It will take practice, but those that become adept at using it will be much safer."

Growling Bear swung up on his mare and reached for the shield placing it in front of him. He rode down the side street and returned riding swiftly, to embed an arrow in the center of Matt Morgan's blacksmith sign.

"It is good," he said, "but for some it will be difficult."

"What could be done to make them better?" Matt asked, dreading the thought that he might have to change all of them.

"The best warriors are strong. The weight will eliminate those that are not."

Father Bob frowned.

"God has the say, not us. They are just what I asked for Matt."

"Good, do you want us to load them up?"

"No not yet. Can you shoe all the horses so we can leave tomorrow?"

"Father Bob, I will do whatever they need. Has that mare ever had shoes on?"

"I don't know," said Growling Bear. "She is from the herd of the people and she is fast and strong."

"She will run faster if she has shoes on so that her hooves are protected." Growling Bear stayed in the shop and watched the process as the mare's hoof was shaved flat and the iron shoe was heated and hammered to fit. He winced as Matt nailed on the first one.

"It doesn't hurt her. The nail goes into the dead part. See, like this extra part of your nail on your finger. What is her name?" Matt was trying hard to make Growling Bear comfortable.

"She doesn't have a name. I just call her and she comes to me. She seems happy to have me ride her."

"That could be her name. You could call her "Happy.""

"Most of the horses in the herd are not named, but I guess she can have a name. She is a good horse."

Father Bob was thinking of the steak and fried potatoes at Cookie's café.

"What day is this?" Matt grinned and shook his head.

"It's the middle of the week, sorry Father. I know you wanted to go to Cookie's. You could ride down to the lumber camp while I work on the team's shoes. Growling Bear would probably enjoy seeing that and you can probably get a meal at the same time."

"Matt, that's a good idea. I need to talk to Tom anyway." He swung up on Macho and waited for Growling Bear. He was appraising Matt's work on each hoof of his horse.

"She is "Happy".

"Yes, Matt does excellent work."

"No, I mean Matt named her Happy."

"That's a nice name." She was prancing around not sure of the weight and the way her feet felt.

"Be Happy, be Happy, said Growling Bear considering her actions normal under the circumstances. "I would like to go with you to see the lumber mill, but I think we should go slowly until she gets used to her new shoes."

Father Bob was pleased. Once again the settlement had not disappointed him. The shields were done and just as he had hoped, Growling Bear had been treated well so far.

As Happy pranced down the main street of Silverville, people noticed them and waved. Some of the folks recognized Father Bob, but others were admiring the high stepping brown mare with the fancy decorated saddle.

"Hello Tom, this is my friend Growling Bear. He is the top warrior and hunter of the Blue Stone People, and he is a Christian."

"Hello, Growling Bear, it is good to meet a friend of Father Bob's." He shook hands vigorously and smiled. Not quite comfortable as he sized up this experienced warrior and at the same time wondering why Father Bob had brought him into Silverville.

"Growling Bear is very strong. He is here to help load some things that Matt made for me."

"Oh yes, I know about the shields. That was quite a story he told me. He was here getting the wood to back them. When will you be going to rescue those folks?"

"When God says the time is right, then we will go. For now it is a time of faith and preparation."

Growling Bear was impressed by the finished product but felt intimidated by the noisy fast spinning, saws. He had not known they would be that loud or be that dangerous when Sharp Knife and Singing Wind had told of their adventures. They walked through a forest of stumps so that he could watch as a pair of men worked their crosscut saw through a tall standing tree. The trunk gave way and they yelled "timber," as it came crashing down making the expected sound and rolling cloud of dust.

Back in the center of camp, Cookie had prepared them each a plate of beans and biscuits. He wouldn't be cooking meat until the evening meal. The food was flavorful and ample, but Father Bob had prepared his taste buds for a steak. The cup of strong coffee was the first that Growling Bear had ever tasted. After Cookie added a generous amount of fresh cow's milk, he downed it and brought back his cup for more.

"Thank you, this is very good food," he said. He was already eager to be back in camp to tell everyone about his exciting activities.

Father Bob arranged for two windows to be made ready for him and two doors along with another load of lumber.

It was the middle of the afternoon when Macho stood at the railing waiting his turn to have Matt check his shoes. Father Bob and Growling Bear went across the street to the trading post. Sam and Helen were both definitely glad to see them. Growling Bear was impressed when he saw all the goods available.

"Sam I want to take back all the canned fruit that you have, and another fifty pound bag of beans. Give me a case of tomatoes and a string of those onions, and the whole jar of peppermint candy. I need four more tins of lamp oil and I see you have the wooden matches. I can think of many times that I have wished that I had those. We will take two boxes of those. We will take six bolts of the fabric. Growling Bear what colors should we take?"

"This one is like the sky. Big Flower will like it."

"We will take the blue and Helen would you please select five others and pick the brightest ones you have and twelve spools of thread."

Sam was writing as fast as he could and grinning the entire time.

Also add fifty pounds of sugar and fifty pounds of flour, a bag of salt and three bags of the coffee."

That's the instant that he remembered to ask if he had any mail. He was holding his breath. His heart was pounding as Sam turned and looked in the little square cubby holes that held the received mail.

"We have only had one delivery this spring. Let me look through this pile. Yes, here it is." Sam leaned over closer, hoping to find out any news that was in the envelope, but Father Bob folded the letter in half and slowly placed it secured in his pocket. His face didn't reveal what he was feeling.

Thank you Sam and Helen, I will be here in the morning to pick all this up and it will need to go on the front of the wagon and be tied on tightly. The back of the wagon will be full, so add a couple ropes to that list. We will need to stack the things up so they don't get wet when we cross the Silver.

Waiting outside the store was Reverend Brown.

"Hello, Father Bob. We heard that you were here and we want you to bring your friend and come to supper."

"Hello Jim, this is Growling Bear and he has come to help load the shields that Matt worked on this winter."

"Growling Bear, I heard that you are the best hunter and the leader of the warriors for your people. With your skills, I know that you will be able to rescue those poor folks that have been taken. I wish that I could go with you. Many men here have heard about it and feel the same. Have you talked to the Major at the fort?" He had addressed the question to Father Bob but was trying to include both men in the conversation.

"No, I didn't Jim. This is something that the people want to take care of themselves. They are not comfortable in the presence of the soldiers and wouldn't want me to insert them into a situation that they feel they should handle." Growling Bear was frowning but stayed silent. "Will you both come eat with us? Melanie is cooking up a storm!" They all laughed at that.

"We will come in just a few minutes. Thanks for having us. I need to talk to Matt and then we will be there."

"Matt we will be back here a little after dark and will bed down in the hay if that is alright with you. We will need your help loading the wagon in the morning. I placed a big order with Sam and it will need to be kept dry so I plan on stacking it high."

"I am almost finished with Macho. There that was the last nail. You can use him and Happy and when you come back just put them in back through the gate and they will have feed and water back there with your team."

"Thanks Matt. We have everything we will need for the night, don't give us a thought. We will see you in the morning and settle up our bill then."

"That's fine. Hope you enjoy your evening." He walked to the back of his shop and headed to his house as Father Bob and Growling Bear rode down the street.

CHAPTER ELEVEN
THE CHOSEN

As soon as Growling Bear opened his eyes, he was ready to get loaded and be underway. He had brought both saddle horses around to the front and was leading the first pair of the work horses through the gate when Matt stepped out on to his back porch and greeted him.

"Good morning Growling Bear, would you like a cup of coffee?"

"Yes, I had a cup at the lumber camp and I like it with milk in it."

"Was that the first time you had a cup of coffee?"

"Yes, we usually have tea."

Liz brought out a tray with a big fresh pot of coffee and a plate of biscuits and strawberry jam with a spoon in it. She had included a small pitcher of milk. She eyed Growling Bear warily, but smiled and poured coffee for Father Bob and Growling Bear.

"Liz, this is my friend Growling Bear. Growling Bear this is Matt's wife Elizabeth, but we call her Liz."

Growling Bear nodded at her and took a swallow of coffee and then offered a small comment.

"She makes good coffee." He had drained his cup and returned to the gate where he brought out the last two horses of the team. Their bedrolls were tied on Macho and Happy. Father Bob noticed the pump beside the left wall of the blacksmith shop and moved the handle up and down until a stream of fresh water, ran over his hand.

"That's nice. I don't think that was here last fall when I was here." He filled Growling Bear's and his water bags with the clean well water.

"There are several pumps here in town now."

139

"Well, Matt, how much do I owe you?"

"Six pair of shoes at twenty five cents each, that's a dollar and a half."

"Don't forget to add the cost of the shields. You did a wonderful job on those Matt."

"I'm glad that I could do it, but you don't owe for that stuff. Some of the folks in Silverville contributed generously to the effort. They didn't want me to give their names, but they wanted to help. We all wish we could do more."

"Thank you Matt. Please thank the folks for us and tell them to pray that we move wisely." He handed Matt the money and a pretty pair of polished stones. See if you can turn those into something pretty for Liz."

"Thanks Father Bob. It is time we got these shields on the wagon. We can layer them with grass between them and that will put the supplies from the store up plenty high enough to stay dry. We can put the canvas tarp over the top of the whole load and that will secure things in place," said Matt.

Growling Bear carried out one in each hand and placed them on the wagon. Matt backed the team into position and had them hitched properly before he noticed that several men were helping with the loading of the shields. Sam, across the street, was busy bringing sacks and boxes out and putting them on the walkway in front of his store. Helen had the paper with the order and was checking things off as Sam brought them out. Henry carried out a bag of salt and then a bag of coffee. He was learning the trade and doing his best to help.

By the time they were ready to ease away from the front of the Trading Post, they had gathered quite a few people. Reverend Brown, Melanie and the children had come to say goodbye and to assure them that the people of the church would be praying for the success of The Blue Stone People and the campaign.

"We appreciate all of you. We will be back when we have news." Father Bob waved and moved the horses toward the Silver and the trail that ran alongside to the crossing. He was already asking God to give his voice the sound of authority so he could get the horses to cross the river with the loaded wagon. Growling Bear surprised himself when he waved and smiled widely. He had been treated well and could honestly say that he had enjoyed the visit to the white men's settlement. Times are changing he thought. It is as Chief Dark Wolf said. We must change, too.

Father Bob was holding the reins high and sitting stiffly.

"Relax, Father Bob. You look like you think the horses are going to do something unexpected. They know their job and are doing it well."

You are right. I am nervous about the crossing. I have never driven the wagon across the river. I had Tom's help last time."

"Now you tell me! Should we be worried? Do you think God has all this planned out and then He will just let the shields sit in the water? I don't think that sounds like the same God that made the beautiful snowflakes that you pointed out to me."

"You are right Growling Bear! God will pull the horses across if it is necessary. Even a Priest needs reminding sometimes, how great our God is."

The crossing was much easier than Father Bob had expected. He hollered and whistled and smacked the reins the way he had seem Tom do it, and the horses pulled hard all the way across and up the other side, without a hesitation.

When they were a short distance past the river, he directed the team into the shade of a large stand of trees and stopped. He was as tired as the horses.

"I allowed myself to worry needlessly," he said with a sheepish grin. Let's rest and have something to eat while they rest." He filled the bucket from the barrels they carried and Growling Bear took it to each horse and let them drink.

"I have a surprise for you," Growling Bear said. "Helen said that Ben and Jed from the S. and J. Ranch were in the settlement a few weeks ago. There was still snow on the ground then, but they brought in some furniture they made during the winter. They left this package for you and she told me to tell you to open it on the trail home."

Growling Bear was curious about its contents, until he held it to his nose. He could smell the sharp cheese inside. Father Bob cut the string and pulled back the brown waxed paper.

"This is cheese. The women on the ranch make it from their cow's milk." He cut a thin slice with his knife and broke it in half, offering it to Growling Bear, who promptly shook his head no. "It tastes better than it smells, you should try some," he urged. Growling Bear walked over to his saddlebag on Happy and pulled out a large slice of dried meat. He offered half to Father Bob.

"Men should eat meat. That cheese smells bad," he declared.

Father Bob laughed and cut another slice before carefully wrapping the cheese and placing it back under the seat on the wagon. He rested his back against a tree and closed his eyes. Growling Bear did the same. He would never admit it but his back was sore from lifting the shields and riding on the wagon was aggravating it.

When they were ready to move out, he said he wanted to ride on Happy.

"That's fine, let's move out, we can eat again later when we stop for the night."

Father Bob was eager to get back to his church. He had discovered a second little bundle in with the cheese. He was sure that it contained a note or letter from his friends at the ranch. He had not opened the letter in his pocket yet either and savored the thought, but he wanted to be alone when he did.

They traveled another two hours before sundown.

"We can unhitch the horses and stake them here in the grass." After they were watered again all of them bedded down for the night. The two men enjoyed talking together and Father Bob didn't start his evening prayers until they were both comfortable in their bedrolls.

At first light Father Bob was up struggling to hook up the team. He felt inept but with Growling Bear's untrained help they managed. Macho was rubbing his muzzle on Happy's neck and Growling Bear seemed amused.

"Macho is whispering to Happy. It is spring," he said laughing as they moved along the wagon trail. "We are getting near. I see the start of the big rocks ahead."

Later, as they drew near, the guards greeted both of them with joy. Falling Stones, Standing Bear, and Two Feathers, came riding out of the woods in time to turn and lead the wagon into camp. The area was buzzing as more people came to cheer their arrival. They slowly pulled onto the sheep's hill behind the church. Father Bob took a deep breath and gave a sigh of relief to be back and breathed a prayer of thanksgiving for the safe return and success of their trip to fetch the shields.

Falling Stones and Coyote unhooked the team and Singing Wind removed Father Bob's saddle and carried it into the church. Bending Grass took Happy behind Growling Bear's tent and gave her the attention that she deserved. He had taken on the job of aiding Growling Bear at every opportunity, as if he would gain status by association. He noticed that the mare now wore the metal shoes that the white men put on their horses. He wondered about that and made a mental note to ask about it.

Father Bob directed the unloading and had most of the supplies taken to the big tent. The shields were covered and remained where they were for the time being. Chief Dark Wolf looked grim as he walked over and asked him to come for the evening meal in his tent, after he had rested.

"Thank you, I will come. We have much to talk about," he replied.

"Yes, much has happened here while you were gone." Father Bob frowned when he heard that. He wondered what else could possibly happen.

It only took a few minutes to put the things from his saddlebags away. It was reasonably quiet and he was alone for the first time in days.

He slid his hand into his pocket and placed the letter on his desk, next the folded smaller pack from the S. and J. Ranch was placed beside it. He sat down on his stool savoring the moment. He decided to open the one from the ranch first. Carefully he opened it, feeling the little bump in the corner. As he did, a small stone rolled onto the desk top. Scrawled in big letters were a few simple sentences. "Even this gray little stone tested positive! You will have what you need for the people and so much more. Congratulation Father Bob! We are all praying for you and know that you will win the good fight. We send our love."

144

He folded the paper but then he unfolded it and smoothed it out holding it in his hand, wondering where he should put it. He stood and walked to the altar, where he slid it into the pages of the large Missal. The prayer book rested there in a place of honor.

"Father this is confirmation of your work. It's all because of you." That added sentence repeated in his mind. It made him feel humble. No, he thought, not me, but the Holy Spirit. He still held the little gray stone in his fist. He lit one of the candle stubs and made a puddle of wax on the back corner of his desk. There he pressed the little rock firmly in the center. It will stay secured and I can see and touch it, he thought.

When he blew out the candle stub he noticed how dark it was inside his little room. He lit the lantern above the desk, and sat back down, staring at the letter. He knew he was stalling. The back address on the envelope read Antonio Clementi. It's odd that Uncle Tony would be writing to me. I hope nothing is wrong at home. The envelope came open with little effort.

"On this, the fourth day of December, in the year of our Lord 1873."

"I send you greetings from your family,

Your Aunt Gabriele wept with joy when she read your letter. Your parents are well. Your brothers are all married and have children, and your sister Georgina has joined the Dominican order and is a teacher. She took the name, Sister Mary Margaret. I know we should have forwarded your letter on to your parents unopened, but we could not resist opening it and reading your news first. It has been such a long time.

Your father took a position with the railroad and they live in town near the rail station now. I will send your letter on to them. I promise.

Your Grandparents are still here with us on the old homestead farm and they are glad that you are doing so much to spread the faith to the Indians. It must be difficult for you in such rugged conditions. We would send you a little money, but I'm sure you would have no place to spend it.

We send you our love. Our prayers for you will continue each night.

God bless you, our dear Roberto and stay well. Uncle Tony and Aunt Gabriele"

He felt let down. The anticipation had been greater than the amount of news inside. Everyone is alive and well. I should be grateful. I should feel happy, but there are so many unanswered questions. Why is Uncle Tony on the farm and where do my brothers live? Who did they marry and when?

He stretched out on his sleeping furs and read it again. It is all good news. I need to be satisfied with that. He jumped back up laying the letter on his desk and then rubbing his thumb over the little wax covered rock. He turned down the lantern until it was a faint glow and then headed for Chief Dark Wolf's tent.

Sweet Grass smiled and said she was glad he was back. She carried a heavy jar of water on her shoulder and ducked quickly into the big tent to be rid of the burden. Others hurried their step to give themselves the opportunity to greet him as he passed on his way.

Chief Dark Wolf stepped out of his tent and motioned for him to enter. He ducked back in. Moonflower was not there, but a pile of fresh corn cakes rested on a plate with shredded meat and a pot of soup was staying hot near the small inside fire. They ate together and had a hot cup of mint tea.

"We will have to have a communal fire but I told the women that it would be tomorrow. The men have had the same dream again. They expect you to tell them soon, who will go."

"Yes, I know they are all eager. How can I choose when I haven't been told? The Great Spirit will reveal the names to me. So far He has only given me the number thirty. That is why we have thirty shields."

"Are you pleased with the shields?"

"Yes he made them exactly as I asked. They are very shiny and strong. They will protect our men."

"Father Bob, did anyone tell you that Debon and Sheltah came back two days ago? They want to be accepted back as Blue Stone People. They insist that they were forced to go by Kier, Gamier and Okallah. Sheltah said she didn't touch the raw stones and that Gamier cut the back of our tent and took the stones."

"What do you plan to do?"

"I haven't decided yet, but of the six, they were easiest to live with. I have put them in the big tent. They wanted to go back to their empty tent, but I didn't allow it."

"Maybe they can give us much needed information. If we question them separately we will be able to see if they are giving us a made up story or the truth. They may have been sent back here to spy on us again. Their Chief may perceive us as a threat still."

"Rightly so, but not for the aggressive reasons he is probably assuming. If they think the supply of blue stone is gone, why did they come back?" Father Bob was puzzled.

"Debon did volunteer that Standing Crane had made the poison and taught their men to dip their arrows in it for war. They don't do it if they are hunting. Where they keep the poison, should be one of the questions we ask them." They talked long into the night. Moonflower stayed the night with Snow Star. She knew that it was important to not interrupt their conversation.

It started to rain softly and continued all the next day. The communal fire was postponed. Father Bob was glad.

CHAPTER TWELVE
WE ARE READY!

He knelt near the altar and prayed most of the day, asking for wisdom and guidance and strength for himself and for Chief Dark Wolf and the people. He said the morning Mass there in the church with the lumber crowding in around him. He didn't want to see anyone or talk to anyone. He ignored his empty stomach and continued to fast, allowing himself only a drink of water before he went to bed that night.

When he curled up on his furs, he doubted that he would sleep at all. He worried if the continuing rain would ruin the shields. I should have covered them with my greased canvas as soon as I returned. He puzzled over the return of Debon and Sheltah.

He thought about Growling Bear and about how important it was to him to go with them. He thought about the friends he had in town and on the ranch. He found his mind picturing what the church on the Hickory could look like, if he left all the huge ancient trees.

"What am I doing?" He sat up, asking the question out loud. "God knows better than I do what needs to be done and who needs to do it. I am not going to do another thing on my own. You need to show me, and until you do, I am staying in here and I am not going to eat a thing!"

He lay back down and wondered what he thought he was doing. You can't give God an ultimatum! No, I have to inspire Him to act! He jumped up and started pacing the narrow space left inside, along the wall of the church. He pulled his rosary out of his pocket and began to pray out loud fingering the prayer beads as he paced. He continued on pacing and praying, until he was startled by a voice behind him.

The small area where he had stood to say Mass was filled with a massive lion. Its tail swayed back and forth as if it was timing the pacing of the priest.

"We are ready. You will leave tomorrow morning. You will take the thirty oldest warriors in camp, with two exceptions. Take Two Feathers and Debon as the first two. Debon will answer your questions truthfully. I have sent him to you. Each warrior is to take one pack horse. I will lead you. Follow me when you hear my voice. You must camp where I say, for as long as I say, for the victory is mine! I am "The Lion of Judah!"

Father Bob sunk to his knees shaking all over as the words he had heard filled his mind with the full realization of the meaning of the vision.

"We are ready. We are ready! WE ARE READY! He bellowed. Thank you God, Thank you God. He repeated with each step as he ran to the Chief's tent. The sun was just peaking over the horizon. "We are ready," he shouted as he neared the tent.

"Father Bob. Good morning, what were you yelling? I couldn't understand the words."

"We are ready! We leave in the morning! I know who is chosen!"

"What? Did you have a dream? What are you trying to tell me?"

He said the same words again. This time he said them a little slower. The Chief stood and asked the names.

"I can't give you the names. God said that He sent Debon and that he will tell us the truth, and that I am to take Two Feathers and Debon. After that I must take the twenty eight oldest warriors in camp."

"Am I to go? I am not young you know."

"I believe that you should go."

"We must have a meeting of all the men right away. I will send Pine Berry to get the men of the night guard. Most of them will be disappointed. Cat Claw can tell the rest." He stepped out and signaled for his messenger. "Cat Claw, you must go get Pine Berry right away."

"Yes, my Chief."

Within a few minutes men began to arrive in front of the Chief's tent.

"Our meeting will be held here by the communal fire." He pointed as two more hurried near him. Debon and Sheltah stood just outside the big tent and Sweet Grass stood there with them. He signaled. "Debon come." The young man hurried to join the others, fearful that this meeting might be bad news for him. He wanted to stay. God had placed it in his heart that he was one of the Blue Stone People.

As more men gathered, some of them worked to light a small ceremonial fire, bringing dry wood from the big tent supply that was covered. It was traditional to have a fire for an important meeting.

They all felt a stirring inside that this would be the news that they had been waiting for all winter. Each man had prepared his weapons and each woman had made satchels filled with dried meat, nuts, berries and other fruits that could be eaten on the move. Travel cakes had been packed and the leather clothes of the men had been polished with fat on the outside so that rain would run off and the wearer would stay comfortable. Each warrior had prepared their saddle and one for their pack horse. They planned on returning with people they had rescued although they had no concept of the distance they would travel or the length of time they would be gone. Every person in camp had seen the map hanging in the big tent, but only a few understood the journey it represented.

Chief Dark Wolf stood before the men and the area grew silent. He raised both his hands and asked the men to do the same and then looked to Father Bob. The Chief understood that he needed to pray with all the men so that they would accept the news that he was about to give them.

"We know, Great Spirit that you are wise above the wisdom of all men. We know that you have created the huge mountains that we labor to climb and that you made the forest that requires much work for us to cut down just one tree. We do not understand your ways or your power. We cannot comprehend the reasons for your choices or your favor that permits us to march with you against evil. Help us to accept your will and guard us as we follow your plan."

Father Bob lowered his hands and saw the anticipation in the faces of the men. He announced loudly.

"The Great Lion of Judah has stood before me! This is His plan. It will be His victory! He will lead us! I need all of you to form a line in the center of camp, starting with the oldest here in front of me, to the youngest. Figure it out. I will wait." Chief Dark Wolf and Growling Bear found they were in line behind Sky Fire. Standing Bear laughed and changed places twice and many others shuffled around trying to decide just where they should be standing. "This is important. Be sure you are in the right place." He waited.

"Two Feathers will go. Also, God has sent Debon to us. He has information that we will need. He will go." Many men murmured. They didn't trust him. He was the enemy.

"He is Abalinah! We can't trust him," said Sky Fire.

"God sent him. He must go."

Now he stood waiting for another objection, but there wasn't one. The entire camp knew that Two Feathers and Willow had taken the name of "The People of the Lion."

There was a hushed awe in camp as the many men made the connection. Father Bob placed Debon in line in front of Sky Fire, and then he put Two Feathers in front of him.

"Now, I must count the thirty men, starting with Two Feathers." He counted slowly and loudly. "Sky Fire is number three and then Chief Dark Wolf is four". His count included Night Hawk, Snapping Turtle, Falling Stones and Standing Bear, Roaring Water, and others, all experienced warriors, and finally Young Blood is number thirty," he announced.

The next in the line was Flying Eagle, son-in-law of the Chief. He would be Chief of the Blue Stone People one day, but he was not among the chosen.

Father Bob looked into the eyes of the young man.

"Flying Eagle, until our Chief returns, you are the oldest man in this camp. God has chosen you to stay and guard His people. He has honored you with this responsibility. Will you accept it?"

"I will." His answer was said in a way that betrayed his desire to be the Chief permanently, but it also showed a tint of disappointment that he would not be going.

"Those not going are here to guard this camp and its people. When we return, we expect to see tall corn and happy people," said the Chief.

"Each man that is among the chosen is to prepare his horse and a pack horse with a saddle and plenty of extra food and water. Take an extra, empty water bag. You will fill it for your horses later on. Take an extra rope. Take your weapons and be ready to fasten a blanket covered shield on your pack horse at dawn. Now go." Father Bob headed back toward the church. The men scattered to their tents. Each repeating the list of things they needed to gather, in their heads until it was collected and ready.

Of the original three trackers, Night Hawk, and Young Blood would be going. They pulled the map from the wall and rolled it up in preparation for taking it. Sweet Grass handed them the copy she had made.

"It isn't exactly like yours but I tried to make it the same. I thought with many men going, it might help to have a second."

"That was very thoughtful of you Sweet Grass, and we all appreciate how talented you are."

"Thank you Young Blood." She had prepared a thorough inventory of medicinal supplies including bandages and healing salves. She carried it to the church and gave it to Father Bob. She explained what the things were and how they were used.

"That's a well thought out help and I will take care that it is kept clean and dry. Sweet Grass, promise me that you will open the big tent early every morning and pray for the warriors and the people we seek to rescue. Also pray for the people to be protected by the Great Spirit. He is everywhere and he will be here with the guards left behind."

"We will pray Father Bob, don't worry about anything. You have a big job to do for God. We will also be praying for you."

Two Feathers left the center of camp and walked directly to Willow. He Scooped up Water Bug from the crotch of a tree as he went and sat him down beside her. She was in front of the tent making their evening meal and trying not to show the turmoil she felt.

"We all need to talk. I was the first one that Father Bob counted! I am chosen! Willow do you understand what that means? I am going to be gone a long time."

"Yes, I know Two Feathers. Isn't that what we talked about? I knew he would take you after you were baptized."

"It's more than that Willow. The Lion appeared to Father Bob and told him who to take. I was the first one he named. I don't understand why I am favored. He has been helping me since my three day journey. Do you think that he will help me find Water Bug's first mother?"

"Yes, I do think so and while you are gone, I hope to be able to prepare space in our tent for her and my cousin if you will accept them. They have no one else and I don't want her to take Water Bug to live with other people at the summer meeting. It would be terrible for us to lose him now."

"I agree with all you have said. We will work it out. Water Bug, I will be leaving in the morning and I will be gone many days and many nights. You must help Willow all that you can and you must do what she says. It will be hard for me to go away. I will miss both of you very much." He turned to her and touched her cheek softly. Willow while I am gone promise me that you will consider becoming my wife at the summer meeting. I love you as much as any man ever could. Don't answer now. Just promise me that you will think about it."

"I will," she said with a big smile. "Now let me help you get ready. Which horse will you take?"

"I need to take two, one to ride and a pack horse. I will ride Friend and use the brown stallion for the things that I will take. He is strong and the shield is heavy. He may also be carrying a person on the way back."

The two horses were made ready and their saddles and all the satchels and packs were placed beside them behind the tent. Willow led them to the lake and let them drink their fill, and then she moved to the back of the lake and filled the water bags with fresh water. She had the food packed. She made sure it would be enough for a full moon or longer. One pack was a change of clothes, in case he got wet and at the last minute she slipped in one of her longest shirts, thinking that one of the rescued women might need it. Great Spirit, is there something else we should pack?" She was worrying that she had forgotten something. Every woman in camp was feeling the same concern.

As the light of the false dawn filtered through the trees and into the open tent flap, she realized it was nearly morning and she hadn't slept. Deep inside, something urged her. Send your love with him.

"Two Feathers are you awake?"

"Yes, I haven't slept."

"I will marry you, but not at the summer meeting. I want Father Bob to do it, here and the way the Christian people do it, with God's blessing. I do love you Two Feathers. Please come back to me unharmed." He rolled over to her on her furs and held her close and then for the first time, he kissed her, not as a brother, but as a man in love.

"I wish we were back already! Your promise will make this trip seem much longer."

He forced himself to get up and to start readying his horses. He could hear others moving about talking in camp. It wasn't long before Father Bob appeared in the center of camp riding Macho and leading one of the big work horses.

Chief Dark Wolf was also ready. He was amused at Father Bob's choice of the big horse, until Father Bob explained that he wanted to be sure they could bring the shields back and this big fellow can easily pull a heavy travois if needed.

When the thirty warriors had assembled in the common area of camp seated on their mounts and holding the leads of the pack horses, Father Bob dressed in his priest's robes raised his right hand high and blessed the men and the camp. He held the cross that he had filed into a knife.

"In the name of the Father and of the Son and of the Holy Ghost, may this camp and all who are in it, be protected by the Holy Spirit. May we ride to the camp of the Abalinah, with the Lion of Judah as our leader and guide. We will witness His victory. He will successfully free the people held captive there. We will be His instruments in this battle against sin. Amen"

"Amen." All the people gathered there, responded. The women tried to be brave, but had to quickly wipe away tears. There was always concern and worry when their men went to war. They wondered whose husband would not return and who would be injured. The winter long anticipation had made it worse.

Father Bob walked his horse slowly out of camp, passed the lake, the church and without entering the meadow; he led the warriors into the north woods. Two Feathers rode beside him on his right. He noticed that the crucifix, made into a knife was now fastened on top of the bundles on the huge work horse for all to see and remember. Debon rode on Father Bob's left. Chief Dark Wolf and Growling Bear rode in the third position in the column. In front of them were Sky Fire and Young Blood. Without a word said, the men were riding in the positions they had seen in the dream. It was comfortable, and felt right. How strange, thought Chief Dark Wolf, I feel as if I am being protected, and he was. God had placed him where he needed to be.

The men and horses moved along smoothly, without strain and an odd quiet rode with them. They sensed this would be a war like no other they had ever been in.

None of them had ever ridden such a long distance to declare war on an enemy that they would find, outnumbered them three to one.

They rode, stopped, ate, rested and rode some more. Days passed. The mountain rumbled as they neared, as if to object to their presence in the area. They continued on until finally the scouts stopped their progress to warn the men that they were nearing the area where Night Hawk had been shot with the poison tipped arrow. Father Bob turned the column into the nearby trees.

Now it is time to let God show us His plan. We need a couple men to look for and capture their sentry. Debon will be able to help with that. The rest of us will wait here in the trees.

"I will go with Debon," said Growling Bear. "You said capture. You want him alive?"

158

"Yes Growling Bear, we need to talk to him. Don't kill him."

Debon smiled nervously as he loosed the burden from his horses and tied them where they could reach grass. He watched to see what Growling Bear was doing and did the same. He poured water into a deep cooking pot and set it where both his horses could drink. He waited and filled it again.

"Let's go," said Growling Bear. "Where are the sentries?"

"They have a post on that highest ledge. I don't know how we can get him down without him seeing us coming."

"Do they have only one guard?"

"Yes, they are very comfortable thinking they are safe here. They count on their wall protecting them."

"I think they will soon regret that," said Growling Bear. "When does that guard come down?"

"He comes down just before it gets really dark. There is a path. I'll show you."

Staying close to the rocks they crept silently to the place where Debon indicated that it was the start of the guard's path. Growling Bear still had not spotted the sentry and said so.

"Where is he? I can't see him."

"Look toward the setting sun. He is up and to the right. He should be coming down soon."

"He will wish he hadn't when I get my hands on him," whispered Growling Bear.

"Remember, Father Bob wants him alive."

"I know."

They waited impatiently until it was very dark.

Finally they could hear the guard coming down across the rocks and onto the path near them. Growling Bear stood and leaned against the rock with his knife drawn. He wanted badly to use it but he didn't. Instead he reached out his arm and encircled the sentries' neck, placing the sharp blade against it.

"Do not make a sound," instructed Debon. They slowly moved back to the trees where the men of the people waited. Father Bob pointed to the ground near their small camp fire and Growling Bear pushed him down against the base of a tree nearby.

"What do you want us to do with him?" Debon asked as he sat down beside the man. "I know him well. He is my age and has a wife and one child. His name is Soren. He is a good man and has done nothing wrong. Don't kill him."

"We hope that it is not in God's plan to kill anyone. God does not punish those that are righteous. Proverbs 11: 8 NIV says, "The righteous man is rescued from trouble, and it falls on the wicked instead." Father Bob knelt near the fire and the chosen men knelt with him.

"Father God, Proverbs 11: 21 NIV says, "Be sure of this, the wicked will not go unpunished but those who are righteous will go free."

We have come here to follow your instructions. We want to set those people free that have been captured and held as slaves. We leave punishment to your hand. Our Father who art in heaven," He continued praying until he knew that they were to rest there and wait for more guidance.

"Debon, explain to him, why we are here and tell him that if he cooperates, we will not harm him. Growling Bear, Sky Fire and Chief Dark Wolf have many questions for him. Tell him that he must answer them truthfully."

They questioned him, late into the night until they had drawn a detailed map of the Abalinah camp and knew where everything was and where the slaves were kept and where the warriors were. Soren willingly answered the questions, but pleaded for the lives of his wife and daughter. Debon translated an assurance to him that if he did as he was told, they would be spared.

"You must hang this white branch on the outside of your tent near the doorway. Tell your wife to go inside with the child when you know that we are coming. If she does, they will not be harmed. Say nothing of our being here. If you do, we will be able to tell and we will not honor our promise to spare your family," said Father Bob.

"You will need to explain why you are so late returning." Growling Bear hit Soren hard on his face, causing him to fall. "Tell anyone that asks that you fell and just now were able to make your way back. It is the truth."

They banked their small fire and rested. Chief Dark Wolf and Father Bob talked as they ate their breakfast.

"After the men finish eating I will say Mass and we will pray. Then the men must make ladders so that they can easily and quietly climb to the top of the west wall."

"Why would you want them to do that? The doorway in the wall is on the southwest, they can go in there."

"No, God has directed us to put our men with the shields on top of the west wall tonight." Sky Fire and Growling Bear thought that this was peculiar. "We will need to capture the guard that watches the herd and the guard that climbs down the rocks tonight at dusk."

Growling Bear laughed.

"I will do that. Now that I know where they go, it will be easy. The Abalinah are not strong warriors." Debon volunteered to capture the herdsman.

"He knows me and will allow me to approach. He will think that I am returning from a journey as before."

"Two Feathers, you should go with Debon tonight. Tie the young man to a tree where he will be out of harm's way."

"Yes Father Bob, but will I then go on the wall with the others?"

"No, next you will help Falling Stones fasten as many of their horses on our ropes as you can catch. You both have a way with horses. You and Debon will then enter the camp from the back where they are working on the wall. Prepare the slaves to run to the back wall at our signal. Open the seams in their slave tents so they can burst through and all leave at once. Tell them to take what they must. They will not be coming back. Lead those people all back here through the trees and around the lake. They will be frightened. Treat them kindly. Debon and Two Feathers, God has given you the responsibility and honor of freeing the people that we have come to rescue."

"Chief Dark Wolf, as soon as Growling Bear sees him; he will secure the guard to a tree, and with him and the rest of the men, you must climb the wall, handing up the covered shields. It is imperative that it is done silently and that the shields stay covered until the signal. Once you are up there, lie down on top of the wall and just wait. Don't talk, not at all, not one word."

"Night Hawk and Snapping Turtle will be with me. We will lead our horses and theirs swiftly around the outside of the wall making as much noise as we can. We will tie pans and cans on ropes to their horses so that they clang as they move."

"The signal for all of us to move is when the sun breaks over the trees in the east and touches the top of the west wall. Then stand with the polished shields and reflect the sun onto the Chief's and warrior's tents."

"When you see the sun reflecting from the shields, Two Feathers and Debon, take the slaves out the back partial wall and into the trees. Do it quickly because the horses will be coming around swiftly. We don't want them to be injured by the horses. None of this makes much sense to me either," he said as he looked at the puzzled faces of the warriors. "Remember, we are just setting the stage for God. This is what He has asked us to do and we must do it willingly and not question His wisdom."

"Aren't we supposed to take our weapons up on the wall? What if they shoot at us?" Standing Bear asked the question that they all wanted answered.

"I don't know what will happen. It won't hurt to take your guns or bows, but remember it is all to be taken up there silently. The shield has to be ready when the sun touches the wall."

Everyone was restless and eager to begin. Yet they thought it all sounded like something that would last just long enough to roust the Abalinah warriors and they wondered what would happen when they had to fight them from the top of the wall. Sky Fire wondered how they could get down fast enough to fight them inside the wall of the fortified camp.

"We will need to pull our ladders up so we can come down inside when the time comes."

"I don't know about that, Sky Fire. God didn't mention it," Father Bob said with a smile. "I am going to sleep for a few hours until it is time to start." He curled up on a hide near the tiny fire pit and soon was sound asleep.

Debon and Two Feathers were unable to relax and so they went through their temporary camp gathering any ropes that were left after the men had lashed together six tall ladders. The ladders were fastened on oiled hides and formed a slippery skid for the big work horse to pull to the base of the wall when the time arrived.

Father Bob stood up and stretched.

"It is time. We are ready," he said, getting up on Macho and nodding to Growling Bear who had accomplished his task of dispatching the guard without a sound. The guard had struggled against his ropes for a while but realized that at least he was unharmed and accepted that he could not get loose. Falling Stones, Two Feathers and Debon coaxed ropes onto the necks of many of their horses and were ready to hand them over to Night Hawk and Snapping Turtle when the time came.

The men moved around the lake slowly each one knowing that they were part of something very special. They attached their horses to the long ropes that Father Bob, Night Hawk and Snapping Turtle held. The ladders were in place and men scurried up and across the top of the thick wall. Growling Bear stood at the bottom of one of the ladders handing up the covered shields.

The men had managed to take their positions without discovery, although Father Bob thought that they had been anything but silent. He watched the trees in the east take on a yellow glow knowing that by now, Two Feathers and Debon were in the slave tents, preparing the people for their exit. He held as many ropes as he could. One of them had the noisy collection attached. Night Hawk would lead the third batch of horses, Snapping Turtle the second and Father Bob would bring the first group with the long rope of noisemakers bouncing along behind them. He had fastened his cross knife to his chest. He felt it had to be near his heart.

The beam of sunlight hit the shields with such intensity, that its power was magnified as it reflected back to the area within the camp. The men on the wall could not open their eyes. They tipped their shields and tried to hold them so that the beams of sunlight would reach the tents that were their targets. The bright light made it impossible to see what they were doing. They balanced the shields with one hand and covered their eyes with their other arm.

As the magnified light beamed across the camp, Two Feathers and Debon knew without a doubt that this was the signal. Men, women and one very small girl ran to the unfinished back wall screaming. Propelled by fear they entered the woods in time to safely watch galloping strings of horses stampede around the exterior of the wall, while sounding like hundreds of riding warriors.

It was from those trees surrounded by the rescued slaves that Two Feathers saw the men and women of the Abalinah kneeling in the dirt with their backs to the chosen men on the wall. They had no idea who was attacking them but the blinding light and sound of the huge number of their horses had brought them trembling to their knees. They covered their faces but the light had already burned their eyes. He could see Hondor and Okallah, cringing with the rest as their tent burst into flames behind them and the large fire pit in the center of camp began to smolder. It kindled adding its heat, as tent after tent ignited.

A small tent stood separate from the rest, against the back wall, with a white branch against its doorway. Debon hollered loudly.

"Soren, come with us. Bring your family and come." Hesitantly Soren pushed back the flap and stepped out. He did not look to the camp but kept his eyes on the trees and the people in them. He motioned for his wife Cumae and daughter Obona to come and instructed them not to look at the camp but to watch the people in the trees. He stayed between them and the awful light until they had all crossed the short row of rocks that was the start of the back wall.

Behind the taller portion and then finally protected by the stone wall that stood between them and the camp of the Abalinah; the escaping people followed Debon.

The sound of the horses was gone. Father Bob had taken them fully around three times. Night Hawk and Snapping Turtle had led some of the familiar riding horses into the woods where the captives were relieved to find they did not have to walk around the large lake. He led them all to the temporary camp after allowing them to drink at the edge of the lake. In the trees the horses stood in the shade, sweating but happy for the exercise.

"Let's walk them down a ways and then bring them back so they can cool off," said Night Hawk. Father Bob and Snapping Turtle agreed.

"We should take most of the horses when we leave. I don't want things to be easy or to ever return to normal for these wicked people," said Snapping Turtle.

Father Bob rode to the west wall taking the string of the men's favorite saddle horses and signaled for the men to lay their shields down and cover them. Growling Bear came down the ladder carrying two and quietly placed them on the grass. Others handed down the shields and with everyone working as one, they came down as quickly and quietly as they went up. The ropes were removed from the ladders and the poles scattered in the trees. The men rode back to their temporary camp with the shields resting in front of them, for the first time.

CHAPTER THIRTEEN
SAVED OR PUNISHED

Chief Dark Wolf was frowning as he rode into the trees and started to rub down his horse. Others were doing the same. They continued to work until all the horses were comfortable.

Two Feathers appeared soon after; and Debon came last, with a look of horror on his face.

"What is the matter Debon?"

"They are burned! All the adults are burned. The little children seem to have been protected but the adults are blind!"

Father Bob understood the distress.

"Debon, God has punished them. They will heal and live, but they will not inflict their terror ever again. He has chosen to allow them to live. I must admit that I thought that He would kill them all."

Growling Bear walked around muttering.

"What is it?"

"He did it all, and we didn't use a bow or gun. Their village is destroyed. It lies in ashes. The only tents standing are the slave tents. They will now have to use the single walled tents that these poor people were forced to live in during the cold of winter. It is good," he said with a heavy sigh.

The rescued people straggled into the trees hesitantly; a few at a time and the men suddenly realized that they should immediately provide what was needed. The last woman sank to the ground and wept. She carried a small girl and her body revealed that she would soon deliver another child. Two other women sat near her. They spoke so softly that their words could not be heard.

Sky Fire searched the faces of the slaves, hoping to see his son or daughter that had been taken.

Father Bob directed that food and water be given to them immediately. He noticed many dark bruises and cringed when a young man turned his back to reveal fresh lash marks not more than a day or two old. Quickly he thanked God for the medicine packed by Sweet Grass and brought it near the fire. One at a time the rescued people were treated and given food and water. The shields were placed face down so that many of the blankets could be used to bring comfort. They all ate and then rested. The little girl cried, but the mother had no milk to offer her. She was very thin and so was the child. Father Bob got out some travel cakes and warmed them in a pan with water. As they heated, the broth they produced was rich and tasty. Using a big cup with just a small quantity, he blew on it and swirled it and blew again until it was just warm. He gave the cup to the mother for the little girl. He filled a second one for the mother.

When Sky Fire walked through the camp a second time, he found his children. They sat huddled together. They were starving and had been badly abused. A scar ran across the boy's shoulder and several stripes were still healing on his back. None of the slaves had ample clothing.

When they finally realized that they had been found by their father, they both cried and clung to him. His tears flowed, as holding his daughter and son tightly, he told them that they would be well again and that God had rescued them all. It was the first time that Sky Fire had actually acknowledged out loud that he believed in a saving God and truly meant it. He had been baptized, but he had done it to be able to go.

"God gave back my children. They were dead to us, but now they are alive. Thank you God," he shouted and wept.

His girl looked very frail. They had come just in time to save her life.

Two Feathers hoped that one of the women would be Water Bug's mother. He didn't know what she looked like and didn't know the boy's Sentu name.

"Who is Sentu?" He said loudly. "Is anyone here from the Sentu camp?"

"I am," said the woman with the little girl. "They took two of us that day. My son was in the water but they didn't even hesitate so that I could get him.

"Who else is from the Sentu?"

"She is dead. She would not yield to Night Crier and he beat her. He was head of their warriors. He was more vicious than Chief Gray Fox. She died during that first night in their camp. I prayed that someone in the Sentu camp would live and find my son. I had to live for him. I did what that beast required, to live."

"I can see that you will have another child soon. When will it come?"

"I don't know, but you are right. It will be soon."

"Are you well enough to ride?" I don't know. I will have to be. Won't I?"

"We will take care of you and your children. What is your name?" I took the name Clover, when I got here."

"That is a good name." He sat down beside her and wondered how to tell her that she could live in his tent with Willow and Water Bug. He didn't want her to think it was obligatory to stay there. It was crucial that he said it in a way that she would feel wanted.

"I have some good news for you. I am from the camp of the Sentu. I was on my three day journey when they raided

169

our camp. When I returned, I found a young woman. She took the name Willow. She was caring for a toddler that she had named Water Bug. She had held him in the brush willows during the raid. She has taken very good care of him and he is well and strong. He lives with us. Willow has agreed to be my wife soon. I believe that Water Bug is your son."

The woman looked stunned. She was staring at his face but seemed not to comprehend what he had told her. "Clover, I think that the little boy we found is your boy!"

"It can't be! They killed everyone. I saw him swing his club at my boy's head! God saved my boy?! I prayed that somehow He would save him."

"Clover, I think he missed him completely. He was in the water unharmed and Willow is in our tent right now taking good care of him. She is making room for you so you can be with him. We have been praying every night that you would be found."

"My boy loved the water. It was just a trickle where I let him play while I worked. Could it be?"

Father Bob had noticed the intense conversation going on between them and walked over.

"Is everything alright here?"

"It is better than that, Father Bob I believe that this is Water Bug's mother."

"Oh Two Feathers, God is so good! How did you discover it?"

"I was asking for anyone from the Sentu and there she was. Willow was sure that we would find her. She is making room for her in our tent."

"You are specially blessed my son. I don't know what God has planned for you but I feel that it is something greater than any of us can imagine."

Soren shyly approached the priest and Debon near the fire. He asked what would become of the herdsman and the night guard that Growling Bear had tied to a tree.

"I'm not sure but perhaps Chief Dark Wolf will have a word of wisdom for us."

"I heard my name. Did you need me?"

"We are pondering a question. What should we do with the two men that we have tied to trees?

"They are both very young. Perhaps it would be best if we send them back to their camp and tell them to care for the children until the parents can."

"Yes, I think that is a good thing. That whole camp has an opportunity to learn compassion. Maybe it will start with those two," said Father Bob. "I want to pray for them and then talk to them before they are free to return to their camp. Debon, come with me. They will not understand me. I need you to interpret."

Soren felt displaced, until Cumae, like any mother noticed needs that the men didn't. She called Soren to her and asked him to inquire if any of the men had extra clothing in their packs. Moonflower had placed a half bolt of tan cotton on Chief Dark Wolf's pack horse. He was annoyed at the time. He saw no need for it.

Now he watched as it was cut in sections that reached from knee to shoulder and back again. A strip torn from the side became a belt and a slit allowed the wearer to pull it over their head and bind it at their waist. He was amazed at Moonflower's wisdom. Men that had not had the benefit of a shirt for a long time, now gladly pulled a shorter version of the garment over their heads and tied it, smiling. He was glad that she had chosen to send tan and not bright or flowered fabric.

Some of the people were eating and resting well, but a few were extremely weak and it was obvious that the rescue was nearly too late. They lingered in the temporary camp for two days to allow all of them to gain a little strength. Sky Fire and Young Blood did not wait until it was suggested. They carefully constructed a travois for Quiet Dawn and another for Clover. They padded them and had them ready when Father Bob said that it was time to leave for home. Eighteen people traveled with them that the Blue Stone warriors had humbly served, and helped to save.

Two Feathers chatted with Debon and Soren as the long column of people and pack horses slowly moved toward home and freedom. Some days, in the beginning, they were only able to travel a few hours. Each day, each step the horses took brought the knowledge to the rescued, that this was real. They were free from the Abalinah.

Chief Dark Wolf occasionally rode to the side and watched as the column passed. He was amazed that God had done this; using his warriors without war. No one was killed during the rescue.

Father Bob had discovered a woman that had been taken when her wagon train had stopped for the night.

"They covered my mouth and carried me away. I was young and pretty then. I kicked and bit but it did no good. One of the men hit me so hard that he knocked me out. When I woke up it was night. After a few times in the tent with him, I felt ugly and old and dirty. He had a wife but he wanted me anyway. She hated me and soon put me in the slave tents. I was glad. We all preferred being there to living with the Abalinah. We worked hard and our food was minimal. We carried all the wood for the fires and the water pots from the lake. We were required to fetch the horses when they wanted to ride a particular one. We had to process the meat and hides when the men hunted, and we all worked carrying stones for the wall. Their women did very little and gave orders easily. Some of them were worse than their men. Do this! Get that! Whack, they would hit us with a stick or whip if they didn't like the way we did our work or thought we were not fast enough. Many of them killed the children of slaves at birth. I had one boy. He was better off in heaven than living with me in hell." Father Bob took a deep breath and gave a sad sigh.

"I am so sorry, Sylvia. You will never be treated like that again. The men that came for you are from The Blue Stone People. They are good men and they believe in God. None of them would ever harm a woman or child. There are no slaves in our camp. When there is work to be done everyone helps. You will see. If you want to go, I will take you to Fort Connor when you are strong enough. Do you have people back east that you would want to return to?"

"No! Who would want me now?"

"You will think differently when you are healthy and rested. What is your full name, the one your parents gave you?"

"I am Sylvia Warren."

"Sylvia, you are still beautiful. You are a child of the living God. You will feel beautiful again when you are healthy and strong. Do not doubt it."

"Father Bob, I have scars on my body, and inside my mind and heart where no one can see them. They will never heal. I can never have a real family."

"You may think that now, but look what God has done already. All things are possible with God." Tears made their way down her face as she rode along. She made no attempt to brush them away. She seemed not to notice the tears as she offered him a small smile that didn't reach her eyes.

*****

"Sarah, are you sure you should be doing this?"

"Yes Ben, I will be fine. I feel wonderful now that the morning sickness is gone. I am glad to be out in the warm sunshine. Winter seemed long this year."

"David are you sure that you can keep track of the three milk cows and their calves and Sarah?" David laughed.

"You know we will all be moving slowly. The calves are young enough that they tire easily. That will give Sarah a chance to rest each time we stop."

"The wagon will be good to take because as usual, Sarah has decided to take some of everything on the ranch!"

"David you know that having chickens will improve their diet. We have plenty now and I don't mind sharing. I will show them how to milk the cows, and how to care for the chickens. It is good that you are sending young Bully. He is a handsome young male and will be glad to be the only Holstein bull around."

"Just be sure you stay away from him Sarah. David knows how to handle him and he didn't get that name just by his gender."

"Yes Ben, I know. I will stay away from him. He does have an attitude sometimes. Are you sure that the two barrels hold enough water for all the animals?"

"Everything is taken care of. You have more than enough of everything. The food is there and the bolts of cloth are there under the oiled hides along with the gifts you made and the things we are sending for Father Bob. He will be glad to get his mail. I put it in that pouch on the side along with the drilled nugget. Be sure you give him our love and let him know that we are continuing to pray for him and the campaign."

At the last minute David added his small hunting tent to the pile in the wagon.

"That's just in case it storms. We have a hide for the chicken cage but I don't want Sarah to get wet and chilled."

The family stood on the other side of the crossing waving and yelling goodbye, as the strange group started out on their journey. Sarah had not brought a riding horse. Instead she was on the seat of the wagon. Jed and Ben had improved it by adding a backrest and the seat was padded. Under the seat she had stuffed her knitting and carefully wrapped in the basket with it, was her Bible.

The horses plodded along at a slow walk. David rode Blackie, watching the calves for any sign of tiring. Ben had given him that horse as part of their wedding gifts.

"Your people will be surprised to see you and the size you are," David said with a grin.

"Never mind about my size, you have gained a few pounds, and you can't use my excuse! What do you mean my people? They are your people just as much as mine."

"I guess that's true but I always think of you as the Chief's daughter."

"David, do you think that Father Bob is gone to war with the Abalinah? If they did they should be back by now."

"I don't know. It was something that Father Bob seemed mysterious about. Like he thought God was going to direct him or something."

"He was certainly listening and getting directions when he put Matt Morgan to work making thirty shields."

"It is hard to picture the Blue Stone warriors carrying shields and why only thirty?" Sarah was puzzled.

"The whole thing is certainly strange. I think when it is over; Father Bob will have a story to tell that is different from anything we have heard before!"

"David I think we need to stop. The calves are falling behind again."

"At the slow pace we are traveling, it will take three days to get there."

"I don't mind. Do you?"

"No not really." David pulled the group up to a small stand of trees and watered the animals. Sarah took his hand and stepped down carefully.

"I almost think that it is easier to ride on Moon Boy. The wagon seems to move from side to side continually. Let's stay here and move out in the morning."

"That's fine. This is your idea anyway. I'm just here to babysit all of you."

"David that sounds like you didn't really want to come."

"I just think it would have been better to wait until you had the baby."

"I have been going crazy worrying about the people tangling with a vicious big bunch of warriors in the Abalinah camp and you have, too. It is better for us to know what is going on than deal with our imaginations." Sarah walked back to a calf that was nursing while her tired mother munched on the prairie grass. "I'm glad that you picked these three cows. They are the gentlest ones in Jed's herd and it will make it easier for the women to learn how to milk them and care for them."

She plopped down on a blanket that David had spread in the shade. He carried over a big food satchel and a water bag.

"We could stay out here a long time with all the food that Beth and Mary packed for us. This brown bread is really tasty with the new cheese." David was an avid fan of the girl's efforts to make various types of cheese. Sarah smiled but knew that he would enjoy arriving and visiting at The Blue Stone Camp as much as she would.

Once the calves were satisfied and the cows had eaten their fill, they settled in the grass for the night. Bully got as near them as his rope would allow and then he lay down and slept. They were all tired from traveling.

As David predicted, it took nearly three days to get there at the pace traveled by the calves. The guard at the path through the big rocks was Running Deer and he greeted them enthusiastically.

"Sharp Knife and Sarah, it is good to see you. Blue Stone and Happy Song will be glad you are here. It has been a long time since you visited."

"I hope that I get to spend more time with them this visit," replied Sarah.

"Your mother is here and well and Snow Star and Flying Eagle are here. He is in charge until Chief Dark Wolf returns."

"Where is Chief Dark Wolf?"

"He has gone with Father Bob to the Abalinah camp to rescue the slaves."

"Oh David, this could be very bad! How long have they been gone?"

"They left at the new moon. It is a half-moon now. Don't worry Sarah. Father Bob said that it will be a victory and that "The Lion of Judah" was leading them. He appeared to Father Bob in the church and told him the names of all the men that were chosen to go." David was frowning.

"They should be back by now! It can't take this long."

"They will bring back the captives," said Running Deer. "They will have to travel slowly if anyone is injured. It is good that you are here Sarah. Sweet Grass will be glad to have the help when they arrive." With that thought she was grim faced as they entered the woods. Coyote was standing guard at the edge of the trees and was pleased also to have the famous Sarah here when the men returned. He watched the loaded wagon and tired animals following it slowly.

David pulled the wagon near the back of church and stopped. Flying Eagle came at a trot to give hugs and showed his curiosity as he studied the cows, calves and Bully.

"These are different. The big cattle we have seem fierce. These look gentle. "

"Yes, they are easier to handle. Sarah wanted to bring them and will teach the women how to get milk from them, so that the children will have fresh milk to drink."

"The milk cows need to be separate from the beef cattle. Can you assign some men to make them a big pen? Running Deer said you are in charge while the Chief is gone."

"Sarah do you think it would be acceptable to tie their ropes to bushes close to the woods for now? They will have grass, water and shade there.

"After Bully drinks and is away from the people he will settle down, but for now we better warn everyone to stay clear of him."

David led the young bull to the edge of the lake and waited while he drank and then tied him in the trees away from the normal area used by the people.

"We have another gift that will also require a pen. Sarah had placed a hide over their little coop to provide shade as they traveled. Now she pulled it off.

"What are they for?"

"They are a good food source for the children. They lay eggs and will multiply. The one with the big tail is the rooster. He will let you know when it is morning with his crowing."

"The crying babies in this camp do a good job of waking us up, but maybe he can learn to sing them to sleep." They all laughed at that remark.

Several women recognized Sarah from a distance and found Moonflower before Sarah had walked the short distance to the path around the lake. Moonflower and Snow Star came with their arms open for hugs. Snow star carried her second son but still managed to wrap one arm around Sarah. Watching Owl ran to them too, but stayed back. He had been too young to remember them from their visit, but he could see that his mother and grandmother were joyous to see them. Flying Eagle scooped his son up and placed him on his shoulders telling him that this was Sarah and Sharp Knife. David was amused that Flying Eagle used the white man's name for Sarah but reverted to his Blue Stone name.

Moonflower patted Sarah's belly and laughed out loud.

"We are going to have another baby soon!"

"Yes, I think it will be just one more moon, but I need to see this little one. Snow Star he is handsome. What is his name?"

" Little Hawk is a big boy already, but how did you know that my baby is a boy?"

"I like the strong chin and big eyes. He just looks like a boy. When did he come?"

179

"He was born only one moon ago." Sarah kissed the baby's forehead but didn't take him. She needed to sit down and rest.

"You must stay in my tent. The men will bring back people soon and they will need to use the big tent for them. Look, it is bigger now. We have added a few of the hides from the cattle. Come sit. You must be tired," said Moonflower.

"I am tired, Mother, but I would like to unload the wagon first and then we can have some tea."

As soon as she said that, a surge of women headed to the area behind the church and the work of unloading was done quickly. The big boxes and pouches, satchels and packages were all placed on the grass beside Moonflower's tent.

Like children they hovered near, wanting to see what was inside.

Dancing Willow came with Blue Stone and Happy Song toddled beside her adopted grandmother, Smiling Moon; holding tight to one finger. They hugged and talked and laughed, spreading blankets and making themselves comfortable. Sweet Grass joined the group and soon Morning Dove appeared too.

CHAPTER FOURTEEN
THE ARRIVAL

David slipped away to find some men to talk to. He knew that as soon as he started to work on a chicken pen, that he would have lots of help, so that was what he did.

The atmosphere in the village felt strange with so many men gone.

Moonflower built up her outdoor cooking fire and while Sweet Grass brought a big pan of steaming sweet tea, she made corn cakes and heated some shredded meat to roll inside them.

"You look well, Sarah. Are you hungry?"

"It seems that I have been eating a lot since I got pregnant, but I can always eat more. The baby is growing fast. I can tell. He kicks hard." They laughed and Moonflower couldn't resist rubbing Sarah's tummy and then hugging her again. "I had to make myself this big dress to wear," Sarah complained. "All my clothes were tight!"

"Soon I will have another grandchild to hold." Moonflower couldn't stop grinning.

Sheltah and Willow finally came over, seeing the women gathered, talking and laughing. Moonflower introduced them and told them that this was Sarah, her daughter. Willow held Water Bug's hand but he was more interested in seeing what the men were doing and wanted to get closer to the new animals he could see. He asked to be released and she finally let him go, knowing that the men would keep him from approaching the animals too closely.

"Willow and her son Water Bug survived the raid of the Abalinah on the camp of the Sentu. Two Feathers found them and together they are starting a new people called

The People of the Lion. The camp of the Sentu is gone," explained Moonflower. "Sheltah and Debon are from the Abalinah, but we have accepted them, because God sent them to us. Debon was the first man chosen by The Lion of Judah to go with Father Bob."

"Mother this is all very confusing. Are you telling me that all our friends and our cousins in the Sentu camp are gone?"

"Yes Sarah, Willow hid the boy in the brush along the stream and saved his life. She has taken care of him since then."

Sweet Grass could see a change in Sarah's complexion. The news of the raid on the Sentu had upset her. Wisely the healer quickly crumbled chamomile blossoms in a pan and added a scoop of the sweet tea and put it close to the fire. She felt concern for Sarah. She is tired from the long trip here and the pregnancy. Now the stress of the bad news is showing, she thought.

"Moonflower, I have some good news that I can tell," said Willow proudly. "Two Feathers asked me to marry him and I said I would, but not at the summer council. I want to be married here by Father Bob." It would always cause Willow great pain to hear any talk about the camp of the Sentu. She was glad to have something nice to tell, so she could change the subject.

"Oh Willow, that is wonderful. Do you know when?"

"No, because he just asked me the night before he left. I have been praying constantly that he will come back to me uninjured." Sarah looked at the young woman and smiled.

"Did you know that I was married here by Father Bob? I was the first Christian bride here."

"That's really nice. I am so glad to meet you Sarah. I have heard a lot about you." Sarah continued to smile, but she wanted to know more about Sheltah and Debon and about the Lion talking to Father Bob.

"Sheltah, how were you brought back here by the Lion? It all seems mysterious. Where were you?"

"We had been here for more than a year, sent here, with two other couples, by the Abalinah council, but we were to spy on The Blue Stone People and find out where the blue stones were and to take over the leadership. Kier heard the workers chipping the stone on the bluff. They were getting upset because they couldn't find any more of the blue stones, so when he told Okallah that they had depleted the supply of the stones, immediately they decided it was time to leave and they made us leave, too. We didn't want to go back there, but Kier told us that the soldiers were coming to raid this camp because the Blue Stone hunters had stolen cattle from a rancher and that if we stayed here the soldiers would kill us! It's just all a big mess."

"As soon as we returned to the camp of the Abalinah, we knew that this was where we belonged and the longer we were there the stronger the feeling grew until Debon told me he wanted to leave the Abalinah and come back here if the people would let us and I said I wanted to come back. We didn't know if the soldiers had come or not. We wondered if the people here were still alive. We were worrying about them."

"The Blue Stone People always treated us well and taught us many things. We knew that the way the Abalinah treated their captives was horrid but we couldn't do anything to stop them. We took food and left it in their tent a couple times but I got caught and I thought that Chief Gray Fox was going to kill me or make me one of the slaves.

He said if I ever went there again, that he would kill me!"
Sheltah continued.

"We brought a water bag and some food and left that
night. The priest here was praying because he wanted God
to tell him what to do, but I don't think he knew that The
Lion of Judah would come to him in the church."

After that, he told everyone that Debon was brought
back here by The Lion to help the men so they could rescue
the people in the slave tents."

"Oh Sheltah, I didn't understand. You have been
through so much. I shouldn't have asked you," said Sarah.

"It is alright that you know. Many people here still
don't understand and they mistrust us, because we are
Abalinah. I am sure that they doubt what I say and are
suspicious. They have been lied to and the Abalinah have
hurt many people here. I hope that one day they will
forgive us for our deception."

Sarah's face was paler than usual and she was upset.
She had no idea that she would be sipping tea with one of
the Abalinah. She wasn't sure if she believed this girl any
more than the others did.

"Moonflower, I think Sarah is very tired. I would like
her to drink this chamomile tea that I made for her and
then she should rest for a while." Sweet Grass had learned
to take charge just as Sarah had when the occasion called
for it. The other women took that as a strong suggestion
that they all go back to their tents, and each stood and gave
Sarah a little hug and moved away as they thanked
Moonflower for the tea and corn cakes. Blue Stone held her
gently and whispered that she would have plenty of time to
visit now that she was home. Smiling Moon hadn't said a
word but patted Sarah's shoulder and grinned as she left.

Dancing Willow and Morning Dove said they were glad that she was back and that they would see her tomorrow.

Soon Moonflower found that she finally had Sarah and Snow Star all to herself. Sweet Grass had slipped away to do some more work in the big tent, to ready it for the expected arrival of the rescued captives.

"Sarah let's just relax for a while," said Moonflower. Is there anything in your packages that will be harmed by leaving it out tonight? It isn't going to rain. The sky is clear."

"Yes I brought some cheese for you to try. I don't want an animal to carry it off. There are two loaves of fresh brown bread there in that tin box. That should be brought in, too."

Snow Star sniffed at the cheese package and said she thought it was spoiled.

"No it is supposed to smell strong like that. Open it and take a taste."

Hesitantly she loosened the string and folded back the brown paper. "Just cut a tiny piece from the corner."

Moonflower wrinkled her nose but took the package from Snow Star.

She sniffed at it and said that maybe she would taste it later. Sarah laughed at them and suggested they remove the bread and put the cheese in the tin.

"You don't want the whole tent to smell like that."

Mary had wrapped the bread in brown paper. It would stay fine without the tin.

"This is good. I will use this," said Moonflower, but she began to frown as she saw Sarah grimace and arch her back.

"I think I should lie down. The wagon ride has made my back hurt."

Sarah entered the tent and Snow Star said she was taking Watching Owl and Little Hawk back to her tent so that it would be quiet.

"I'll talk to you in the morning," she said as she left. Moonflower crawled in close to Sarah and said they should just enjoy being together as they rested.

After a few minutes they both relaxed and Moonflower went to sleep. Sarah couldn't sleep. Her pain had diminished but later returned with a sharp grip that sprang through to her front. She clenched her teeth and waited. It softened and finally was gone. She told herself that it was just her muscles practicing for the real thing, but when another pain gripped her, she gasped and the sound woke her mother.

"Sarah, are you ill?"

"No, but I think that you will see your grandchild before we leave. Please get Sweet Grass." Moonflower dashed from her tent to the big tent shouting.

Sweet Grass had delivered several babies since Big Flower had her twin boys. She had a big bag that she kept prepared. She came immediately and helped Moonflower clear away the sleeping furs and placed an old soft, oiled hide in their place. Armed with willow bark tea for Sarah, they sat the vigil.

It was quite dark when David came to tell Sarah that the chickens were in their new pen and that he had instructed several people on their care. No one had thought to tell him that Sarah was in labor! First he was concerned but then he became angry.

"Why didn't you send someone to get me?"

Moonflower, apologized, but it didn't seem to calm him down.

"There is nothing that you can do here David. Have you eaten?"

"No, I am not hungry." Flying Eagle came near and suggested that David come with him to their tent. As they sat outside the tent and talked, David did eat and ended up spending the night just inside the flap of the big tent where he would be close to Sarah. Snow Star stuck her head in the tent once and told him that it wouldn't be much longer.

It was dawn when the first cry of a new born baby was heard. Snow Star ran to tell David and bumped into him. He had heard the baby and had come running.

"What is it?"

"A baby!" said Snow Star. "Sarah will tell you when you see. You can't go in yet, but it will just be a few more minutes."

David paced back and forth until Moonflower came out smiling and walked away, then Snow Star, and finally Sweet Grass stepped out and allowed him to enter.

"Sarah, how are you feeling?" His voice was just a whisper.

"I feel much better now that she is here," she laughed.

"Sarah, she is beautiful. She looks like you. We need to think of a name for her."

"I had only planned names for a boy. I was sure our first child would be a son," she said. "She is small, but strong."

David turned to the door. They could both hear someone shouting. Pine Berry had been guarding the north wood near the meadow. He jumped on the nearest horse and rode through camp yelling. "They come! They are coming and they have many people and horses with them!" He jumped down and ran to Flying Eagle's tent, delivering the message again.

"Good Pine Berry, go bring in the night guard. They will want to be here", said Flying Eagle with a huge sigh of relief, he hurried in the direction of the slowly advancing column.

Father Bob and Two Feathers walked their horses side by side and behind them came Chief Dark Wolf and Growling Bear, next Sky Fire and his son Young Blood. Behind them came the young lad, Son of Fire, riding a good-looking paint. He led a pack horse that pulled a travois with his recovering sister, Quiet Dawn.

The women of the Blue Stone Village quickly gathered in the center of camp as soon as they heard the news that the chosen men were returning.

Sweet Grass immediately took the rope on the first pack horse and led it directly to the big tent. Sky Fire slid down from his horse and he carried his daughter into the tent and put her on the first of many pads that Sweet Grass had prepared and waiting. Rippling water burst through the flap and squealed with joy as she realized that her husband was back uninjured and he had brought her children back to her. She first clung to him and then each of the twins, wetting them with her tears of joy. Her young son, Son of Fire, winced when she hugged him but he didn't pull away. He had longed for her embrace. Rippling Water knelt beside Sweet Grass as she offered Quiet Dawn a cup of medicine mixed with tonic and rich beef broth. Her instinct and good training, had led her to have ready, several brews with different medicines. She noticed the young man's discomfort and signaled him to come to the second pad. She helped him removed the improvised shirt and handed him a cup of brew containing willow bark and broth. She placed a large pot of salve she had made, in Rippling Water's hand.

"Smear it on thick and be gentle," she said as she hurried out the door to receive the next patient. Clover was embracing Water Bug in a tight hug that was quite disconcerting to the youngster. Willow stood close and had wrapped her arms around Two Feathers. He picked up the little girl that clung to the hem of Clover's crude garment.

"Willow, this is Water Bug's half-sister, Cricket. Our family will be large now and even bigger soon. Clover is expecting another child shortly." Willow held her arms open and accepted the frail girl and added her love to the hug that Clover was giving Water Bug.

"Clover, I am so happy that you are here and that you and your family have survived. We have been praying for you every day and night. Two Feathers knew that he would find you and bring you back to us. You are my sister. I love you and remember you from the days you worked near the water so that your son could play in the little stream." Willow could feel the need for Clover to rest. She was shaking. Sweet Grass placed her arms around Clover from the back as her knees began to buckle. Two Feathers grabbed her just in time to keep her from falling. He helped to take her in the big tent and she was placed on the third pad.

The center of the camp was a confusion of voices and dust stirred by so many horses. Coyote and Night Hawk pulled gear from the horses as fast as they could.

As soon as families had been greeted by returning warriors, the men helped to take their own favorite horse to the back of their tent and unloaded the pack horses and led them to the meadow.

As the captives were made comfortable in the big tent or on blankets near the communal fire, their horses were also removed from the common area of the camp.

189

Huge pots of rich stews and stewed apples with sugar were placed near the rescued people and victorious returning men.

Father Bob prayed a loud prayer of thanksgiving to the Great Spirit.

"Lion of Judah, we all give you the praise and glory for this wonderful victory! We thank you, for bringing all our warriors back unharmed. We thank you, for the healing that you have begun in the bodies of our new friends. We all thank you for your wisdom and leadership during this campaign and we thank you for the provision that has made this camp and these people strong enough to be used by you to help rescue the captives."

"Amen," A resounding reply was heard; as quickly the women served ladles of food into bowls and handed them to the new people seated around the small ceremonial fire. A large kettle of stew was taken inside the big tent and Sweet Grass found that she had all the help she needed.

While all this was going on Sarah had insisted on being moved out on a blanket near Father Bob. She proudly cradled her newborn daughter in her arms and as soon as Moonflower had managed to collect herself after hugging the breath out of Chief Dark Wolf, she proudly told him that he had a new granddaughter to name. He beamed a wide smile as he peeked into the soft white flannel that swaddled her. He placed a kiss on Sarah's forehead and gave David a strong hug.

"She always comes home when something big is happening! She amazes me. I can see you are taking good care of her, not that she needs taking care of. Thank you Sharp Knife. I will think of a good name for her," he said proudly as he hurried to hug Snow Star, Watching Owl and Little Hawk. He hugged Flying Eagle with enthusiasm and then asked if everything in camp had gone well while they had been gone.

"Yes my Chief." Just that quickly the symbolic staff of authority had shifted back to the Chief.

"Thank you Flying Eagle. I knew that the camp was in good hands. The people we brought are all in a weakened condition. We should do all we can to get them healthy so they can go to the summer meeting. Many of them will join other people there. Some will stay with us and that is good."

"The chosen have done well. I am eager to hear the story of the raid on the Abalinah," said Flying Eagle.

"I will have a meeting but not tomorrow. I need to talk with Father Bob and Sky Fire at length first. It is good to be back." He patted his son-in-law on the shoulder and returned to the fire, to sit near Sarah and Moonflower.

Snow Star had taken Sarah's baby and was carrying her and showing her to everyone. Blue Stone smiled and after looking at the baby girl, she came to Sarah's side. I want to be the first to give a gift to your baby. She opened her hand and in it was a relatively small blue stone, suspended on a piece of yarn.

"Running Deer made it to look like mine. We thought at the time that it was for Happy Song, but now I know it was meant to be hers. What are you going to name her?"

"Oh, thank you Blue Stone. I will treasure this for her until she is old enough to also hold it dear. Father has claimed his right to name her. I wonder what name he will choose. I can still remember how petrified I was on the day Rising Eagle gave me the name Brave Sparrow. Now it won't be that way. It will be a day of celebration for so many reasons!"

"I am so glad that you were in camp when your baby was born. It is a memory we will all hold in our hearts, Sarah."

As soon as the new people in camp had been fed and their wounds attended, by Sweet Grass, they were encouraged to bed down in the big tent. The chamomile and willow bark tea she had served them helped them to relax and by dark the tent was full of sleeping people. Rippling Water had snuggled in-between her children and she spent the night there.

Moonflower was so happy to have all the men back and Sarah in camp with a new baby that she couldn't go to sleep easily. She had heard some of the true stories of the nightmare existence that these people had survived; and they also filled her mind. She thanked God that he had used her husband and the men of their camp to help free them. She wanted to know the whole story of the raid, but was a little afraid to hear it.

Willow had worked hard during the absence of the chosen men. Moonflower had given her several big hides to add to her tent. Sheltah had helped and they sewed the heavy leather until their fingers were sore.

Moonflower had felt sure that Two Feathers would return with Water Bug's mother. She thought that the possibility that she had a child to return to would help her survive. Of course she couldn't have known about Cricket or the expected baby, but with quick and clever repositioning, Willow had made enough room.

Willow brought Water Bug to the big tent often and he and Cricket played well together. He was gentle with her and seemed to realize that she was fragile. Clover watched them in amazement.

"I never really thought that I would get to see them together," she said. "God spared me, for them. Several of the people in the slave tent helped me to hide her. She was a toddler before Chief Gray Fox knew she existed. He caught a glimpse of her one night and for some reason, she smiled at him. He thought she was cute. When he picked her up I feared that he would kill her, but instead he carried her around camp and brought her back to me. God softened his heart toward her because she is his child. Now we are safe from him. Thank you God," she sobbed.

Many tears were shed by the rescued and the Blue Stone People, when they heard their stories; as the healing began. Sarah advised Sweet Grass to use a little of the sleeping herbs in the tea she served them.

"They will heal inside, as they sleep. Rest is the best medicine of all."

"God brought you back here for more than having a baby. I am so glad that you are here at this special time."

"Thank you Sweet Grass, but you are a good healer. Don't ever doubt yourself," said Sarah.

CHAPTER FIFTEEN
THE EIGHTH DAY

Every one of the Blue Stone People had a job and they were busy doing it.

With Sarah's instruction and the three yeast balls that Sarah had brought; the women of the camp were learning to make several big batches of bread dough. Sarah had coaxed the women of the ranch to part with their bread tins. Ben had promised to replace them all soon.

In a covered tin she had also brought five pounds of butter. With the three milk cows in camp the women would soon be making their own butter. Father Bob would have to help them with that when the calves were big enough to be weaned but for now, Sarah was excited to add fresh baked bread with butter on it, to the feast that was being prepared. For most of them it would be a new food. Father Bob had told Sarah that he could milk the cows. That he had done it daily as a boy, so he would be teaching them that skill.

The modified oven was perfect for baking the bread and several of the women voiced a desire to make another oven for communal use.

Sheltah had frowned when she returned to camp to find her oven had been modified, but now she was glad.

"I will help you build two new ovens, and one will be for pottery,' she said laughing.

The guarantee of a supply of meat had made the village of the people a secure place to live. For the first time since their capture, the new people had more than enough available to eat.

It was wonderful to know that they would grow strong and healthy.

As Moonflower sat with her daughters and their children under the trees, she saw Willow hurrying; carrying Cricket and Water Bug was trotting along beside her as she ducked into the big tent. Her face was flush and she seemed worried.

"I wonder what is going on at Willow's tent." Sarah stood, handing her baby to Moonflower. "I think I will go ask if Sweet Grass needs help with anything." Moonflower was glad to take the sweet baby girl.

Just as Sarah arrived at the big tent, Sweet Grass darted out the door with her big bag in hand.

"Clover is getting ready to have her baby. Sarah I can help her. If we run into a problem, I will send for you."

Sarah smiled as she returned to the shade under the trees.

"It sounds like Clover is about to add to The People of the Lion!"

"Strange, but I never thought of it that way. I imagine when the time comes, they will move their people away from us, and some of the young people will go with them. I'm sure we will lose Debon and Sheltah and I noticed that there is a new family of Abalinah that Father Bob and Chief Dark Wolf have accepted and they have been staying with Debon and Sheltah."

"I suppose the Abalinah are like any village of people. They can't all be bad. I wonder what their names are," said Snow Star.

"The woman and her child were at the lake when I was there earlier. Her name is Cumae and her little girl is Obona. She said her husband's name is Soren. I told her she was welcome here. I figure if the men let them come, they must be special. Father Bob would discern it, if it wasn't right," said Moonflower. "I was never completely comfortable with Okallah or Gamier, but this woman has a nice way about her. I liked her right away. She is a little shy though."

"Hmm, Cumae, I have never heard that name before, but it is pretty. It has a nice sound to it. I wonder what name father will choose for this little one," said Snow Star taking the baby from Moonflower.

"I don't know. He hasn't given me a hint."

"Well, I hope it is something that Ben and the rest of my family will like, or she will end up with a nick-name."

"What is a nick-name?"

"It is a shortened or changed version of a name. My brother's wife, Mary, wanted to name their last son Nathanial and Ben said it was fine, but within a couple minutes he was calling the baby Natty and he has been Natty ever since!" The women thought that was funny and laughed about it.

"Do you think they will be upset when they find out that you had the baby here?"

"Well, it isn't as if I planned it that way. They will just have to be glad she is healthy."

Morning Dove strolled over and smiled.

"The cow is in the pit and it is covered and roasting. The bread that the women are baking smells so good I can hardly wait. Father Bob said we all have to wait to taste it. He is hovering over that oven like a hawk!"

"I'm glad that he is there and capable of watching it so it doesn't burn," said Sarah. The baby began to fuss and Sarah took her and nursed her. "You will have a name tonight, my little girl. Your father is as eager as I am to know what it will be. I haven't seen much of him today."

"He is helping with the building of a fence for the milk cows. Some of the men helping are ones that they rescued.

They seem to be getting well but they are thin. They will gain weight now that they can have the food they need. They are eager to work to earn their keep I think," observed Morning Dove.

"You are probably right. It is much better to work when no one is forcing you to do it." Moonflower winced when she heard that. She had seen the whip marks on Son of Fire's back.

"Some of them cannot understand our language. They must have been quite young when they were taken. They speak Abalinah to each other," said Moonflower. "It is important that they learn to trust us and to speak a few basic words of our language before the summer meeting. Most of the people that attend the meeting can speak and understand our words. It will help them to find their people or new people to go with."

"It was easy for me to learn your words, but the trust came slower," said Sarah.

Moonflower looked at her for a moment and her eyes filled with tears.

"I am so sorry Sarah, I never thought about it before but you must have felt like those poor people did when they were taken. You didn't know us or what our intensions were. You were just a little girl wanting your family!"

"Mother, don't cry. You gave me love and you were a good mother. You were never cruel. You treated me just as you did Snow Star. It was different with me. Yes I longed for my family for a long time and when I figured everything out, I held resentment, but I was adopted, not enslaved. This has been an emotional time for you, with worrying the entire time father and the men were gone and then hearing about the new people and some of their stories.

Next you got a granddaughter and you didn't even know she was on the way! Dry your eyes and smile. We are preparing for the biggest celebration ever in this camp!" She leaned over and hugged her. "I love you and someday, some way I am going to have you meet the rest of my family."

Morning Dove nodded approval and smiled.

"I think I will tuck this little one inside. She is sleeping. Mother will you watch her? I want to walk to Willow's tent and check on Clover and her baby. The walk will be good for me."

"Yes I will be glad to watch her but don't put her in the tent, give her to me so I can hold her."

"She will be spoiled before I leave here," said Sarah with a little laugh as she handed the sleeping baby to her mother.

When she arrived at Willow's tent, she heard the tiniest of cries. The baby had arrived. It was very small but appeared healthy. The women inside the tent were doing their best to make Clover comfortable. Two Feathers was pacing outside like an expectant father. Sarah suggested that Willow come outside and help her raise the sides of the tent a little while Sweet Grass helped Clover.

"What is it? Is Clover all right? Is the baby all right?"

"She is doing well and the baby is a girl. It is small but I think it is going to be fine," said Willow. She hugged Two Feathers tightly. Our family is growing, Two Feathers."

"Can I go in and see them now?" Sweet Grass heard his request and stuck her head out.

"You can come in now. Don't stay long though, because Clover is very tired."

"Thank you," he whispered. "Clover, may I come in?"

"Yes Two Feathers, come meet the newest member of your clan," she said weakly. He reached down to gently move the blanket back from the babies face and as his finger touched the baby's hand, she automatically gripped his finger. It only took that small instant for her to steal his heart.

"Clover, she is absolutely beautiful." He looked at her for another moment and then asked if Clover was going to be alright.

"Yes, Two Feathers we will all be fine now that we are here with you and Willow. Thank you for everything you both have done for us." He smiled and stepped out smiling.

"We have another girl." He said it with such pride in his voice that a passerby would have thought he was the father. Willow felt a small pang of jealousy just for a moment. Forgive me Father. I am not remembering all that this woman has been through. He has bonded with her and just feels protective. Sarah started back without disturbing the new mother and Willow walked with her.

"Sarah, will you give me some advice?"

"Yes, if I can. What is it?"

"I wonder if having Clover and her children in the same tent with us is such a good idea. Just now when Two Feathers acted so pleased and proud of her baby, I felt jealous. I want to be his first thought. I think it should be me and someday my baby he is proud of. What is the matter with me?"

"Didn't you tell us that Two Feathers asked you to marry him? His feelings for you have not changed. He is simply feeling compassion for her and joy at the success of their mission. He is not in love with her any more than he is the other people that were rescued. It is natural that he has invested some emotion in her and her children because he got to know her as Water Bug's mother. That boy has been his son. He has watched him grow and learn, just as you have been his mother. Willow, what you are feeling is your heart trying to sort out all the emotions and fears for the future that it feels. I promise you that you are doing the right thing by welcoming Clover into your family and your heart."

"Thank you Sarah, I feel a lot better."

"You should talk to Father Bob about the wedding and maybe you and Two Feathers can announce your intention to marry tonight at the celebration."

"You are right; I will walk over there right now!"

Willow turned down the path by the lake but stopped. She could see Father Bob and Chief Dark Wolf sitting in the shade of the church. They were in a deep discussion about something. Without a hesitation she turned and walked into the cold water of the lake. Her cotton dress clung to her legs and then spread out around her as she submerged. If this doesn't clear my head nothing will, she thought as she rubbed her scalp and body. She came out slowly letting her soggy clothes settle in place as she moved to the sun warmed grass. This is nice she thought, and then just for an instant a jolt of worry entered her mind before she remembered that Water Bug was with the story mothers in the shade pavilion. He is so hard to keep track of these days. It will be good to have another woman to look after him. She was still lying there beside the path in the sun when the Chief stepped between her and the sun's rays, casting a shadow.

"Willow, are you all right?" She bolted upright.

"Yes, I am good. I mean I am fine. I was just drying off and waiting for Father Bob to finish his meeting. I need to talk to him."

"I think if you go to the church now, you will find that he will be glad to see you."

"Thank you, my Chief," she said respectfully, but as she walked the path she was thinking that he wasn't really her Chief. If Two Feathers and I are starting a new people and we are The People of the Lion, then really Two Feathers is my Chief. I must think about this some more.

Father Bob greeted her with his usual inviting smile.

"You have come to visit. This is a lovely treat, Willow. My recent days have not been spent in the company of a pretty, smiling young woman. You are wet. Let's sit here and the sun will finish drying your clothes." He rolled the short piece of log that the Chief had vacated into the sun and moved his to the edge of the shade. "Now tell me what is on your mind."

Willow talked for several minutes, first about the wedding but then branched into her feelings of concern over the presence of Clover and her family and how it could affect her relationship with Two Feathers. He listened attentively and sympathetically.

"These are not going to be easy days ahead for the people. Even after the summer meeting when some of the new people choose to follow others to their villages. We all will need a happy distraction. Their stories are of pain and cruelty. Clover's is especially vivid in that she forced herself to survive on the chance that her son was alive. Willow, if you could look into her heart, what do you think you would see when you opened the place that has your name on it? I don't want you to tell me, but I do want you to pray about it."

"Also, are you sure that you and Two Feathers want to announce your wedding tonight? Maybe it would be good to wait until the next celebration. I know that the Chief will talk about the rescue tonight and he plans to give Sarah's baby her name tonight. I wouldn't want your announcement to be overshadowed by all that."

"Yes, Father Bob, you are right. We should wait and make a happy celebration later on, but I do want to be married to Two Feathers before the journey to the summer meeting."

"We can work hard and make it happen." He smiled his biggest smile then and she knew it was time to go back to her tent to check on Clover and collect Water Bug from the story tellers on the way. He is probably hungry by now, she thought.

The entire camp was full of good scents coming from the cooking fires. She coaxed him away from the group of children and offered him his lunch. She peeked in on Clover to see a bright smile.

"Hello, Sister Mama, we have come to see how you are doing." Clover's smile beamed at the two of them and said she was doing well.

"Sweet Grass was just here and she brought me some tea and soup. She changed the baby and I fed her. Look Water Bug, this is your baby sister," she said. She couldn't resist the urge to touch the boy's face as he moved closer to view the sleeping baby. He quickly kissed the top of her head and then darted out the door. "Willow he is a precious boy. You have done a good job with him."

"Thank you Clover. I love him as if he was my own. I think I better follow him. He needs an eye on him. You rest now. We will be back later."

She rushed out to see him running down the path to the meadow. He stopped just long enough to allow Coyote to open the gate and he continued on to the middle of the herd. With so many new horses added, Willow found the little boy was soon visually lost to her. She yelled his name and the startled horses moved away from her causing dangerous movement. Realizing that she needed to calm down and stand still, she saw that with nothing but his hand on her shoulder, he was leading Grandmother to the fence so he could climb up onto her back. He had permission to ride her, but adding the new horses had increased the possibility that he could get hurt in the meadow.

Once he was on her back, he was safely up out of the way of the big feet of so many horses. She waved to him and motioned for him to come to her.

Slowly the old mare walked to the gate.

"Water Bug, I want to ride with you. Can you see Lady?"

"She is over there getting a drink."

"Let me get her and we can take a ride together. We haven't done that for a while."

The herdsmen were thoughtful and always kept several old blankets and soft bridals near the gate for anyone to use. Coyote helped her with Lady and soon, she and Water Bug were headed out between the big rocks where the lingering aroma of the baked bread made Willow's mouth water. She hadn't eaten today and had only given Water Bug two corn cakes with a little soft meat inside. They would eat tonight at the feast.

Once they were free of the rocks she rode beside Water Bug.

"I like it here," he said. "It isn't so clogged up."

"What do you mean?"

"Well, like our tent now is so squished up. When are that lady and the baby and Cricket going to go away?"

"They are not going away, Water Bug. They are going to stay with us now."

"No, I don't want them!" He stormed. "I want Two to talk to me. He came back and now he talks to her and we are all close up. I don't like her!"

"Oh Water Bug, I am so sorry. No one has taken the time to explain to you what is going on. Let's sit down here in the grass and let the horses eat for a little while. We need to talk."

She sat close and tried very hard, using words that he could understand. She told him where Two Feathers had gone and why. She explained who the people were that he had brought back and why they now lived with him in the tent.

"Jesus has blessed you with two mamas and two sisters. We have a big family now. It is your job to take care to always be gentle with your sisters and to love them and your other mama. She is a gift to us from God. Clover is her name, but it would be nice if you would call her Mama, too. She was there when you were born. You were a tiny baby just like your little sweet baby sister but she had to go away. Now we are so happy that we have her back. Promise me that you will not be angry anymore and that you will try to be glad that they are back with us. I am happy and Two Feathers is happy. Promise me. Please tell me that you will be a good big brother and that you will be happy." He was frowning the whole time she was talking to him.

"I want to go back now. I am thirsty." Jesus, please help me to make him understand what is happening. He resents the attention that has been focused on them. Maybe I should talk to Two Feathers about this, she thought. She helped him up and they rode back.

She looked at the small boy and thought that he didn't understand. He just knows that his world had been turned upside down.

"Water Bug, we are going to have a big celebration tonight."

"I know," he said glumly.

"Father Bob is going to help our Chief tell about all the new people and about Clover Mama, too and your new sisters. The Chief is also going to tell the name of Sarah's new baby girl."

"What is my baby sister's name?"

"She will get her name from the Chief in seven more days."

"He should call her tiny because she is so little. Was I really that little when I was born?"

"Yes, you were." Willow felt joy. I think he is at least getting part of what I told him.

"I'm going to go see Mama Two. I want to know if Tiny is sleeping." He ran through the center of camp and was stopped from running into the tent by Sweet Grass as she was coming out.

"Boy, you have to slow down. The new baby is sleeping and so is your Mama, too. Cricket is in the shade with the story mothers. Why don't you go talk to her? I think she is lonely."

"I guess I will but I want to see Tiny first." He slipped past her and stood inside quietly looking at the baby when Willow caught up with him.

"Water Bug, come out here," whispered Willow. Your mama and tiny sister are sleeping now. We will visit with them when they wake up."

"I am a big brother. I don't have to take a nap."

"Sometimes big brothers get very tired, but you don't have to take a nap today." Willow was so pleased that he had accepted what she had told him that she would have agreed to almost anything.

"Mama Two is sleeping. She is tired and Tiny is tired. I am not tired." He babbled on using the new names he had for the new people in his life. Suddenly it all seemed fun and exciting to him. Willow wondered why he called Clover, "Mama Two" until she replayed their little talk in her mind. She had said, "She is your Mama too." He had accepted that and then took it upon himself to name his baby sister Tiny, since the Chief would wait days before he gave her a name. Thank you, God, for helping me with Water Bug's change in his attitude. I am grateful that he has decided to be joyful. It will be better for all of us.

She watched as he ran to the edge of the grass near the lake. He bent and picked a yellow flower. With his hand extended he slowly approached Cricket smiling. She could hear him launching into a long, one sided conversation as he gave her the dandelion.

The three grandmothers that sat there in the shade looked up at her as she approached.

"Do you have eyes enough to watch him again? I will go help with the feast if it is alright."

One of them nodded and rested her hands in her lap for a moment and then continued her work on a large basket.

CHAPTER SIXTEEN
A WELCOME CELEBRATION

Chief Dark Wolf had stayed busy all day, some of his absence from his tent was necessary, but some of it wasn't. He was troubled. He was to name his granddaughter at the feast and he still couldn't decide on a name. Every time he thought of a name, it didn't seem quite right for Sarah's baby. He was sure that Sharp Knife would not object, no matter what name he gave her, but Sarah might not be pleased. Still he kept coming back to the same name.

As was the custom of the people, gifts were prepared to give the mother of a new baby. In Sarah's case it was good that she had a wagon to cart all the gifts home.

As the fire was lit and the roasted meat piled high on platters and covered, other foods were added to the feast until the amount was far more than even a village this large could eat. The women had worked hard to make the food they brought the very best they had to offer. It was important that the rescued captives knew that they were celebrating them and that they were welcome in this camp of bounty. Groups gathered around the fire and the level of noisy voices told Chief Dark Wolf that it was time to start the first portion of the evening. He nodded to Father Bob.

Father Bob stood with his Bible in his hands.

"For those of you here that are new to our ways, this is a very sacred book. It contains the words of the one true God. The Lion of Judah is one of many names we use for Him." He paused long enough for his words to be translated for those who could not yet understand him, and then he continued. "In this Bible, is a section called Proverbs. In Proverbs 11 verse 8 NIV, it says "The righteous person is rescued from trouble, and it comes on the wicked instead."

"In that same Proverbs 11 verse 21 NIV it says, "Be sure of this, the wicked will not go unpunished but those that are righteous will go free." At that the entire gathering stood and cheered and applauded until Father Bob decided only to finish with a simple statement of fact.

"We have seen these verses proven true. Thank you God, thank you Lion of Judah, for leading us; for yours is the glory and the victory!"

The Chief stood and finally the cheering and clapping quieted.

"It was my intention to give a detailed story tonight of the entire campaign against the Abalinah. The results of that effort are seated here tonight, with the exception of Clover. She added a baby girl to our camp this morning." He waited until the people quieted again. It is joy that we should talk about here. We celebrate success and life. God has blessed us all. He has given new life to The Blue Stone People."

Debon and Sheltah were doing their best to translate what was being said.

"Although the captives came to us hungry and weak, now they grow stronger each day, because God has blessed us and we are able to gratefully share our bounty. These wonderful people have brought us an appreciation for life that was not there before. They have shown us how precious life really is. We all thank you for that." He waved his hands over the heads of the rescued people sitting together. "This summer, during the hottest days, we will all make a long journey to the summer meeting. There you may be able to find the people that you were taken from. If you do not find anyone that you want to stay with, we welcome you back with us. God has shown us how special you all are to Him and you are very special to all of us, too."

"Now something else that is joyous. Sarah and Sharp Knife please come up here and bring the baby." Sarah was surprised to find that she was shaking nearly as much as she had as a little girl when she stood for her naming ceremony before Chief Rising Eagle. Chief Dark Wolf asked her to remove the blanket that covered her baby daughter. He took the pretty baby girl in his arms and examined her with his eyes, thoroughly enjoying the moment. She had a tuft of golden hair but her eyes were not blue like Sarah's. They were dark but he wasn't sure what color they were now or would be when she was grown.

"This child is the newest member of my family, and I as Chief, accept her as a member of The Blue Stone People." The noise of cheers and applause erupted, startling the baby and she started to cry loudly. He cradled her close and walked slowly all the way around the fire so that everyone could see her while she quieted. He stopped in front of Sarah and David smiling. "I name her, Pili Lioness Sharpe. It is tradition in the camp where Sarah and Sharp Knife live, for a child to take the name of their father.

I had a talk with Father Bob and he told me the name Pili, means miraculous in Hebrew, God's special chosen people. Could anything be more miraculous than what we have seen happen in the past few days?" He continued to talk and walk slowly around. The baby nestled and felt safe in his strong arms.

"Pili Lioness, to revere the Lion all her life, that has honored our people by allowing us to be His hands in the work he has done to free his captive children. I will probably call her Kitten," he said laughing, as he handed her back to her mother. "Her parents are fond of nick-names," he said winking at Moonflower. Once again the applause of approval woke the baby and Sarah walked a short distance away. David was smiling broadly. Sarah was crying, overcome by emotion.

"I like it. Do you?"

"Yes David, her name is perfect."

One by one the women brought gifts and placed them beside Sarah on her blanket. She had returned to the place next to Moonflower.

The scarcity of animals in the region made the gifts of soft furs more precious.

Willow and Two Feathers came near and Two Feathers spoke loudly so that all could hear.

"We invite David Sharpe, Sarah Sharpe and Pili Lioness Sharpe to become honorary members of The People of the Lion. You will always be welcome in our camp, when we have one of course."

The people laughed and applauded again.

"Two Feathers made this for you and I colored it with dye," said Willow. She handed it to David rather shyly. They had created a shield the shape of those used on the campaign, but a lot smaller and in the center was carved a fierce lion with his right paw raised. In that paw was held Father Bob's cross blade. It wasn't perfect, but the message that it conveyed was.

"This is beautiful. Its significance is powerful."

David held it up for everyone to see.

"We accept your invitation and thank you for this unique and sacred gift." David handed it to Moonflower to see up close and she in turn handed it to the Chief and he to Father Bob until it slowly made its way around the fire. The people had grown quiet as the object was passed around.

Father Bob said that he was ready to say a prayer of thanks for the food if anyone was hungry and his suggestion was met with great enthusiasm.

During his prayer he included thanks that they had two healthy new baby girls in camp and asked a special blessing on the life of all the children in the camp. He made the sign of the cross on Pili Lioness Sharpe's head.

During his prayer the shield was returned to David. He immediately carried it to Moonflower's tent and slid it carefully in his satchel.

The feast was delicious and the fresh bread and butter were in itself a new treat.

As the people ate and became quiet, one of the youngsters spontaneously started singing the bell song. It surprised Father Bob and Singing Wind but they joined in and so did Willow and Sarah and Sylvia Warren. The Blue Stone People were warmed by their memories of their first Christmas as they sang the Alleluia Holy Holy and the night ended with small groups removing some of the food and covering the leftovers.

The rescued people moaned with their stuffed tummies and laughed at each other's wonderful discomfort.

Father Bob hurried back from the church bringing a plate buried in one inch long pieces of cinnamon candy sticks. He had finally remembered them.

Sarah and David had told everyone toward the end of the communal fire that they would be leaving in the morning. They had enjoyed having enough time to visit and David had taught the people how to care for the new animals. He knew they would benefit the people and felt that they would receive good care.

It was mid-morning by the time all the gifts were safely in the wagon and everything was protected in case it rained on the way back. A few gray clouds rested on the horizon.

Growling Bear rode out ahead of them along the bluff to make sure they had a clear path for the wagon. Nothing obstructed their way and soon they were out of the trees and ready to roll slowly across the prairie grass. He wished them well and waved, noting the absence of a guard at the edge of the woods or the path into the big rocks. It felt good to know the people were safe in their camp without all the extra measures.

Big Flower met him with affection knowing that never again would she take it for granted that he would always be there for her. His absence during the campaign had sharpened her awareness of his vulnerability and hers. She was glad that he had been chosen to take part in the rescue. He had regained his self-esteem.

*****

Adam cheered when he saw the wagon and rider coming slowly across the prairie. He forced himself to climb down the bluff carefully, but once at the bottom he rang the big bell that Ben had put up after Sarah and David's departure. "Clang, Clang, Clang," it went bouncing off the lake and surrounding trees as it announced to every corner of the S. and J. Ranch that someone was coming. Adam felt very important. He was the first to officially use the bell. Ben had talked with Jed and they had determined when and how it could be rung. They instructed the boys that kept watch at the lookout.

Mary with Eli and Natty, and Beth with Lily, stepped out of their houses for the short trip to the crossing. Ben, Jed, Johnny and Joshua hurried, thinking that it had to be

Sarah and David. They had been expecting them back for several days.

They were met with a barrage of questions. Ben and Jed were eager to hear about the war with the Abalinah, but all the questions stopped when they saw the baby that Sarah gently handed to her brother's arms. He took a deep breath and swallowed hard, blinking back tears.

"What is her name?" He asked while holding her as if he thought she would break.

David answered proudly.

"Meet Pili Lioness Sharpe. Father Bob said Pili means miraculous and Lioness is to honor the Lion of Judah and Sharpe, well that's because I am her father." He chuckled nervously. No one was saying anything.

"You can all call her Kitten, we do." Then everyone started talking at once.

"That was one of those "like being in church moments," wasn't it Mom," said Adam.

"Yes son, this baby has been given a very special, blessed name."

Eli pulled on Ben's arm wanting him to lower her so he could see her face.

"Awe, she is cute," he said.

"Aunt Sarah, where did you get her?" Adam asked with a frown.

"You can ask your Mom about that later. She knows all about it."

"Adam, don't be dumb," said Johnny

"I'm not dumb. You're dumb." The two boys argued while climbing up the bluff hoping for another excuse to ring the bell.

"If someone comes, I get to ring it next," said Johnny.

"No you don't, the one on watch gets to ring it, and I'm on watch today."

"So what, I can beat you down anytime?"

"No you can't. If you do you will get punished. Dad said no one hurries down the bluff for any reason!"

"So then I'm not going to stay up here with you. You can just stay up here alone." Johnny came down carefully knowing that Adam had been right. Since his fall and the broken arm that was the result, Ben had warned that the bluff be treated with careful respect, or he would use corporal punishment. They knew what that meant!

As Jed and David rolled the wagon off the big raft and took it to Sarah and David's cabin, Mary reached for the baby.

"You have held her long enough. It is my turn. Come here little kitten. You are so precious." Mary had cuddled many babies as her boys joined the family, but this was different somehow. Mary had held Lily, too, but this baby seemed so special that she couldn't express it and wouldn't with Beth standing near, waiting for her turn to meet the new member of their family.

Beth was eager to touch her but she could see that this was not a time to rush Mary. Slowly Mary gently transferred the baby to Beth.

"We need to eat together tonight, Sarah," said Beth. "We can all come down to Ben's place. It is closer for you and bigger for all of us. The men still have chores to finish and so do we, but we are all anxious to hear what happened with Father Bob and the war, and we want to hear about this little ones arrival, too."

Sarah took Pili into her arms and rode with Mary on the seat of the small wagon. Sarah smiled, at Eli and Natty. They were in the back of the four-sided wagon.

"I think those boys have grown in the few days we were gone. Is it possible?"

"Eli is a big help to me. He tries to keep Natty entertained and out of trouble. That's a big job. Natty knows no limits and never stops unless he is asleep, like now."

The women laughed and were glad to be back together.

"She is beautiful, Sarah. I am eager to hear all the news. Wait and I will help you down."

Mary took the baby while Sarah got off the wagon. David came out to meet them.

"I took everything inside but you will have to figure out where we should put it."

"Thanks for the ride Mary," she said as she carried Pili and took her in their house for the first time. "Pili Lioness Sharpe, you are home. She is a miracle isn't she?"

"Yes, and so is her beautiful mother. I am very blessed." David kissed the baby on her cheek and then Sarah on her lips. "I will bring in some wood and get a small fire going. Is there anything else you need me to do?"

"Yes, Daddy, you can change Pili's diaper and put her in her new cradle for a nap."

"What? I can't do that!"

"You need to learn. School is in session."

"Sarah!" He didn't want to do it, but he muddled through with Sarah's instruction.

"Now pick her up and gently put her in the cradle and turn her on her side. You can make her cozy with this quilt that I made."

David felt clumsy as he handled his little daughter, but sighed happily when he saw her close her eyes contentedly. She went to sleep without a fuss.

"Is there anything else?"

"Yes. I need you to hold me."

*****

Ben looked out the window and then walked out the front door of his house. His work was done for the day. Mary came out and said that supper was ready. She handed him a cup of coffee and sat down beside him on the smooth bench. From their front porch, they could see the trees that lined the river and a field with Dart Away and two beautiful mares with good bloodlines.

"Where are the boys?" Ben was fully aware of the whirl wind that Natty had become.

Joshua took Natty for a ride to let Jed and Beth know that we are ready when they and Sarah arrive. David stopped here a few minutes ago and said that Sarah was still asleep. She is worn out from everything. The rest will do her good. I told him not to wake her. We aren't in a hurry. If they get cranky, I will feed the boys.

"What are you cooking?"

"I have a kettle of beef and mushrooms and I made big egg noodles to put it over. We have lots of dried vegetables so I made a big pan of those and just put in a mix of onions, green beans, green peppers and tomatoes."

"I may get cranky soon and eat with the boys, that all sounds extremely good to me."

Jed and Beth pulled up in their wagon with Lily in the back.

"Where's Johnny?"

"He went up on the bluff to get Adam. He could have yelled but wanted to climb up. Josh took Natty to our barn to see the new foal. Sarah doesn't know about Pretty Mother's baby yet. It will be a surprise for her. They always come back with amazing stories. This time we have something to tell," said Jed.

Josh rode up and carefully transferred his little brother to his father's arms before riding to the gate and putting his horse in the side field with many others.

"Dad, that foal is really beautiful. She is cream color like her mother though. I was thinking it would be white like Cloud."

"She is healthy and strong and the odds are that her babies will be pure white." Mary stood up and smiled.

"Here they come. Let's save the foal as a surprise for morning. It is getting dark already." David helped Sarah down from the wagon and then he carried the baby in the house and everyone followed him wanting another look at Pili. The smaller children formed a ring on the living room floor and after grace they each received a bowl with their meal inside and a spoon.

"Remember," said Mary, "the bear rug doesn't eat real food Lily, only pretend food." Their fresh cold milk was put in cups at the end of the table where it could be supervised.

Beth leaned over and quietly asked Mary why she had said that to Lily.

"After you took her home yesterday I found that someone had fed a sugar cookie to the bear rug. I guessed it was her." Beth laughed.

"This meal looks delicious Mary," said David. "We had a big celebration feast our last night in camp and we were eating leftovers from that on the way back." David always appreciated Mary's cooking.

"We missed both of you while you were gone. This ranch just isn't the same. Sarah the baby is so sweet, but she is a little small," said Beth as she cuddled Pili. "I think

217

she came early. Didn't she?" Beth's question was very direct.

"Yes I think you are right. The motion of the wagon bothered me even though we went very slowly. We took three days to get there. Usually it is a day and a half or maybe two if you're not in a hurry," said Sarah.

"That isn't the only reason. Sarah got very upset when she was talking to one of the Abalinah women. Then Father Bob came back with all the warriors and the captives and it was an emotional time for everyone. I felt it. The Holy Spirit is strong in that camp and Father Bob is so anointed that I think he could do almost anything."

"David, why are there Abalinah people in the camp of The Blue Stone People? Aren't they the ones that caused all the trouble in the first place? That was the impression we got when we talked with Father Bob, his last visit here."

"Jed, you know there is good and bad people everywhere. The woman that Sarah was talking to is Sheltah. She is the wife of Debon. The Holy Spirit sent them back to our camp after they left, so that he could give Father Bob and Chief Dark Wolf all the information that they needed to rescue the captives."

David had talked at length with Two Feathers and other men from the campaign while they worked together building the fence for the cows and calves and the chicken pen.

Sarah had not had an opportunity to know the details of the raid and listened intently.

Mary asked him not to tell anymore of the story until she and Beth came back.

They took all the small children in and washed their faces and hands and tucked them in bed.

CHAPTER SEVENTEEN
TELL US EVERYTHING

Bringing a platter of cookies and the coffeepot, the women returned to the table.

"Now we want to hear every detail," said Beth. "Start with when you left here."

"I have to go back farther than that. Father Bob took his load of lumber back last fall and they stacked it in the church. It is still in there."

David patiently related all the events as he knew them. He told about Father ordering the thirty shields. Ben said they had been to Silverville and knew about those.

"Matt Morgan had them in his shop. I saw them stacked against the wall. They were so heavy. I couldn't see how they would work for a warrior to carry."

David continued with his story. He told them that the people of the camp had all been baptized and had been praying all winter for direction."

"We were all praying here, and lots of people in town knew and they were praying for the success of the raid. Reverend Brown told me," said Ben.

"The Lion of Judah appeared to Father Bob in the small space he had in front of the altar.

When David started to explain that he had been saying Mass outside or in the big tent, his listeners became impatient.

"Two Feathers told me all this. He said that Debon and he were chosen by the Lion of Judah and that he had directed Father Bob to have all the men in the village form a line in the center of camp, from the oldest to the very youngest. He put Two Feathers in front of the line and then Debon and then counted thirty men and the next one in line was Flying Eagle, the Chief's son-in-law! He was in charge of the camp while they were gone. All the experienced warriors went, including the Chief of the Choyinaw, Sky Fire, but he is not a Chief in the camp of The Blue Stone People. Father Bob had been directed to take only thirty men with him and they followed a map that was drawn by three scouts that Chief Dark Wolf sent. Before he sent the scouts, two important things happened that I forgot to tell you."

He stopped and took a drink of his coffee. Mary slipped in and made sure all the children were asleep and returned quickly. Six Abalinah people had been sent there to the camp of the people to gain knowledge of the supply of the blue stones, and to take over the power of the camp, but one of them heard that there were no more stones in the bluff where they had been extracting them. That's when one of the Abalinah women, Gamier, decided to steal what stones were left and she cut open the back of Chief Dark Wolf's tent and took two containers of the rough stones. All six hurriedly left the camp and went back to the Abalinah, thinking that the blue stones were depleted and that the soldiers were going to come because Growling Bear and the night guard had taken the cattle from the ranch; but as you know, no soldiers were sent there.

Once it was known that the six Abalinah were gone, Sky Fire told Chief Dark Wolf the whole truth that his village had been held hostage by the Abalinah warriors and that was why his men rode into summer camp with war paint on. They were overpowered and outnumbered and forced to do it to save their families. Most of them were killed. Sky Fire told about the Abalinah taking slaves and that they had taken two of his children. He told of the vicious ways of the Abalinah.

Chief Dark Wolf had three scouts trail them and they made the map that was used later for the rescue.

The Lion had given Father Bob exact instructions on what they were to do when they got there. The glory and the victory was His alone. The shields were not intended to be carried into battle. The men were instructed to take them silently to the top of the west side of the fortified wall that surrounds the Abalinah camp. The shields were polished to a high gloss, so when the morning sun reached the shields, it was magnified thirty times by the thirty shields. The Blue Stone Warriors couldn't see from the brightness, so they covered their eyes with one arm and just held their shield in the direction of the tents in the camp. Debon and Two Feathers helped the slaves escape while the heat of the intensified light burned the tents of the Abalinah. The Abalinah adults were blinded. An exception was made for a young guard named Soren that they captured. He was helpful and didn't like the ways of the Abalinah. He was told to place a white branch on his tent door and his tent was not burned, and neither were the children in the camp. God spared them. Soren, his wife Cumae and his daughter Obona are now in the camp of The Blue Stone People. A herdsman and another guard were captured and tied to trees but they were released by Father Bob when they left. He told them to care for the children in camp until the parents could.

I forgot to tell you one part. While the light was blazing and destroying the camp, Father Bob and two other men took the horses of the Blue Stone warriors and their pack horses and caught the Abalinah horses and strung them all together on long ropes and they ran them around the outside of the wall of the camp. Two Feathers said it sounded awesome. He said anyone inside the camp would have thought that the largest band of warriors in the whole world was attacking their camp.

The captives were taken to a temporary camp where they were cared for and fed and given clothing and when they had rested for a few days they were brought slowly back to the village.

The Abalinah have no idea what happened but they know that it was a power greater than they were or ever will be. God punished the wicked and set free the righteous."

It was silent in Mary's kitchen.

"David you are right. That story is about the power of the Holy Spirit. Did I understand it? No one was killed?" Ben finally asked.

"Not one person in their camp was killed, and not one warrior of The Blue Stone People was injured."

Jed shook his head in awe.

"You couldn't make up a story like that, but it is hard to believe that something like that actually happened! What an honor for the men in The Blue Stone Camp to have been chosen by The Lion of Judah to do His work."

When David looked at Sarah, he realized that she was crying.

"What is it Sarah? What's the matter, why are you crying?"

"Now I fully understand the special name that Chief Dark Wolf gave our baby," she said between sobs.

"This has been a difficult time for Sarah," said David, "I think it is time that I took my little family home." Standing up, he moved away from his bench at the table and helped Sarah.

"Just a minute David," said Ben. He walked into his bedroom and returned with the well-worn Bible. He opened it to a center section that held family names and dates. He slowly and carefully wrote in it.

"Pili Lioness Sharpe, daughter of David and Sarah Sharpe, born early summer in the year of our Lord Eighteen Hundred and Seventy four."

"That's nice Ben. I didn't know that section was in Father's Bible. I see that you put our wedding in there too! Yours is above ours and you wrote Jed and Beth's in there too, and all the children. That's wonderful."

"It's tradition Sarah. That is our family history. Goodnight, sleep in tomorrow. We will see you later," he said as he gently touched the baby's face and smiled at her mother and father as they left.

"This has been a night to remember. After that story of God's might and power, I won't be able to turn my mind off enough to get any sleep," said Beth.

"It's hard to absorb that things like that are still going on. Some folks think that the time of miracles is over. The world is getting so modern."

"You only have to look at that beautiful baby or the new foal to know He is active in our lives each day."

"You are right Beth. Our daily miracles are not as dramatic, but it is easy to see His hand at work. We are surely blessed." Jed picked up Lily and held her close as he walked to the wagon. Johnny jumped up on the soft hay in back as Beth turned the wagon and drove back to their house by moonlight. She and the horse both knew the path very well. They had memorized every foot of the way. Johnny had not said a word since David had ended his story.

"Dad, he didn't tell us if they found Sky Fire's children and he didn't say how many people God rescued. I think there is more to the story."

"We can ask them all to come to our house tomorrow night and maybe David will tell us more. I'm wondering why Sarah was so upset by Debon's wife that she had the baby early."

"She is very emotional," said Jed. "It's not like her to be that way."

"That's normal right after a woman has a baby, but you have to admit that is really a dramatic story he told and then the Chief named her baby so she will always be reminded of the whole thing. It's obvious that she didn't know a lot of the story. She was listening as closely as we were."

"I don't think I will need reminding," said Jed. "That's not something a person would ever forget."

*****

A soft rain was falling when the people on the ranch woke up. Mary fed all her boys and reminded Adam to be careful going up and down the bluff.

"Adam, the chickens still need feeding and Josh you should probably help in the barns. Dad said he is going to bring Blaze and Star in and do their shoes today. Uncle Jed would appreciate the help in the cow barn. Check with Aunt Beth and see if Johnny is going to help clean stalls."

"I will Mom," said Josh as he kissed her cheek and hurried out the door pulling on his slicker.

"Adam, where are you?"

"I can't find my shoes!"

"Look under your bed."

"I found them!"

"Don't forget. Dsio the chickens, both pens and then be careful on the bluff."

"Mom, I am going to leave my shoes off. They will just get all muddy. They are getting tight anyway."

"Out you go," she said, kissing the top of his head as he went.

"I want to go out and play in the rain," said Eli.

"Will you stay here in front of the windows where you can see me in the kitchen?"

"Yes, I will. I promise."

"Alright, go out. Do you want your slicker on?" He ran out quickly. He was out dashing around in the grass with his tongue out trying to catch rain drops on it. He hadn't heard the question. She picked up Natty and handed him the last half slice of breakfast toast and treasured the time alone with him when she could treat him like the baby he still was. She knew that he would soon grow up and he would not want to be held or cuddled. He would, all too soon, be big enough to run outside and play or work with his brothers. I have quite a miracle of my own, she thought, four wonderful boys.

"Slim, we are doing well. Ben is good to all of us and he is a good father. We love each other and this ranch is a perfect place for our boys to grow up, but I still miss you and love you." She was watching Eli out the window and softly talking to Josh and Adam's father. She couldn't help but laugh out loud when Eli slipped on the wet grass and lit on the seat of his pants. She opened the back door.

"Eli, are you alright? It is time to come in now and get some dry clothes on."

He got up off the grass laughing and came in shaking his hair like a wet puppy.

"Here rub your face and hair with this and drop all your wet clothes right there before you go in the bedroom and put on dry ones."

"It's a good rain Mom. Our garden is happy and growing right now."

"Yes, I think you are right. I have some work to do. Would you play with Natty for me as soon as you are dressed?" Mary lifted from the closet shelf; a big wooden box filled with blocks and set it on the floor near the living room window. She pulled out two quarts of canned wild cherries from the storage room and smiled. I am going to make pies she thought. I could make deer stew with potatoes, carrots and peas also.

Just as she started to make the pastry for the pies, Johnny politely tapped on the back door and she yelled for him to come in.

"What do you need Johnny?"

"Nothing Aunt Mary, but Mom said to tell you that supper is at our house tonight so you don't need to cook today."

"That's good. Are you going back near the house now?"

"I'm going to the cow barn. I have some stalls to clean."

"Please stop long enough to tell your mom that I said thanks and that I am bringing two cherry pies."

"Yum, they are my favorite. I'll tell her." He closed the door and she watched through the kitchen window as he swung up on an old brown mare and headed for the path home, to deliver her message. She is doing a good job with that boy. He is polite and responsible, she thought.

She glanced at her boys playing on the floor and saw Natty, swatting down a four-block tower and both boys laughed.

David waved at the house as he rode past heading for Jed's barn. He is late getting started today. It must have been a rough night with the new baby. She chuckled to herself. We had a lot of those.

The sky cleared and the day became bright and cheerful. She looked in the oven, but the pies were not done yet. I better slice some of the roast and make sandwiches. My hungry men will want lunch before long. Ben came in with Josh and Adam, just as she was pulling the golden pies out of the oven.

"They look delicious! Are we taking those to Jed's tonight?"

"Yes, you must have been talking to Johnny."

"No, Jed told me as soon as I got in the barn."

"Have you told Sarah about the new foal yet?"

"No, David said he will take her to Jed's barn before supper. If she falls in love with that foal, like I know she will, we may have to all eat in the barn! She won't want to leave her to go eat."

"I want to go over there early tonight so that Eli and Natty can see the foal. I saw her the night she was born. She sure is pretty."

"Boys if you're done eating go ahead and go back to your jobs. I need to talk to Mom for a few minutes."

"Is something wrong?" Josh looked concerned.

"No son, I just need to tell her something. Adam, remember to be careful climbing the bluff. It will be slippery now." The boys left closing the door.

"What is it Ben? There isn't much we talk about that they can't hear."

"I just wanted to let you know that I will be going in to Silverville to see Tom about the logs for the cabin by the spring. I think if he delivers them right there, we can have it built before we tell the boys about it. We can work on it this summer. Next spring is the deadline for improvements on your land. We have to get a well dug too, but that shouldn't be hard with the spring there. We can dig near that and then just cap it."

"I'll ask Sarah and Beth if they need anything and make sure they don't spill the beans to the boys. Supplies are always needed. Maybe Sarah needs something for the baby."

"I doubt that. She has been sewing and making stuff all winter, and they came back with a wagon full of gifts for that baby, but it won't hurt to ask. You didn't say when you plan on going."

"Maybe tomorrow, I need to get some advice from Matt while I'm there. I am still not very good at doing shoes."

Ben stepped out the back door and was gone without another word. He has a lot on his mind, she thought. It seems that this ranch could use a few more hands. We have at least two dozen mustangs that have never been worked with and so many more that should be ridden to keep them saddle ready. Three men and three boys just can't do it all. I'm going to suggest that Ben post for some help when he goes in. Maybe we can get a new family for the cabin by the lake. I liked it when Rachel and Margaret and Zack were there. I wonder how they are doing. We should go see them.

"Mary? What are you thinking about?" Sarah had tapped but when Mary didn't answer, she stuck her head in the front door.

"Oh, nothing really, I was just thinking it would be nice to visit with Rachel and Margaret. If I could I would wish them back here. They were a good help."

"We do need some help. Ben just left my place and said he has to go in to Silverville in the morning. Do you think he could put a notice at the Trading Post for someone?"

"I was just thinking that very thing," said Mary. "The mail boat brought down a family late last fall. They must need a place and work until they figure out what they will do."

"Mary, that was six or more months ago. They have to be settled somewhere by now."

"I suppose you're right. Let me hold that little kitten." Mary cuddled her close and longed for another baby of her own.

"Mary, I know that look. Don't be thinking about having another baby. You have plenty of work to do now. I don't know how you do it all."

"You are reading my mind. I would enjoy having another baby. It seems like it is just a routine now. One more wouldn't add that much work."

"I think you have forgotten. David and I were up more than we were down last night. When we go to sleep, she wakes up. I am really tired. I know he is."

Mary laughed.

"I guessed that was it when I saw David leave. He is usually up and out before Ben wakes up."

Mary handed the baby back to Sarah.

"Get her dry and fed and then you should both nap and just in case no one told you, always put her in her own bed. If you put her in yours, she will still want to sleep with you when she is seven!" They both laughed.

"See you at Beth's tonight." Sarah yawned and closed the front door. She walked the short distance back to her house and took Mary's good advice.

*****

"Don't worry about me; I may be gone for a week or more. I plan on visiting friends. Thanks Night Hawk for hitching up the team for me." Father Bob looked behind him in the wagon and appreciated the people that had made sure he had all he might need and more. Night Hawk made the sign of rotating his wrist which Father Bob knew was a reminder to grease the wheels often. He checked under his seat and the big pan of grease and brush were right where he expected them to be. "Thanks again, Goodbye, I'll see you all soon."

He slowly turned the long wagon and headed down the trail beside the bluff. Suddenly he remembered his first experience with these woods and the mountain lion that he shot spooking his mules. He laughed at the thought. What a greenhorn I was then. He looked at the horses pulling the wagon and saw for the first time that they were younger and appeared in their prime. This is not the team I have been using. I wonder if they came with the Abalinah horses. There was so much happening then that I don't remember seeing them. He stopped at the little pool and made sure that each horse drank its fill and checked to see that his water barrels were full and fresh.

When he looked up at the spot the men had worked, he felt sad that the blue stones were gone. I must ask Chief Dark Wolf about it when I come back. He said he knew where there was a new supply of blue stones. He drove along the bluff until he was out of the trees and onto the bright sunny prairie. The recent rain had brought a few wild flowers and he thought the scene very pretty.

"Oh my," he said out loud. "I stuffed my mail that Sarah and David brought for me, in my pocket days ago and I have been so busy that I still haven't read it. I could have written an answer to take back." He carefully opened the first envelope. Sarah and David had brought that one to him from the ranch. He felt the lump in the corner of the envelope and shook the nugget into his palm. "Now that is undeniably gold," he said to the horses. They plodded along at a sensible pace, not caring what he was commenting about. He read the short note and thought that he would enjoy answering this in person. I did open the cheese and eat a bit of it. I have some with me to snack on.

After folding the note around the nugget and putting it back in its envelope, he stuffed it in his pocket and brought out the second envelope. This one was far more formal.

He hesitated, glancing up to give the horses some gentle guidance, and then as if almost afraid of it, he opened the second envelope.

It was from the bishop, brief and to the point. It stated that he was glad to finally hear of some success with the Indians. He was sad to learn of the sudden death of Father Peter O'Riley, and had chosen one of the seminarians to replace him. He had sent him on his way and that he would be traveling down the Silver River and should arrive in late spring. It was signed with regards and God's blessings, etc.

"Well, what do you think of that? I've got myself a baby brother on the way!" He pulled the horses to a stop and loosened their bridles and fastened them two on each side of the wagon. "Lunch is served my big fellows; you have all the grass you can eat. Enjoy yourselves. I'm in no hurry. After they each had a long drink from the barrels, he picked out a sandwich from his satchel and a slice of the strong cheese and sat with a cup of water in his hand watching the sunset.

I wonder what day of the week it is. I need to buy some wine to use for saying mass. That café had wine on the menu. Cookie must keep his supply there. I wonder if he would instruct me, so I can make some for the church. I know there are grapevines near the camp. I saw them. In his thoughts he traveled the town thinking of the various places he would stop. Tom will have the windows ready for the church by now and Jim and Melanie will like hearing that their prayers were answered. I should go to their church on Sunday and tell all the people about the campaign. I wonder if that would be appropriate. Certainly it must be acceptable to tell of God's victory. Yes I think so and I will tell them of Sarah's baby girl, too. I have to stop and tell Matt how God used the shields that he made. The Trading Post will spread the story of the rescue. I just hope they get it straight. I will go there first and give them my order but they can hear the news in church. When I leave Silverville, I will have to go the long way across the Silver, but I want to go to the S. and J. Ranch for a short visit. They are wonderful people. He was sitting on a thick blanket that he pulled up over his chest. He had trouble quieting his mind before he slept contentedly until morning.

When he looked at the horses and the tangled lines he was wishing he had not released them. This is a confusing mess. I hope I can get it all back on the right way, he thought.

After he watered them again from the barrels, he managed to sort it all out and with a little help from above he got the big horses back in front of the wagon, hitched and ready to do their job. They were well on their way when Ben saw him in the distance as he pulled the wagon very slowly across the strong little bridge his family had made. Even though the cattle were close to the fence, Father Bob was no longer intimidated by them.

"Multiply you beauties, so you can feed the people," he said as he drove along.

CHAPTER EIGHTEEN
A BROTHER

Ben gave a shrill whistle and Father Bob pulled the team to a stop. He looked back to see Ben riding a new horse.

"Hello Ben. What a wonderful surprise to see you now. I was planning on stopping at the ranch before I head back."

"Hello Father Bob. I am so glad to see you. David told us about the campaign and we are all so happy and relieved that it went well. He told us about your adventure in the Abalinah camp. I am glad you are all unharmed and the captives are now free."

"Yes, thank you. God did it; I just followed a few simple instructions."

"So we heard," said Ben laughing. "You all did a lot more than that."

"Well, it certainly did go according to God's plan. Thank you for the prayer support. I could feel the grace pouring on the men, the entire time."

"Ben that is a magnificent animal you are riding!"

"This handsome guy is Cloud. I bought him and two white mares from the army more than a year ago. Sarah's mare that she calls Pretty Mother just had a foal by him. The mares I bought were in a field with my white horse, Buddy and Sarah's Moon Boy, but I had to take Buddy out because they started to get a little aggressive with each other. I am hoping to create a pure white bloodline with stamina and a smooth gait. I know I will find a market for them. The officers like riding white horses."

"You know I could never understand why they did that. It seems to me if they go into battle it would make it easier for the enemy to target the officers."

"I can't answer that but you are right. It sure is easy to spot a white horse. I brought Cloud in today to see if Matt would check his shoes. I have been doing some shoes at the ranch and I did his. I am wondering if there is something we can do to make his walk a little smoother. Maybe one foot is different or something. I needed to go to Silverville anyway so I rode him. I need to order some things from Tom.

"I am going there too," he said, stating the obvious. "He has some windows for the church."

"Did you notice the new cattle on Mary's land?"

"New? What do you mean new?"

"They brought us a hundred head two weeks ago. They will be nice and fat by fall. The men that took them last time can come get them and we will help them get as many as they need, headed in the right direction. I sent word up river and it is going to be a consistent supply."

Father Bob smiled and thanked Ben for his generosity, and then silently, he thanked God for His provision.

"Ben, Chief Dark Wolf appreciates all that you and your family do for the people. The milk cows and chickens are a good addition, too but the beef cattle kept them alive and healthy last winter. The people pray God's blessings on you and your family."

"Well we sure can use blessings. Thanks! It's good to know that your influence has brought The Blue Stone People close to God."

"Ben, your sister Sarah was the first to speak the word of God to them. She was just a young girl but spoke bravely of what she believed. If she hadn't, perhaps none of the

234

wonderful recent events could have happened. I was the first Jesuit to find them and they already were aware of His power. They had learned that the Great Spirit was the creator of all things. They were learning to believe."

"I knew that she had kept her faith but I didn't know that she had done that much to influence them."

As they passed the falls they stopped and gave the horses a rest and a drink, while they shared a meal.

"It is so beautiful here," said Father Bob. "Oh I didn't tell you, that I received a letter from the Bishop. It said he has sent a seminarian down the Silver and he is assigned to help me. I hope that he is big and strong. We have physical work to do as well as the spiritual."

"He probably took the railroad as far as he could. I would like to ride on a train someday and go back to see the rest of my family," said Ben.

"That would be quite an adventure, but you might be disappointed. Things change and people change. It wouldn't be the way you remember it from your youth."

"I think you are probably right but it would be exciting." They rode quietly for a while. Each man lost in his thoughts.

"Here we are," said Father Bob. He stopped at the bridge.

As usual Sam came out and stood close enough to the river to see and hear everything that was going on. He waved but didn't cross the bridge to help with the horses. Matt strolled over and he unhitched the first pair. He and Ben led them across, one at a time and then with little effort he rearranged the rigging so that one horse could pull the nearly empty wagon for Father Bob and the fourth horse came on a long rope, led by Ben on Cloud.

"Thank you for your help Matt. You will be amazed at the story I have to tell you. The shields were just perfect. Thank you again for your hard work on them." Matt led the team to the railing along the river after putting the wagon out of the way beside his shop.

"Do you need me to check any of them? Their shoes should still be fine."

"Yes check them, because I don't think this is the same four that I brought last time, and I need to borrow a riding horse while I am here. I need to talk to Tom at the mill and a few other folks."

"Sure, I have a nice little mare I acquired recently. I would like to have your opinion on her." He went to the side gate and slipped on a soft bridle and saddle.

"She responds to the name Betsy."

"Are you going to be busy later? I would like to come back and tell you that story."

"No I don't think so, unless your team needs shoes. If someone brings in something they need done right away, I can work and still visit with you."

"Good, thanks for letting me use Betsy." Father Bob patted her neck and gave her a few scratches before swinging up into the saddle. "Matt, what day of the week is it?"

"It's Friday, May the twentieth.

"Thanks, I lose track out where we are." Ben had heard that and made a mental note. Sarah must have had Pili on or near the sixth. I will put that date in our Bible.

"Ben, hello, how are you?"

"Good, Matt. It's good to see you again."

"I recognized this horse as soon as I saw him. You are getting a reputation for always riding a big horse. This is the big guy you bought from the army."

236

"Yes Matt and I have practiced a lot on making and putting shoes on my horses until I think I am doing it properly, but his gate isn't smooth, would you take a look and see if I have one of them wrong or something?"

"Sure Ben, here is his problem. It's not anything you did. But it may be why they sold him. His front hoof grows out crooked. If you put his shoe on flat it just increases the problem. Let's shave it down a bit on the outside and then thin that shoe down some on the outer edge and build it up slightly on the inside, so his hoof sits straighter." Ben watched intently, wanting to learn all that he could.

"Never do a lot of correction on a hoof the first time or the horse could pull up lame. We'll do a little this time and when he needs new shoes, you can do a little more to correct it, each time until it is completely level. He probably injured it when he was young."

"Thanks Matt, you are a good teacher. I want to let Cloud rest a bit here. I have an order for the store and then I will come get him to ride to the mill."

"You can tie him beside Father Bob's team if you like; he will have grass and water there."

"Matt, what do I owe you for the correction on his shoe and the lesson?"

"Not a thing. See you shortly."

Ben went to the Trading Post and gave Helen a list from the women and told her to add some candy if it wasn't already on there, and a bolt of white cotton flannel. He glanced around and added a dress length of pink cotton and another of blue plaid.

"I'll pick it up on the way back through," said Ben starting toward the door.

"Father Bob was just here with a list, did you see him?"

"Yes, I rode in with him."

"Well, isn't that nice. How are Sarah and David?"

Ben knew that he was not behaving the way he should. He felt angry. Sarah has forgiven her, why can't I forgive and forget?

"They are fine. She had her baby. Its name is Pili," said Ben before he darted out the door not giving her an opportunity to ask further questions. Let her think on that and make up another story, he thought bitterly as he pulled Cloud's reins loose from the rail and headed out to Tom's.

Father Bob was on the way back. He waved as he headed down the side street where Melanie and Rev Brown's house stood proudly; looking loved with its window boxes starting to show flowers and the small lawn out front trimmed and dark green. Father Bob knocked but got no response. He knocked again hearing voices and laughter. He waited and finally Melanie opened the door with a big smile and a giggle.

"We thought you would be here today or tomorrow. Hello, Bob. Your young friend is being held hostage by my children. Follow me," she said pleasantly. The kitchen door stood wide open and on the back lawn tumbled a wiry, bean pole of a young man; wrestling with her children. He growled and they squealed as he played with them tickling tummies and rolling them over on the grass.

When he realized he was being observed he stood quickly scooping a child under each of his arms and with their legs dangling loosely he shook them vigorously, side to side, causing another peal of laughter.

"That was to get the loose grass off so it doesn't end up in the house. Here we go, one, two, three," he counted warning them before he literally rolled them into the house across the throw rug and jerked off their shoes tickling their toes before they could crawl away. "That's all for now. Let's say hello to the man standing in the kitchen."

Violet hadn't noticed him until that was said. Immediately she ran to Father Bob and hugged his leg. Willie had gone into the living room where he could look at the visitor from a safe distance. Father Bob picked her up and kissed her cheek and then carried her to her mommy and gave her a peck on the cheek, too.

"Hello, I am Father Bob and I am assuming that you are the seminarian that the Bishop has sent."

"Yes, it is nice to meet you. I am Timothy Sunning." Father Bob placed the little girl on the floor and shook the young man's hand. Willie had come one step closer, showing a little smile with his thumb in his mouth.

"How long have you been here?"

"Since the boat dropped me and the mail off on Wednesday. The Bishop assured me that all I had to do was look for the church and I would find you. He gave me the impression that you had a church and had converted the Indians.

"That is true, but our church is not here. It is near the camp of our congregation. Melanie, where is Jim?"

"He isn't here. We have an older parishioner that he visits on Fridays. He left early this morning. Tim and I have been getting along well and he and the kids have been having a lot of fun."

"When will Jim be back?"

"It is a long way to their place. He will probably not be back until it is nearly dark."

"Do you think we could talk to him in the morning?"

"Yes of course, but you are not taking Tim now are you? He is a great help to me and I promised him apple pie for supper. I would love to have you eat with us. You know I always make plenty. Will you stay?"

"Thank you Melanie, I would love to enjoy your cooking again, but I can't stay here until then, I have other things I need to do. I will come back about dark if that is acceptable. Until then I will leave Tim to lend a hand with the children."

"Thank you Melanie for the invitation. I look forward to coming back. Tim, it was nice to meet you. I am glad you are here. Does this arrangement for the day, meet with your approval?"

"Yes, of course."

"Good, then we will all see you this evening," Melanie smiled another big smile as he left. He saw her pick up Willie. "It is time for your nap young man," she said as he closed the front door.

Father Bob walked to the hitching rail where Betsy patiently waited.

"You are a nice young lady, Betsy. I think I will see if Matt will sell you to us for Tim to ride. Come to think of it, I'm not sure if he can ride a horse. Well if he can't, you will have to teach him. Won't you?" With that thought in mind he rode to Matt's shop, happy to see that no one else was there. Matt was putting new shoes on one of his team.

"Hi Matt, I can see that you decided that the new team needed new shoes. How bad is it?"

"Not that bad but it was time to change them. Did you get all your business done already?"

"No, but I did talk to Tom. He has the windows ready and I want to take another load of lumber that he had cut ahead so that sure helps with the timing. Now that I have Tim to help, we will be able to add onto the church and start the school."

"If you are referring to that slim lad I saw get off the mail boat Wednesday, I don't think he will be much help. He is immature and seemed rather lost when I talked to him."

"Yes, he is young, but so was I when I came out here. The Bishop gave him bad directions and that didn't help any. I was thinking if you are willing to sell Betsy, she might be a good horse for Tim."

"No, she is not right for him. He is a tall kid and needs a bigger horse, so as he fills out it will still be a good fit. I know that Ben Slater is in town, and he has lots of horses. You should ask him if he has one that is right for Tim."

"As usual you have good advice. Matt you are such a good friend." Liz came out of the house with coffee and a tray of snacks that included some cookies with jam in the middle.

"Hello Father Bob, I thought Matt should take a break and when I heard your voice I just added a few things to the tray. Matt came in and told me you were here and that you were coming back this afternoon to tell him how the shields were used and what happened. Do you mind if I stay and listen?"

"Of course not, we will enjoy your company."

"I'm not sure where to start with the story, but it's important to tell you up front that the shields were the key to the whole campaign."

He launched into the tale with enthusiasm, but deliberately left out many of the details knowing that he intended to tell the complete story in Reverend Brown's church on Sunday, if he would allow it.

"The captives were in bad health and it is God's wisdom that took us there when He did. They are healing and gaining strength in the camp of the people. They will go with them to the summer meeting and perhaps some will find their people there, but if they don't they are welcome to stay with our camp and become one of the Blue Stones."

"That is so amazing, but I have a million questions," said Liz.

"Please save them, because I'm sure they will be answered in church on Sunday. I will try to include all the details then. My invitation for supper was for dusk, so I better get going. Is it alright if I bed down later, here in the hay at the back of the shop?"

"Yes, of course but you could use our couch if you want to. Or we can put you in the children's room and put one of them on the couch."

"No thanks, I am used to rustic surroundings. I slept well here last time. When I come back I will put Betsy in the field out back."

"That's fine and you will find your team out there, too. I will move them in there now."

"Thanks Matt, and thanks for the coffee and sweets Liz." The afternoon had flown by as they had talked and Matt had finished the shoes on the team. Betsy was waiting for him when he came out. He offered her a double handful of grain from the big bin and she gratefully munched through it. He smiled at her and scratched her ears. He was getting fond of her.

"You are such a sweet girl," he said.

When he arrived at their house, Jim was home and the table was set for four. Melanie had fed the children and was busy giving them a bath. They came out to say goodnight, smelling of sweet soap and powder. She tucked them into bed and returned to put the meal on the table in just a few minutes.

Father Bob saved his request to tell his story of "The Lion of Judah," until the meal was over. They sat in the living room enjoying another cup of coffee.

"Jim, I would like to share the story of the Abalinah and the rescue of the captives with your congregation. I would like to come to your church this Sunday and tell it all, in detail." He waited. Jim didn't say anything for the longest while.

"I would like that. Some of my congregation will be shocked, but maybe it will be good for them. Please come at seven and that will give us time to pray together before the service."

"Since you won't need to spend tomorrow preparing a sermon, I would like all of you, children too, to come to Cookie's Café at noon as my guests. You have fed me many times and it is time that I returned the favor."

"Oh that is not necessary at all, that will cost you a fortune," said Jim.

"Please, I want to do it and Melanie deserves to have a meal she didn't have to cook."

"Well, if you are sure, we will meet you there at noon." Tim had listened quietly most of the evening and said very little. He looked exhausted and stifled a yawn now and then."

"Tim do you have a bag here?"

"What? Oh, yes I do. Good, you will be coming with me tonight, so you should go get it and make sure you have not left anything behind."

He stood looking around for a second and then stepped down the hall where his carpet bag was behind the door.

"I have some boxes and other things on the grass by the store. Sam said I could leave them there and if it rained he would put them inside."

"We will collect those when we pick up our order at the store. Thank you Jim and as always Melanie, the meal was excellent. Thank you so much. I am looking forward to seeing you at the café at noon tomorrow."

"Tim, do you know how to ride a horse?"

"Yes, I have ridden a few times. It was before I went in the seminary. I don't know how well I will do now though, that was at home with my dad's old horse."

"Say hello to Betsy, I borrowed her from Mathew Morgan the blacksmith."

Tim ran his hand along her neck, and rubbed his forehead on hers. He stood scratching her ears and talking softly to her.

"She is a wonderful horse. I think I need to get one a little taller, with my long legs, but she has a nice disposition. I can tell that right away."

"You're right. Hook your bag on the saddle horn and we can walk back to the blacksmith shop."

"It will be good to walk after that big meal. They are really nice folks and treated me like family. I love those babies. I like all children really. I think that is my calling Father Bob, to bring children to the Lord."

"That's great Tim because we will be picking up a load of lumber tomorrow from the mill. It is the start of a school for the Blue Stone children."

"How much did the Bishop tell you about me?" Tim asked, sounding concerned.

"Just that he was sending me a seminarian to help. He didn't even tell me your name."

"Well I may as well confess that he sent me here to sort things out. I didn't finish. I have a year to go."

"I want to do the Lord's work. I don't care how hard it is, but I need to see the people and children and be genuine and real and just teach them with actions. I didn't care much for the psychology, and philosophy or theology. They were having me study all kinds of books that seemed irrelevant. We were all reading books that didn't speak to me about the Lord at all. The bishop was determined that I needed to grow up. I think I did that a long time ago. We just didn't agree on much and he isn't going to change what they teach because I don't like it; that's when he asked if I wanted to come out here and I jumped at the chance. Are you disappointed? I am not a priest yet. I haven't taken my vows."

"No, not at all Tim, I am pleased that you are open with me and willing to work hard. I think we are going to get along just fine. Here hold onto your bag, I'm going to put Betsy in Matt's field."

"Goodnight sweet girl," said Father Bob. "I really like that horse. I just wish she was a bit taller."

Father Bob led Tim into the shop and asked him which stall he preferred.

"I have some leather clothes you can use to sleep in, if you don't have anything suitable for sleeping in the hay."

"I have these and they will do just fine," said Tim. He pulled a ratty pair of farm trousers from his bag and a flannel shirt. Father Bob slipped out of his cassock and into his well-worn leather clothes.

When they carried the light to the back stalls they found blankets and cups and a jug of water standing beside two cheese sandwiches wrapped in wax paper and a stack of cookies.

"It looks like someone has taken care of us in grand style." He said with a grin.

They knelt in the hay and prayed, giving thanks for the day they had enjoyed and the exciting future that lie before them. Father Bob thanked God for sending him a pair of young and willing hands to help with the growing faith of the people. They went to sleep quickly and slept soundly. Matt quietly opened the back door of the shop and saw that they were still asleep. He took pleasure in returning to the kitchen and telling Liz that he had changed his mind, and that he would have that second cup of coffee with her.

The second time he went out, he found Father Bob in his priest's robe and Tim in black dress pants and a white shirt. Both men were clean shaven and they had devoured the breakfast that Liz had left for them.

Lunch at Cookie's Café, was wonderful fun and Violet stole the moment by preening her hair and then telling Cookie that she liked his braid. His smile was reward enough but he returned to the table with a small pudding for her and one for Willie.

"I like this pretty little girl," he said grinning broadly. The food was delicious and their friendship would have encouraged them to linger, had the café not been so busy.

"We will see you at the church at seven in the morning. Rose might be in the front practicing shortly before eight, but we will have time to pray and get organized by then."

When they left the restaurant, Tim asked if he could change back into his work clothes.

"Yes, I think I will too. We need to hitch up our team and go pick up the lumber and our order at the store, and your boxes so that we can leave as soon as church is over in the morning."

"I doubt if we will get away with that. I am guessing that we will be asked to stay to a potluck dinner after the service," said Tim. "That's usually the way it goes."

"Well we will eat then. A man has to have lunch. I hope you are right." They laughed together easily.

Tim proved to be an expert at handling the big horses and hitching them to the freight wagon efficiently. They headed first to Tom's mill where he introduced Tim as brother Sunning and the men carefully loaded the wagon making sure that the windows stood up between walls of lumber and were protected by a cushion of tightly packed sawdust on both sides.

"Tom you haven't seen the work God is doing with the Indians but be sure you come to Reverend Brown's service tomorrow. I am going to tell about a recent event that will amaze everyone."

"We will be there."

"I almost forgot to ask you. Can you get me two pumps and the pipes for two wells?"

"I have them now if you want them. We can pile those on the sides and you will still have room for some supplies from the store.

Tim stood on top of the loaded wagon and as supplies were handed up, he placed them securely; making sure the load was balanced and stable. His boxes went on with the rest of the sacks and bundles and finally after placing his own bag and Father Bob's satchel near the front, they covered the load with the white canvas and tied it on tightly.

"There we are. I think we have done a good days work, Tim."

"This has been fun!"

Tim drove the team slowly, turning it around and placing the wagon once more beside Matt's shop. He unhooked the team and took all of them at once to the rail by the river where they could graze or drink until dark. Father Bob was amazed at the skill and confidence in the young man.

"What else is in this little town?" he asked.

"The lady that plays the piano for the church lives in the house over there, her name is Rose and the house near the Trading Post belongs to Tom and his wife Gentle Fawn. They have two nice children. The building down there with the cross on the door is the land office. Let's walk down there."

"Why is the cross on the door?"

"I was told that it was used as a church until the settlement built a real church."

The door clanged as they entered and the same scene presented itself that Father Bob had found his last trip. Two men sat against the wall at a small table drinking coffee and playing checkers.

"Hello Father, what can I do for you today? I am afraid I can't give you any more free land. It's one to a customer."

"Yes I know. This is Brother Timothy Sunning. He has moved here and will be working with me. I am just showing him around the settlement."

"I don't have a piece left on the river, but if you want it, the piece behind Father Bob's is still available. I don't know what good it is. It has a lot of rocks and a big bluff back there somewhere."

"Are you saying that you are still giving away land and that Tim can sign for the piece behind mine?"

"Yes, that is why you came in here isn't it?"

"Glory to God! No, not really, like I said I was just acquainting him with the town. You can get a piece of free land Tim!" Tim stood there not sure what he was supposed to say or do.

"Look on the map, you may not want it," the frowning man said. Father Bob pointed out the land he had signed for and where David and Sarah Sharpe's piece was and then he pointed to Ben and Jed's ranch and the Parker place and a few others.

Tim was a farm boy and he was smart enough to know that big rocks and a bluff wasn't land that would grow anything.

"Don't you have any farmland?"

"No, that's all that has been opened up at this time. You have to build on it and put down a well in the next five years and then she's yours all legal."

"I'll do it," said Tim. "The man shook his head and filled out the paper.

"Do you understand son, that this is mostly rocks and a high bluff? It's not farmland."

Tim studied the map for a long time.

"It's this or the mud bog. That's all that's left," he said.

Tim signed the paper and the old man at the checker table didn't even get up. The paper was taken to him and he signed as witness. It was stamped and a copy was given to Tim.

"Father Bob, I know that this land won't grow a thing, yet I felt compelled to take it. It will be interesting to see what God will do with a big pile of rocks."

"Well it is directly behind the piece that I have chosen for a church on the Hickory River. Isn't it strange how things come about? You came out here feeling a little concerned and confused, and now my prayers for help have been answered and we have each been given land. Certainly God has a plan." Tim carefully folded the paper and put it deeply in his pants pocket looking puzzled but excited.

"What's the matter?"

"My father would be appalled that I had taken land that can't be farmed." Then he started to laugh and they both laughed until their sides hurt. "I think the bishop would, too." And the laughter started all over again.

*****

"This settlement needs to grow a bit. It could use a good boarding house," said Tim as they put the team in Matt's field for the night and then dusted their shoes and whacked at the bottom of their trousers trying to make them as clean as possible for church the next morning before draping them over the stall.

"I hope Matt remembers to wake us at dawn. I think I'll open the front door of the shop. That way the light will come in and get us up."

Matt did wake them with fresh coffee in plenty of time. As they walked to the church, Father Bob found that he was a little nervous. Father God, help me to tell the story of your victory so the listeners will give you the glory you deserve. Help me to remember all the details accurately. I want to convey the power that you brought to that camp. He prayed silently. Tim sensed that Father Bob was not in the mood for chatting, and he too prayed that the people would come and hear the real message in Father Bob's words. Tim had no idea of the mighty display of God's power that Father Bob was about to relate.

Reverend Brown, Father Bob and Brother Tim, all knelt on the floor near the front of the church. They prayed that God would use this time to touch the hearts of the settlement. They asked that many people would come to hear what the Holy Spirit had done.

When Rose entered, she saw the three men kneeling, praying with their heads bowed. She sat down in the back of the church and waited. The voices of people arriving alerted her. She went to the front door and asked them to wait. They eased it open and people peeked in but they silently waited. Finally the three opened their eyes at the same time and each saw that the other was wiping away tears. The church was filled with the Spirit so strongly that it could be felt by the people as they entered. Each took a seat and had to move down as others came until people stood in the aisles with no place to sit.

Rose slid onto the piano bench and began to play softly. "Holy, holy, holy God of creation, early in the morning's glory our praise shall come on high."

The people stood and sang as one voice. Never had this church felt the presence of God Almighty as they did that morning.

"God is here. His Spirit fills this church this morning. Before I introduce our guests, I would urge all of you gentlemen in the seats to make room for the ladies that are standing." A shuffling took place as men, with embarrassment written on their faces, stood and moved to allow the women in their full many layered skirts to be seated.

Thank you, for that, and now I recommend that you sit down where you are and try to make yourselves as comfortable as possible. I am sorry that our church is not larger, with more seating. Perhaps after today, we will be planning to build on." Melanie and the children were in the front row and beside her sat Father Bob and Brother Tim.

"Father Bob and Brother Tim, please come up to the lectern."

After their introductions, The Reverend Brown and Brother Tim sat down next to Melanie and like everyone else in the building they listened intently as the story of the Lion of Judah and the campaign against the Abalinah unfolded. He talked for nearly an hour and a half. He told about Two Feathers and the raid on the Sentu. Then he told about the Choyinaw and Chief Sky Fire's people.

When he said that the Lion of Judah had stood before him at the altar of his humble church, he felt it necessary to make sure that everyone knew that he had not been drinking alcohol, or on a long fast. The Lion was there! He was as real as this church and the plan for the campaign came from Him. He gave me the names of all the men that were chosen to go. Father Bob continued, including how Matt Morgan made the shields. Every detail fit together. "The captives are all free now. They are in the Christian camp of The Blue Stone People."

It seemed like just a few minutes to the people gathered there. The windows had been opened wide, but it was still too warm inside. Ladies were fanning themselves, while sweat made circles under their arms and trickled down between their breasts. Men pulled at their collars with a finger trying to make room for air to circulate, but they never lost focus on his every word.

At the end of the story, he told that it all started with one brave little girl that had boldly shared her faith many times and finally led The Blue Stone People to the cross. "Most of you owe her your lives. She was Sarah Slater then. She is married to David Sharpe and they have a baby girl now. Chief Dark Wolf honored her greatly by giving her child the name Pili Lioness Sharpe. Pili, means miraculous in Hebrew, and he gave her Lioness because she was born the very day that the captives were brought to the Blue Stone camp by The Lion of Judah." He paused wanting more than anything to make his message clear. "God can use anyone, at any time to do His work, if they are willing. This all happened. Every word of it is true." The people stood and said Amen as if he had just ended a prayer.

"Thank you," he said as they started to applaud. He applauded too, pointing toward heaven. Rose played "Onward Christian Soldiers and the people filed out into the sunshine. It wasn't until much later that Melanie pointed out that they should have taken up a collection to help with the work Father Bob is doing. Jim assured her that he would next Sunday.

"I don't think that Sunday service will be the same here after that. Do you?"

"No, I don't. I think it changed everyone." He didn't have to wait until the following Sunday. Envelopes started arriving at the parsonage. Some were marked, to expand the church, while others were to help Father Bob.

CHAPTER NINETEEN
BUILDING A CHURCH AND HIS PEOPLE

"It was all too quickly planned, the women didn't have time to make a potluck, but Melanie has a nice dinner in the oven if you would join us, we would love to have you."

"We would but I think we should get under way soon," said Father Bob. Thanks again for allowing me to share our story with your congregation. God has blessed the people and I think they know it now."

As they walked down the planked sidewalk, the windows, of Cookie's Café stood open. Every table inside was full of people from the church. Several couples stood outside waiting. Father Bob pulled on Tim's sleeve and crossed the street quickly.

"I think we just escaped a fate worse than death! I can't stand theological discussions with people who don't know what they are talking about." They hurried along hearing Helen calling after them, but ignored it.

"Now I see why you wanted to be ready to skip out of town right after church. I'll hitch up the team and we are on our way."

They turned the big wagon and headed up the Silver. Tim was driving the team and laughing.

"Why do I feel like I am driving for Black Bart and he just robbed the Wells Fargo?"

They laughed again until their sides hurt and had to wipe tears from their eyes.

"We just went past Fort Connor back there. Just so you know where not to go. I haven't laughed like that in years. Tim you are really sent by God. I am so glad that you are here. I can't wait to see what is in store for us together."

"You know Father Bob; I think our future is built on our history and our present."

"What do you mean?"

"I think our earlier experiences affect our responses to current situations and so one instinctive reflex could change our course and sets a precedent and so our prior intended path is never completed."

"Tim, are you trying to confuse me? For a man who says he doesn't like it, you are good at throwing out textbook verbiage. You are just teasing me aren't you?"

"Yes, and it worked!" Tim started to chuckle and soon they were both laughing loudly again. "I am so glad that you are here. You know we haven't had lunch. I am getting hungry."

"Let's pull up and give the horses a chance to drink and eat a bit, while we have something."

Everything went easier with Tim there to help. He handled the horses, checked the load to be sure it hadn't shifted at all and handed down the packs that Father Bob indicated.

"I hope you like strong cheese and beef jerky. I have some corn cakes here."

"It all sounds good," said Tim. "I'm not from a privileged back ground so you don't need to expect that our living conditions near the Indian camp will be a problem either. Tell me about the church you built. What's it like?"

"The church that I have so far is built of split logs. It isn't as warm as whole logs would be, but since I had to chop the trees alone and had to lift them in place, half is easier than a whole log to set in position. It's very small. The twelve foot lumber just fit in and right now most of the interior is piled high with mill cut boards. I brought that back with me late last fall and the men helped me pile it inside so that it wouldn't ruin in the winter weather. I have a separate area to the right of the altar that I sectioned off for a private sleeping quarters. We have a kerosene lamp and there is just room for two bed rolls. Father Peter O'Riley was a bit shorter than you and weighed a lot more but he managed to fit in there. I made a crude desk after he died and put it there where he slept. Maybe when we get a chance to add on we can allow room for us to have an area for study and prayer."

After the break for the horses and a meal for them, they rolled on until dark.

"We won't get to the ranch until about noon tomorrow. There is no point in trying to travel in the dark. I don't want any of the horses to get hurt. We are near the crossing. We can do that first thing in the morning and everything will dry as we travel."

"I want to change back into my work clothes," said Tim. "I have a package for you in my bag from Melanie. I forgot all about it." As Tim switched clothes, Father Bob opened the package and found that it held a dozen huge sugar cookies and a note.

"Thanks for lending me Tim to entertain the children. He is the nicest young man. We all love him. Please share these with him and tell him thank you again, from all of us."

"Tim, we have sugar cookies and a note from Melanie. I will light the lantern so you can see it."

"They have a good family. I was blessed to find them to stay with while I waited for you." He read the note and smiled.

"Do you mind if I keep this?"

"No of course not, put it in your bag so it won't get lost." They were both eager to be underway and moved on as soon as it was light enough to travel. Tim handled the team crossing the river without a problem. This assistant was just what he had prayed for.

Adam saw the loaded wagon coming and wondered if it was something his father had ordered in the settlement. He didn't recognize Father Bob in his leather clothes and had never met Tim. He prepared to ring the bell two clangs. That was the signal they had agreed upon. It meant someone is coming, not family and doesn't look like trouble. He was proud that he had been the one again to ring the bell. Climbing down slowly; he was gloating inside, knowing that Johnny should have been on watch but had traded because he wanted to spend time in the barn with Aunt Sarah and her new foal. Now he would have to feed and care for the chickens for two days and he didn't get to ring the bell! Adam was laughing out loud as he reached the bottom of the bluff and the cord on the bell.

He ran down the path to the crossing at the big oak. By the time the men of the family had gathered there, Tim was pulling the team to a stop in the dense shade. Ben maneuvered the raft across the Hickory and greeted Father Bob with a hug.

"Hello everyone, this is Brother Tim. He will be helping me at the church. Tim, this is Ben, Jed, David, Josh, and Adam. The ladies must all be busy." He sounded a bit disappointed.

"It's nice to meet all of you," said Tim looking across the water and smiling, as Ben poled the small raft expertly to the spot they used to tie it. Jed held it steady as the men stepped off.

"Adam gave us a two clang signal. That means company coming but not family and not any danger. From now on Adam, let's give Father Bob three clangs, so the girls will come to greet him."

"He is like family. That's what we should do from now on," said Adam trying to sound important. "I didn't know it was you, Father Bob. I am used to seeing you in a black uniform." Father Bob laughed, that long black thing I wear is called a robe, or a cassock. Today we are wearing our work clothes. It is much more comfortable when we are traveling. I hope no one here minds." Tim looked at the raft and the river and the tired horses standing on the other side, still hitched to the full wagon.

"Would one of you take me back across so I can make the team comfortable? That is a big load they have been pulling and I'm sure they would like to get a drink and be free of the harness for a while."

"I'll be glad to help you Tim, climb on." Jed took him back and helped him tie the horses near the river where they had sweet grass and water.

"I'm not sure if Father Bob wants anything from the wagon but maybe we should bring his satchel and my bag, just in case."

"Brother Tim, when did you arrive?"

"Call me Tim, please, and I came Wednesday on the mail boat down the Silver. That river is a lot deeper most of the way and moves much faster than this one."

"This is the Hickory, and most of the time she is no deeper than now. We can cross on our horses and they just get a wet belly, but it can get deep and dangerous especially in the spring when the snow melt is coming down and the rains hit at the same time."

"That's good to know. Thanks Jed for helping me. I wonder where Father Bob went."

"I think they probably went up to Ben's house. Let's walk up there. Jed took Father Bob's satchel from Tim and they strolled up the path. Are you going to be here permanently?"

"I really don't know. I guess that explains why the bishop dispatched me out here. I couldn't commit to taking my final vows so he sent me here to think what I wanted to do with my life."

"I'm sorry Tim, I didn't mean to pry."

"Not at all, I have nothing to hide and quite frankly I am glad that he sent me here, because I have already had a most rewarding experience, considering the adventure of the trip and then listening to Father Bob tell the story of "The Lion of Judah" actually appearing to him and the campaign that followed. I want God to use me like that!"

"Well if you stay around Father Bob, He probably will," said Jed with a nervous chuckle. "We are here and we figured correctly. I hear Ben inside talking." Father Bob stood as Tim and Jed entered.

"Mary this is Brother Tim. He is here to help me."

"Hello Mary, please just call me Tim." Mary hurried to the chair in the living room where Natty was climbing up.

"This is Natty, and he loves to climb anything. Eli is in Jed's barn with our oldest son Joshua and the rest of the children." David extended his hand and reintroduced himself to Tim. I am married to Sarah. She is Ben's sister and she is in Jed's barn, too. The attraction is a new foal."

"Hi David, this must be a nice place to live. We had horses on my father's farm. I love working with them."

"Sarah and I won't always be here, we have land up river that we will build on before long."

"Sarah and David have the piece of land next to the one we have for the church. Do you remember? I pointed it out when you got that piece behind the church land."

"Oh yes, Father Bob, I do remember. How far is your land from here?" he was wondering how far his piece was and wanted to see it.

"Tim, if you are not tired of riding, we could take a couple of horses up there and be back by dark if we hustle."

"Father Bob, would you mind if I went with David? How long did you intend to stay here? I don't want to cause you a delay."

"If you would like to do that, it is fine with me. Ben, do you and Jed know of a horse that would fit Tim. He is thin now but I suspect he won't always be. I would like to get him one that he will enjoy for years to come. I am fortunate that you gave me Macho. He is such a nice horse. I am not asking you to give it to us. I will be glad to pay what the army would, if you have one that you will part with."

"There is no shortage of horses on this ranch Father Bob. Let's go out to the field where there are at least a dozen saddle ready mustangs. Maybe Tim can spot one that he wants to try." They walked to the gate and stood looking at the horses. "Not all of them are reliable yet. We are still working with that big young bay over there, and the dark one over there, that looks almost black, she likes to stop abruptly and tilt her head down so you go sailing over her head."

"Tell me about that bay. What have you been doing with him?" asked Tim.

"First I need to explain to you that we don't break horses here. We gentle them with patient training. We never use whips or spurs and if you take one of our animals, we expect the same from you." Tim nodded listening. He liked what he heard. Ben told him that the bay had carried bundles and was no longer blanket shy." He has had a saddle on and I have gotten on and off a few times but we haven't really ridden him yet. He is only half way through school."

"Is it alright if I go talk to him?" Tim asked.

"Sure, go ahead, introduce yourself." Ben stepped close to Jed and said that he doubted if the Bay would allow Tim to even get near enough to touch him. Tim walked at an angle so that he could approach from the front. He walked to within ten feet and just when the horse looked like it was ready to move away, he sat down in the grass facing the horse. They could see that Tim was talking, but they couldn't hear what he was saying. What they could see was the result. The horse came closer and closer. He stood three feet away when Tim got up very slowly. He held his palm out and the horse sniffed it. Tim pulled part of a broken sugar cookie from his pocket and extended his hand again. The horse stepped close enough to reach it. Tim whispered something to him and scratched his ear as he ate the piece of cookie. He turned his back and walked over to the gate. The bay followed and stopped just a few feet away.

"Ben, I like him a lot. I want to finish his schooling myself, if we can afford him." Tim looked to Father Bob for approval.

"Borrow a different one for now and I'll see what Ben and I can work out," said Father Bob. Ben smiled

"That young man knows horses. He just picked the best horse in the field."

David brought over Blackie and a second horse saddled and ready.

"I am sure that by now, Mary has packed lunches for you both and I will get two water bags. I'll be right back," said Ben. He stepped in the house and came back with the promised lunches." If it gets dark before you come back, stay and return in the morning. We know that you are both safe. Don't hurry back in the dark."

Tim swung up on the saddle holding the reins in his left hand as he stashed his lunch in the saddlebag. They hooked their water bags over the saddle horn and started away.

"Let's cross the river and ride up the prairie side. It is much easier than going through the trees and brush on this side."

They crossed and David set a good pace knowing that it was well past the time when they would be able to reach the land, explore and return before dark. When he thought about it, he slowed Blackie.

"Tim, tell me how you know about horses."

"I'm no expert. I just like horses and I have learned that if you approach them from the front you don't get kicked. I learned that the hard way!" They laughed and Tim continued. "When I was a boy my grandfather told me that you can tell your secrets to a horse and he will keep them and not tell a soul. At first I just thought that was a joke until one day I was entering the barn and there was Gramps with a new two year old he had just brought home from a sale. He was standing in front of it and murmuring softly."

"I asked him why he was whispering and he said, I'm not telling and neither is this horse. I guess the whispering lets them get your scent and sound without scaring them. That's what I was doing with the bay back there at Ben's, trying to let him know that I was not a danger to him."

David looked over at Tim and noticed that he was leaning forward and scratching the ears of the horse he was on. She was moving along looking happy. They stopped for a break and a drink for just a few minutes. Then moved on and finally David could see the dead trees that Father Bob had left lying near the front of the church property.

"We are almost there." He carefully walked Blackie into the ragged grass and weeds, avoiding a thorn bush. "Tim this is the church property and the river runs through it about two thirds of the way back. So yours will start back a little ways further back from the river. We can cross there. The bottom is stable enough so the horses can get there footing." They crossed easily and walked the horses back a few yards and moved around a huge cluster of boulders.

Tim was looking all around trying to absorb everything.

"I love the big pines. I can imagine this being made into a prayer garden. It is peaceful."

"I haven't ridden back here. You are right. I feel it. It is calming somehow." Just then they circled around another clump of big pines and found themselves in front of a yellow and gray bluff that reached far above them.

"Adam would love this. He would be looking for a path up, to make a lookout," suggested David.

"Look over there." Tim slid from the horse and tied the reins quickly to a nearby pine. "I'm going in there."

"Tim, you shouldn't just enter a cave like that. There could be a bear or mountain lion in there!"

"Let's make two torches and explore. You have your pistol, if we find ourselves in danger."

"Trusting soul, aren't you? How do you know I can shoot?"

"You wouldn't be wearing it if you couldn't," said Tim grinning. With torches in hand, they entered the cave, watching for prints of any animal in the dust near the opening.

"I don't see anything but some sand and leaves and pine needles that have swirled in on the wind. This goes back farther than we should try to go today. Look up at the ceiling. It opens up higher and the sides are widening into a big room. Watch the floor, it is tricky right here, and look at that. It is sloping down. It seems like it is cooler down here." Tim moved cautiously around a boulder to find he was walking in mud. David grabbed Tim's shirt sleeve.

"Don't go any further. We need to come back with lanterns and ropes just in case we step where we shouldn't." Tim was so excited that he didn't want to stop.

"We can't stop now! I think there is water ahead."

"There may be Tim, but you could be standing on a layer of eroding sandstone. If you break through, I couldn't help you back up. We need to take precautions."

"David, are you always the voice of reason?"

"I try to be."

"Can you believe that they gave me this land free? I own this cave!"

We need to head out while we can see. My torch is about to sputter out."

"Mine too, let's go back to the horses and get a rope." They were both surprised to see that it was nearly dark when they walked out of the cave.

"I guess we should sleep out here and then we can explore a little more in the morning," said Tim.

"That was fun!"

"We have enough food and water but only one blanket each."

"It is not cold. One is fine. Let's sleep out here in the open so we can see the stars." Tim was grinning. "I haven't done that since I was a kid."

"You act like this is just an adventure. That cave was entertaining, but I am glad that it is not on my land. How can you build on it or put down a well? If you don't, you won't be able to keep it."

"David, you are not going to ruin my pleasure and joy by being practical. I know that God has a plan for such a unique place and it is right beside the church property. I wonder who he intends to live in such a marvelous cave." The bluff ran behind the river properties for as far as they could see. The cave opened to the west. Tim had difficulty falling asleep. He was imagining many different uses for the cave.

Morning dawned to wake them. As they rolled their blankets and David insisted that they should return to the ranch, they could hear whimpering. Just that quickly, Tim was off on another adventure.

When he found the den, three precious pups huddled in the back. They were small and thin. Their mother had managed to return to them, but had been badly wounded. She didn't live. Now they were alone, and starving.

"Tim, don't reach in there. They are not dogs. They are wolves. They will be afraid of you and bite you." Tim ran to his saddlebag and brought out one last piece of cheese he had not eaten.

"The dried meat is too hard but this isn't." He broke it into tiny pieces and placed them on the floor of the den. With courage, the starving babies sniffed and nibbled the new food. Tim made a cup with his hand and poured water in it, they licked at it and as they did it tickled. He giggled and the sound sent them huddling again in the back of the den.

"Tim, it is no use feeding them. You are just prolonging the inevitable. You can't take those back to the ranch. We have foals. Wolves kill foals!"

"There you go again, the voice of reason! Have a heart David. If we don't help them, they will die!"

"Well you will have to take them with you when you go. You can't leave them with us! There was a Den on the ranch and they put rocks in the mouth of it, so the wolves wouldn't use it anymore."

"Did they kill the wolves that were in it?"

"No they didn't have to, they moved on. Jed did shoot one big black one that joined the pack. He was ready to attack Beth on the path. That all happened before I came along." Tim crawled in the den and pulled three little gray fluff balls out and tucked them in his shirt. Tim was distracted by the pups and forgot that he had intended to go back in the cave. He got up on the saddle and they headed back to the S. and J. Ranch. David was not happy.

"You can't show those to Ben's sons or they will want to keep them. What are you going to do with them?"

"I don't know. I just couldn't leave them there beside their mother. Who would do such a thing?"

"I would, if a wolf was attacking one of our horses, but I don't think a man did that. She looked like she had tangled with another animal, a big one."

"It is so sad. It seems that so often, it's the weak and innocent that suffers. Why didn't God make a provision for them?"

"I can't answer a question like that Tim. No one can. At least Father Bob was able to help rescue the weak and innocent from the Abalinah. That's something I will never forget," said David.

"I didn't know anything about that until he told it in church Sunday morning. That story had that whole community stunned. Maybe Father Bob will know how to help these poor babies."

David doubted it but didn't say so. They traveled about halfway back before taking a break. Tim put the pups on

266

the grass and gave them water from a cup that David had in his saddlebag. They both searched and came up with a small piece of bread and Tim got the idea that he would chew the dried meat until it was soft and then feed it to them. The pups knew instantly what it was and fought over it. They both chewed and offered more. David got his finger bitten as a result.

"That's a fine way to say thank you!' He mumbled.

Before they reached the crossing, Johnny finally got his chance to ring the big bell.

"Clang, clang, clang, family is coming home," he signaled. Sarah brought the baby to greet her daddy, and Tim was glad to see Father Bob and Ben on the path coming. David hugged Sarah and took the baby.

"Tim this is my wife Sarah and this is Pili. Sarah this is Brother Tim.

"It's nice to meet you both," said Tim. "I have three babies of my own and quite frankly, I haven't a notion what I will do with them, or for them, but they are very hot inside my shirt!" Sarah laughed and looked puzzled. She could see his shirt moving, and then one baby pushed out the top, popping a button from his shirt.

"Oh, let me take one," she crooned. Adam reached for the second and Johnny took the third.

"They are wolves, boys," said Ben. "Don't get attached. We can't raise wolves around our horses!" He said it firmly and meant every word, but was smiling.

"Be careful, one of them bit my finger. They have sharp teeth already."

"Bring them to my house Tim, I'll find something they can eat." She kissed the little wolf on top of its head and handed it back to Tim so she could take Pili. "David, where did you get three wolf pups?"

"I didn't. He did. I told him we can't have them here with the horses, but he brought them anyway."

"Where is their mother?"

"She ran into some bad luck. I am guessing that it was at least three days ago. The pups are thin and very hungry."

"That's awful." Everyone followed along. Soon Beth came up behind the rest with Lily on the horse in front of her. Jed changed his step so he was beside her and explained that they were all going to Sarah and David's to feed three baby wolves that Tim brought back. Father Bob shook his head in incredulity.

"David, where did you find the wolves?"

"They were in a den at the bottom of the bluff on Tim's land. We heard them whining and Tim turned our trip into a rescue mission!"

"Well the lad has a good heart, doesn't he?" Father Bob was already aware that finding someone to take care of them was not going to be easy.

"David didn't answer. He was praying that Sarah wouldn't fall in love with them and want to keep them. As soon as she stepped in her cabin she handed Pili back to her father. She hurried to the huge pot of stew hanging over the edge of the fire and scooped out a large cup full and poured it out onto a platter where she sliced, diced, mashed and stirred until Adam asked her what she was doing.

"I'm making baby food. They probably want milk, but I'm not sure if cow's milk is good for them. She poured a small amount of milk into a bowl and added water. The food is just warm now, let's put them out on the grass and see if they will eat this." They devoured it and licked the plate clean. "They shouldn't have any more for a while, until their tummies can get used to the change.

Beth gently picked up the smallest one and peeked under.

"It's a girl. She looks a lot like Bold One did. She has the white bib under her chin." Jed was frowning.

"She is pure wolf and don't even think about it! I know that look, Beth. No wolves!"

"Well, I guess he is not in the mood for adopting," said Father Bob, watching Jed as he slipped a soft bridal onto the nearest horse in the field and headed down the path to his barn.

"Father Bob, if you can stay tonight, I have three fat rabbits for supper. There will be more than enough for all of us."

"Thank you Beth, but at the moment, I'm not sure what we are going to do." She nodded understandingly and turned the horse toward her house. Father Bob sat down beside Tim's brood, and soon found his lap full of wiggling furry babies.

Tim laughed and sat beside him.

"They seem to be accepting humans very readily."

"Seriously Tim, what are we going to do with them?" We can't take them to the Indian camp. They have horses, cows, sheep and chickens, too."

CHAPTER TWENTY
DISCOVERIES

The Priest and his assistant sat together playing with the pups and talking.

"Father Bob, what did you and Ben decide about the bay?"

"We will take him with us when we leave. He is yours now. I hope you can train him well. He won't like following that wagon on a rope all the way, but he will appreciate his freedom when he is put in the field at the village."

"Thank you Father Bob. I won't disappoint you."

"Did you see the church land? The ancient trees are so beautiful. I hope that we can build a church there without cutting the biggest ones."

"That whole area has a nice feeling to it. David and I crossed the river and went back on my land. It is as the man said at the land office; rocks, pine trees and a bluff that runs parallel to the river for as far as we could see. The bluff on my land has a cave in it that I would like you to see. The area in front of it feels like a prayer garden. All it would need is a few benches. It is perfect already with huge pines for shade and immense boulders."

"It sounds lovely and the cave is enticing, but I really think we need to head out."

"What about the wolf pups?"

"What about them?"

"I can't leave them here, they don't want them, and I can't leave them out on the prairie to starve or get eaten. I don't know why God had me find them! It hurts to think about it."

Father Bob placed his hands over the pups and prayed for a solution before morning.

"We will stay the night, but we need to head out early," he said as he stood up laughing at the antics of the three furry babies, now chewing on Tim's clothes. Sarah came out and poured another helping of mashed stew onto the plate and placed a pie pan filled with water beside it.

"Has anything been decided about these poor little guys?"

"No, I guess I didn't have any idea how much of a problem they would be." Once again the plate was clean and they sniffed at the water and decided to stand in it as they drank. "It is hot here in the sun," said Tim. I think I should move them to the shade of the trees. Their den was in the shade all the time." Sarah agreed, but thought that Tim needed a way to keep track of them.

"Tim there is a pile of boards by the fence; I have a hammer and nails, if you want to use them to build a little house or den for them. Pili is sleeping in her crib so I can watch them for you while you make it."

"Thanks Sarah, I am not sure how to go about it but I will try." She went inside her cabin and returned with the hammer and nails.

"Just think box, and make it small enough to be cozy." Sarah picked up the darkest of the three and stroked its soft fur. "This one is a boy," she said. "And this one is a girl. So you have one male and two females." She sat on the grass in the shade of a tree and they came one at a time and crawled into her lap. Soon all three were cuddling.

"They look so harmless in your lap," said Tim grinning as he worked. Sarah examined each cub thoroughly, making sure they were healthy. She pulled the water pan closer so that it was in the shade and one by one she washed their faces.

"The little male will be very dark when he is grown. His fur is almost black where I wet it. His eyes are darker too. I think we should give them all names."

"Sarah, David doesn't want you to keep any, so don't bond with them."

"I'm not, I am just having fun. Let's call him Woof, as in bark. The girls can be Little One and Sister. What do you think?"

"I like the name Woof, but not the girl's names. We have to do better than that."

What are you going to name your horse?" Father Bob said you are taking the bay with you in the morning."

"I haven't got a name for him yet either and I need to get this done so I can spend some time with him. What do you think? Will this do?"

"That should do fine. You made a solid bottom. That's good. The sides will let them look out without falling out. They may not like traveling very well, but at least you will know they are safe in there. Should we try it?"

"I'll put the kennel box in the densest part of the shade." He carried it there and thanked Sarah as she put a piece of cloth in the bottom.

"As soon as they sniff at every board, they will settle down."

"Look how cute they are. They are tired. I think they will sleep for a while now. I'm going to take the hammer and tin of nails in and check on Pili," said Sarah. Tim walked to the gate but didn't enter the field; he quietly tapped on Sarah's door and opened it softly.

"Sarah do you have some crackers or cookies I can give my horse?"

"Yes I have just about anything you could want in here. Ben is generous. He and Jed built this cabin for me before I returned from the Indian village. David is a good provider and makes sure that we always have supplies. Here I will put some crackers and a couple of cookies in this pouch for you. Come in and look around."

"This is a nice cabin," he said stepping in and looking at the well-furnished little home. "I guess Father Bob has a lot of work waiting for him back at the camp. He doesn't have a nice place like this yet, but I plan on helping all I can. I want to spend some time with my horse now while it is light. I think I am going to call him Jack. It's simple and seems to fit him."

"That's a good name. He will be a blessing to you. Tim, your face is red. You should have a drink of water before you go back out in the sunshine." He drank the glass of water and downed a second.

With the pouch of treats in his hand he thanked her and walked to the gate. The big bay stood far away, in the center of the field. He repeated the same words that he had said when he met the horse.

"You are a very handsome big horse. I want to be your friend." He recited it softly until he stood in front of Jack. He was no more than five feet from him.

It was then that Tim realized that David's Blackie was coming to him and a pretty female palomino. They could smell the sugar and knew that treats were to be had. Tim scratched each of them, and gave out pieces of the cookie before turning to Jack. He held out the cookie and waited as Jack stretched his neck but didn't step closer. He wanted it but wasn't quite sure of Tim yet.

With time and patience Tim was able to scratch and pet the big bay, using the name Jack often.

"You are Jack. You are my friend, Jack. We are going to have fun together." Tim walked to the water trough and waited. Jack followed hesitantly. He slid up on his back slowly, and got back off. "Good Jack, You are a good horse, Jack." He worked with him until he felt that he had made progress and wanted to end on a good note. He fed him the last half of a cookie in the pouch and whispered to him.

When Tim left the field, he looked back to see Jack standing at the gate, with his big beautiful head hanging over it. He was looking in Tim's direction. He had a feeling of joy until he looked in the direction of the trees and the crate he had built. His feeling changed to one of concern as he recognized the work that the pups would require before they could be returned to the wild.

Joshua had walked down the path and was now petting the pups, and smiling.

"Have you decided what to do with these babies?"

"Not yet, but I know your dad doesn't want them here."

"He's just worried that when they are grown they might hurt one of our animals. We have calves and foals every year and they are vulnerable. Bring your babies down to Aunt Beth's when you come to eat. They have two old dogs that are gentle. Maybe they can be friends. We had four but one died and one just left. I don't know why. We still have Sunshine and Rascal, but they are really old. They will probably like to see the pups."

"Thanks Josh. I will. I am going to take my bag down to the river and get cleaned up. I have been working in the sunshine all day and I think I must smell like a combination of sweat, wolf fur and horses." Josh laughed and headed home to wash and change his shirt for supper.

Father Bob was sitting on the front lawn with Jed when Mary pulled her little wagon close and helped Eli down. She headed him toward Beth before returning for Natty. He had moved from the corner of the wagon to the middle where the crate held the three wiggly babies. He was poking his fingers through the spaces in the sides and was giggling as they licked him. Tim lifted the pen down and put the pups on the grass. Mary sat down holding Natty. She was helping him to pet them gently. Lily and Johnny came out and joined the group on the grass. Adam came saying they had an all clear and scooped up the all gray pup.

"I like this one. She likes me," said Adam.

"This is my favorite," said Beth scooping up the other female. Sarah and David arrived just as Ben came out of Jed's barn leading Sarah's beautiful cream colored foal. It pranced and called to Pretty Mother. She called back loudly. Everyone turned to see what Ben was doing. He led the foal close to the group and just stood there.

"Ben, what are you doing?"

"I thought that maybe this group needed reminding just what this ranch is all about and why we can't adopt a wolf! Look at her! Can you picture her after a pack of wolves attacked her?"

"Ben, take her back to the barn! You are upsetting everyone." Sarah was angry at him, for the first time since she had come to the S. and J. Ranch. "David I want to go back to the cabin. I am sorry Beth, but we won't be staying for supper." She stepped up onto the little wagon and held Pili tightly as David looked back at the gathering, shook his head and drove them slowly home.

Tim felt terrible and Father Bob felt even worse.

"We apologize to all of you. Especially to you Ben for the trouble we have caused. Don't worry about the wolves. We will be leaving at first light and the pups are all going with us." Ben didn't reply. He turned the foal around and walked her back to her mother.

Jed suggested that they all go inside. After washing their hands, Beth sat the children down with plates of deboned rabbit, fried potatoes and biscuits with butter. The adults all bowed their heads and Father Bob said grace. He kept watching the door, but Ben didn't come. Jed knew that something had to be said to ease the tension. He could feel it in the room.

"I think Ben has gone down to Sarah and David's. I'm sure that it will be okay once they talk. She has been emotional ever since she came home with Pili."

*****

Sarah's face was red with anger.

"I know you are concerned about the safety of the animals, but Ben you had no right to drag that foal out of the barn away from her mother like that. You treated her like your exhibit! She is my animal! I have not said no to you at all. You have moved my horses around and put Pretty Mother in with Cloud without even talking with me about what I had planned to do with her. I get a lot more respect in the village than I do here!" She went out the back door and slammed it."

"Wow, I have never seen her that upset!" Ben looked at David and could see that he was also angry.

"I didn't hurt that foal. I would never do that. What is she yelling about?"

"I think she is tired of just trying hard to fit in and maybe it's time that we built our own place, down on my land. Ben I know how she is feeling. She wants to be able to do what she wants. She is a grown woman. You control everything here. You are not wrong. I'm just saying that sometimes the things you want or need for this ranch aren't always comfortable or right for all of us."

"What are you talking about? I've made sure she has everything that she wants or needs."

"I am her husband. Do you think that is comfortable for me?" I want to be the one providing for my family!"

"David, be reasonable."

"I'm always reasonable! You just can't accept anyone's view but your own!" Sarah had placed Pili in her crib and the men arguing had caused her to wake and she was crying. Sarah came back in the back door and went straight to the baby without looking at Ben or David. With the baby in her arms she looked at her brother and spoke very softly.

"Ben, you have done all that any brother could do. Now it is time for us to start being responsible adults. If Rachel and Zack can do it, so can we. You can have David's help four days a week, but the other three days he is mine. We will be moving in the morning."

Sarah took Pili into the bedroom and yanked the curtain closed on the doorway. She busied herself with changing the baby's diaper and then feeding her. Pili was back sleeping in her crib when David stepped into the bedroom.

"Ben has gone home. Are you sure you want to do this? I wanted to build a house down there someday, but are we ready to abruptly leave and start now?"

"David, if we don't do it now we never will. Our lives are getting tangled so tightly with all of theirs that it will be impossible to cut ourselves free. That foal is a good example of what I am talking about. Is she mine or is she half his, because he put Pretty Mother with his white stallion?" He acted like she was all his tonight! David we need to do this before it is too late."

He sat down beside her on the bed and put his arms around her.

"We could build a cabin on the backside of the river and stay in Tim's cave until it is built."

"If we do it right away, we can put in a small garden before it is too late in the season. We can use Beth's plow. David, we have to do this. I don't want to lean on Ben anymore. I love him so much but it is time that we are separate from the S. and J. Ranch!"

She had formed a strong conviction and wasn't changing her mind. As they talked, they became less angry and more excited.

"I want to take the wolves with us. That way they will be back in the area they were born in. I am capable of feeding three baby wolves and nature will help them learn to be independent. Please don't disagree with me. Please David, let's build our own place."

"I am wondering how you decided that I should be here four days and with you only three. What are you thinking? It will take me a long time to build us a cabin and work up a garden. I'm not even sure if there is land clear enough to do either."

"I just thought until they get some help that they would really need you. I probably shouldn't have blown up that way, but to tell the truth I have felt this way for quite a while. We have been here two years and nothing has changed. We are no closer to having our own place than we were the day we got married."

"You are right but I think we need to go back to Beth's now and talk to everyone including Father Bob and Tim. I've got an idea!"

"What is it? Tell me."

"Come on girl, grab the baby and let's go. It is getting late. I don't want us to drag everyone out of bed!"

David could hear voices as he stepped on Jed's porch. He tapped on the door and then turned the handle.

"Is it alright if we come in?"

"Of course David, we were hoping you two would talk things over and then calm down. Sarah, are you alright now?"

Beth asked as if she was afraid of the answer.

"I'm fine but we have something we all need to talk about." At that point, Father Bob and Tim felt like they were intruding, they stood up and were ready to step outside.

"Don't leave, please. We need to talk to all of you," said David with a smile.

"First I need to say something." Ben stood up at the end of the table being very formal. "I apologize to both of you. I didn't think that what I was doing would seem controlling. I was being protective. Please don't leave here tomorrow and go to a piece of land that hasn't even got a tree cut for your cabin or a place to stay in out of the weather. You have to think about the baby. That wouldn't be good for her." He wanted very much to repair their relationship. He wanted things back the way they had been.

"It will never be the same Ben. You shouldn't want us to be dependent anymore. We are adults, and we need to have our own place now. We want to make a home for Pili."

"Sarah that cabin is your home, we built it for you!"

"Ben this ranch is a jumble! No one really owns anything but you. You built that cabin for me? You told me yourself that it sits on your land not mine. The land you put my name on, has a fenced field for your mustangs and the long pen that you used to trap that first herd of wild mustangs when I came here. Mary has land that she would like to build on for her sons one day, but I don't see a cabin or a well. You are running cattle on it! She could lose it Ben if the improvements aren't made and when you built your new house, it sits on the edge of my land. That's what I mean about this place being a jumble. It would be impossible to sort it all out!" Sarah had worked herself back into a temper. Ben stood there with his mouth open but not able to say a word.

David turned to Father Bob.

"Would you be willing to take that load of lumber down to my land? I'll pay you for it of course and Tim, could we stay in the front of the cave while we build our cabin?" Father Bob didn't know what to say. He didn't mind selling the lumber but he didn't want to appear to take sides. Tim looked to Father Bob for guidance but when none came he smiled and just nodded.

"Sure you can use it. It's just sitting there, and I can drive the team down with the lumber in the morning if you are sure that's what you want."

"It is, and we want the pups, all three of them. They will be back in the area where they were born and we will take care of them until they can take care of themselves."

"David, this is an extreme move to make with no planning. You can't do this now without accommodations down there," said Ben firmly.

"I know that it is sudden, but Father Bob, if you will let me have your load of lumber it will help us to get started."

"Yes of course, if you need it, you can have it. Tim can take it there."

"Ben, you have treated us well, and we are grateful for the love from everyone here," said David. "I wanted to do this, but I wished that it hadn't come about so abruptly." He saw the pain in the eyes of the family.

"I will try hard to hire some help in town," said Jed. "David is going to need time for building his own place. I don't know how much help he will be able to give us. We already put a sign in the Trading Post. I hope it gets results."

Ben looked at Sarah, holding the baby.

"I will do whatever you want, if you will just stay and forget all this."

"No Ben. I can't."

"You will need to get a garden in right away," said Beth. Jed and I will come down and help you get it in, won't we Jed?"

"I guess so, as soon as we can figure out the time. You can use the big wagon that's in my barn for your things tomorrow."

Mary sat in the rocking chair near the window, holding Natty and not saying anything. Tears slowly made their way down her face.

Sarah knelt beside her.

"Mary, we are sisters. It will be better this way. I love you and Ben and the boys. You know I do. It's just time. We have lots of things to discuss in the coming days including the buried horses in the field behind Jed's barn."

Ben heard that comment but chose not to respond. Adam looked at his father and sadly said goodnight. He walked home and went to bed. Josh soon followed him. Johnny sat on the couch trying to make sense of what was happening, but none of it seemed right to him.

"You know what I think? I think that you all need to say "sorry"! You tell us to say it when we get mad and we do and then things are back right, but grownups argue and they don't say sorry and it makes everybody sad. Mom is crying and Aunt Mary is crying and Aunt Sarah is going away with Uncle David and Pili. Doesn't anybody want to say sorry?" Sarah wrapped her arms around Johnny and cuddled him close against Pili.

"It's going to be right again soon Johnny. We are not going to move far away. You will come to visit and stay overnight sometimes. I am sorry that everyone is feeling sad or mad now. This is just something that we have to do. Uncle David and I love you and Lily, and your mom and Dad and we will all have good times together again. I promise."

"You can't say that! You don't know how it will be when you are gone away. What if you were already gone when Adam broke his arm? Who would have fixed it? You are supposed to be here. We need you." He hugged her and then dashed out of the room to his bedroom sobbing.

Sarah looked at David from the rug she was sitting on near Mary. Eli slept on the bear rug beside her. She touched his face softly and carefully stood.

"We should go. It is very late and we have a lot of work to do in the morning," she said. David agreed.

"Goodnight everyone, we will see you all in the morning," he said as he held the door open for her and the baby.

Ben looked at Mary and realized that he had held Sarah so tightly that he had driven her away.

"I didn't know that I was making her feel uncomfortable. Mary, I have made a lot of mistakes. At least I will be able to right one of them soon. The men from Tom's mill are going to bring two big loads of the precut logs next week and they will be delivered just outside the fence by the spring, on your land. I checked and we have until next spring to get it done and the well in place. Mary I am so sorry. Have you felt the way Sarah does, that I control everything?"

"Ben, it's different for me. I am your wife and I love you and I am grateful that you love me and the boys. Our lives were shattered and you put them back together and gave us a wonderful place here to live. Release Sarah lovingly, and you will still have a relationship with her. Don't fight this. She doesn't want you to take care of her anymore, and I think you need to tell her that she found the gold and it is hers to have or to share. Explain that it has been paying for the cattle for The Blue Stone People and let her decide." She paused just a moment and then said, "Goodnight everyone, I am going to take the wagon and tuck our little boys in bed. I want to be up to help Sarah in the morning."

"I'm coming too. Goodnight, everyone. Please pray for us. Our family is hurting right now," Ben said in the direction of Father Bob and Tim.

"We will Ben, don't worry. God always has a plan," said Father Bob.

Jed had guided Johnny out to a sleeping pallet on the bear rug and Lily was on the floor of their bedroom with a similar arrangement. Father Bob and Tim knelt beside the beds that the children had vacated. They could feel the pain this family was experiencing, but being outside the family circle made it possible for them to see that perhaps this was what God intended all along. They prayed until their knees told them that they should continue their prayers in bed, where they said a quiet goodnight to each other.

Father Bob remembered that he had asked for a solution for the wolf pups, before morning.

"I could never have imagined such an outcome." Tim felt guilty because he had forgotten them in their crate all evening. He tiptoed out with a bowl of water and several large pieces of soft meat. The meal had not been appreciated by the people it was prepared for but now the hungry babies gobbled it in.

Ben and Mary had come up with a plan that included everyone. Ben helped Josh and Jed to get the milking done quickly, and Adam and Johnny took care of the chickens after checking the lookout. The men of the ranch gathered in Jed's barn to hitch strong horses to every wagon on the ranch. They formed a slow moving parade down the path to Sarah and David's cabin with the women and children riding along inside.

In the back wagon Ben had loaded every tool that he thought they might need, including hammers and nails and some extra rope.

The women worked together to empty Sarah's kitchen. There seemed to be a general consensus that anything within the four walls was going. Efficiently they boxed, crated or stuffed baskets and barrels until it started to sound hollow inside when they talked. The beautiful bed that Ben and Jed had carved was dismantled and wrapped in bedding and placed in the largest wagon. The crib was next and two beautiful trunks that held their clothes and the baby's clothes. The hand stitched curtains were removed and used to wrap anything breakable. The oil cloth from the table was folded and placed between the chairs to prevent chaffing of the wood as the wagon jostled across the prairie. The table was placed top down on a layer of hay along with its benches.

The storage room was emptied into the third wagon along with large bundles that had appeared from both Beth's and Mary's kitchen. Beth sent Josh and Adam back to Ben's barn to bring the forms for making the sunbaked bricks. She knew that Sarah would want to make a new oven as soon as time allowed. Mary tucked in a long length of white cotton cloth, thinking that with Sarah's abilities it could be used for almost anything.

Ben and Jed had already discussed several things including the transport of Sarah's foal. Jed nailed boards together and formed a mini stall within the largest wagon. She could lie down in a layer of hay or stand but that was all. Pretty Mother was on a rope attached to that wagon. She would walk beside her foal. Jed brought Moon Boy and David's Thunder and added them to the column on comfortable leads. Blackie was saddled and restless as he watched the activity. Sarah's saddle and two horse blankets were placed on top of the tools; she would ride on the seat of the first wagon. The plow had been the first thing that Ben and Jed put in the tool wagon. Everything else was fitted around it.

Mary kissed Sarah on the cheek and hugged David.

"I won't be coming down today. I am going to stay here and watch the little ones, but Beth is going to help you get set up. I'll come down when I can."

Sarah hastily scrubbed a tear away and hugged Mary tightly, squeezing Pili between them.

Tim had hitched the big team back to the freight wagon and had removed Father Bob's boxes and bags from the Trading post along with his own crates and ferried them across to the ranch side of the river where they were left. He hoped it would not rain or any animal get into the food supplies while they were gone.

Tim closed his eyes and prayed for protection not for these few goods, but for the people who were setting out to start a new home. He asked that this family be healed and blessed. He knew the story of how Ben had started this place from nothing but a strong will and lots of hard work. Lord it must be very hard for him to let Sarah go. She was separated from him for so long. She had to be strong and independent to survive with the Indians. Maybe that's why she can't accept Ben trying to protect her now.

When he opened his eyes, he saw that the wagons were being pulled to the crossing. They were ready to go. Mary reminded Tim to put the crate with the wolves on his wagon where he could easily tend to them.

"Thanks Mary for the food and tin plate and bowl. These little ones will be glad to be back in their old den."

One wagon at a time was ferried across the river to the prairie side without incident. Tim urged the team pulling the lumber to start and he led the way, with Father Bob on the seat beside him. The wagons rolled along and stopped often to give Sarah a chance to tend the baby without the rocking movement. The pups were let loose for a break at the half point. They were placed on the grass and fed and given a drink. They were enjoying this new activity and all the attention. They could see the trees near the river moving by slowly between the slats in their crate.

When he finally saw the cut trees on the church land, Father Bob's face was lit with a big smile.

"Tim I feel that all this is for a good reason. We are working in God's plan. I can't discern it yet, but we will; all in His good time."

David came close to Tim and asked if he thought it was possible to pull the lumber through the church land and down to the river.

"I'll find a way, while the rest of you build a big raft to take the other wagons across. Don't worry, we will make this work."

Tim smiled, as he cut brush and paced off the width between ancient tree trunks. It is marvelous. We are back here and Father Bob will get to see my cave.

With the new raft built and tethered tightly to the trees on the bank, the smallest wagon was rolled on and its wheels blocked. The men had strung a rope to help guide them and each got on the raft, with a sturdy pole to ease the raft across. Ben had taken the horses over and cleared a graded path up the far bank. David waved at Sarah and smiled as the raft was afloat with its first load. The ropes were quickly tied to old trees and it was stabilized as the wagon rolled safely off the raft and up the bank, with the help of Sundown. He was one of the strongest riding horses on the ranch. Ben thought it was appropriate that Ginger's first son bring the first load across for Sarah. He was still hurting, but he was beginning to see that she needed to be separate and on her own to feel whole.

The bluff peeked out between the huge pines here and there but the cave was not visible from the place Father Bob had agreed to put the crossing.

Only the wagon with the lumber stood on the prairie side of the river, as the whole group moved the other wagons slowly with Tim and David's direction, toward the cave, missing huge boulders by inches and brushing between the trees without breaking branches.

All the work of loading, traveling, stopping to rest and crossing the river twice had taken the entire day. It was late afternoon before Tim spoke excitedly.

"The cave is just around the next clump of pines!"

Father Bob was walking beside Tim. He looked up and saw the open cave at ground level. Then he saw the image above it! He knelt.

Each person in turn did the same. As they rounded the trees they looked ahead and then up. They knelt. Their hearts beat faster than they had from all the hard work. Their mouths dropped open and each face showed that they recognized that they were on sacred ground. Directly above the cave, the sun had illuminated with highlights and deep shadows the perfect image of "The Lion of Judah"!

Tim whispered to David.

"How is it that we didn't see it before?"

"We were in the cave until it was almost dark. I think the sun has to be at the right angle to make the image," David whispered back.

Josh turned to Ben and spoke in a normal voice.

"Dad, I know that you have been worrying about Sarah. I think you can stop that now. She is under the protection of The Lion of Judah."

"Is that the Lion in your story Father Bob?" Adam asked enthusiastically.

"Yes Adam, I believe it is, but I am not sure why we were allowed to see His image today."

"Perhaps this explains why this place has such a feeling of Peace," said Tim. "Oh," he said, sounding sad, "It is gone."

"Father Bob does that mean we shouldn't use the cave?" Sarah asked.

"I think it means that you are blessed, protected and welcome here."

"Quickly let's put your things in the cave wherever we can and then they can be arranged the way you want them tomorrow." Ben suddenly felt like he had very little right to be there. He carried things quickly and kept his head down.

"Slow down Ben. There is no danger of things being damaged by rain. The sky is clear," said Jed.

"Sarah I cannot think of anyone more fitting than you to lodge here. You brought The Blue Stone People to Jesus and He loves you."

"Thank you Father. It is strange though. I keep looking up there thinking that I should be able to see it if I look harder, but it just isn't there at all. I can't wait until tomorrow so I can see it again. It will be there won't it?"

"I think so, but I don't know. Maybe it was a gift to us, a one-time thing."

"Oh that can't be right. The rocks are there and the sun will be there. We have to be able to see it again!"

She sounded like a child teasing for candy.

"Sarah, David and I have set your bed up for you and the cradle is near it. We brought two lanterns and there is extra oil here somewhere. I set one lantern over there on that smooth rock sticking out of the wall; just inside the opening. That jar has a box of stick matches in it."

"Thank you Jed. Thanks for everything."

"Ben and I are going to ferry all the wagons back across and then we will be heading to the ranch," said Jed. "Father Bob and Tim are going to stay tonight and so is Josh. They will help get the lumber unloaded and across in the morning. Beth is leaving with me. Sarah you are going to be fine here. Take a deep breath and know that you have done the right thing. Don't worry about Ben. He is already beginning to understand. How could he not after seeing that this is **The Lion's Den**?"

Beth had been working in the cave putting some of the things in order. She had put bedding on their bed and had set up a kitchen area of sorts near the entrance.

Adam came and gave David and Sarah hugs and said he would be back whenever he could.

"Mom will come and I will come with her," he stated it as a fact. "I like it here." Ben hugged David and Sarah and kissed Pili on the head.

"My Sweet Kitten," he said, but didn't say anything else. It was growing quite dark by the time he and Jed headed back to the ranch.

"Well we have a three quarter moon and a clear sky. I think we will be able to stay in the tracks we made coming if we are careful," said Ben. Jed nodded and started out with the second wagon cautiously. They had always made a point of not using the horses at night. There was always a danger that they might step wrong and be injured.

They stopped at the halfway point briefly, to rest the horses. The empty wagons rattled and banged but were not at all difficult to pull. Father Bob and Josh had agreed to bring their last wagon when they came. Tim had said that he would be swinging by with their freight wagon to pick up the things by the river and they would not be staying. They intended to go back to the mill hoping that Tom would have another load of lumber available and then they would head home on the wagon trail after they crossed the Silver.

Jed and Beth rode along quietly. They were tired from very little sleep the night before, the hard work of loading and unloading the wagons and now this long trip home. This was the first time they had ever been this late with the evening milking. They knew that they would have a barn full of bawling milk cows when they arrived at the ranch. Adam was laying in the noisy wagon on some hay, sound asleep.

Ben watched the trail through tears. I really messed everything up. Forgive me Father. I think they would have been moving there soon anyway. You had it all prepared. You always know what we need and get it ready for us. That was an awesome moment! I know she is safe there with you watching over her. Thank you for "The Lion's Den."

AN INVITATION

If you do not know Jesus, as your savior, but you would like Him to be, please pray the following prayer. Invite Him into your heart. Commit your "New Life" to Him. He will be your constant companion, counselor, comforter, and protector. The Holy Bible tells us that He will never leave you or forsake you.

"Dear Jesus, please forgive my sins. Give me grace Lord, so that I will not commit them again. Come into my heart and strengthen me, so that I can start a "New Life" with you as my companion. I want to live according to your will and commandments. Bless me Lord and lead me in a life that is pleasing to you. In Jesus' Holy name I pray. Amen"

If you sincerely prayed that prayer, you are saved! You are born again. Your soul is whiter than the snow on the highest mountains. The angels in heaven are rejoicing as your name is written in The Lamb's Book of Life!

Get a Holy Bible and begin to read it. Find a good Bible believing church and start attending, so that you can learn more about Your Heavenly Father. What a wonderful God we have.

Sign your Bible and date it as a witness of your commitment to God. Tell someone!

I will pray for you. God bless you. Your sister in Christ, Louise Bouck

About the author

Louise Bouck is a follower of Jesus Christ. She and her husband, Dale, live in Arizona. Together they have raised six children.

Until an early retirement from her fulltime job in 2000, not much time was available to allocate to writing or art. Along with many other interests, Louise enjoys painting on location. The lush greenery of Michigan, her home state and the abundant flowers in her grandmother's greenhouses and flower shop all encouraged her eye to appreciate the colors and beauty of nature.

After moving to Arizona, the rugged landscape of the mountains and desert stole her heart and took her artistic soul in a new direction.

Paintings in many media cover the walls of her studio as she has deliberately turned her creative side more to the discipline of writing.

Hesitantly she withdrew from the art gallery where her work was sold and left the position of resident artist at the local Historical Society Museum. Louise has written a ten book series of Christian; Bible based novels that she is now starting to release for the first time as she works on still another story and another painting.

Book Titles in "The New Life Series"

Book #1   More Than Survival
Book #2   Life's Many Journeys
Book #3   The Land's Heritage
Book #4   The Story of Sarah
Book #5   Together
Book #6   The Blue Stone People
Book #7   Teewahpanyee the Boy, Two Feathers the Man
Book #8   The People of the Lion
Book #9   The Lion's Den
Book #10 Just The Beginning